MELANTHRIX THE MAGE

Borgo Press Fiction by ROBERT REGINALD

THE NOVA EUROPA FANTASY SAGA

THE HIEROMONK'S TALE
1. *Melanthrix the Mage*
2. *Killingford*
3. *The Dark-Haired Man*

THE ARCHQUISITOR'S TALE
4. *The Righteous Regicide*
5. *The Virgin Queens*
6. *The Exiled Prince*

THE PROTOPRESBYTER'S TALE
7. *Brother Theo's God*
8. *Quæstiones*
9. *"Whither Goest Thou?"*

THE HYPATOMANCER'S TALE
10. *The Cracks in the Æther*
11. *The Pachyderms' Lament*
12. *The Fourth Elephant's Egg*

Other Fiction: *Academentia: A Future Dystopia* * *The Attempted Assassination of John F. Kennedy* * *Dead Librarians and Other Shades of Academe* * *The Elder of Days: Tales of the Elders* * *If J.F.K. Had Lived* * *Invasion!* (War of Two Worlds #1) * *The Judgment of the Gods and Other Verdicts of History* * *Knack' Attack* (Human-Knacker War #2) * *The Martians Strike Back!* (War of Two Worlds #3) * *The Nasty Gnomes* (Phantom Detective #2) * *Operation Crimson Storm* (War of Two Worlds #2) * *The Paperback Show Murders* * *The Phantom's Phantom* (Phantom Detective #1)

MELANTHRIX THE MAGE

THE HIEROMONK'S TALE, BOOK ONE

BEING THE FIRST ROMANCE OF NOVA EUROPA

ROBERT REGINALD

THE BORGO PRESS
MMXI

MELANTHRIX THE MAGE

FIRST BORGO PRESS EDITION

Published by Wildside Press LLC

www.wildsidebooks.com

DEDICATION

To the memory of

Dr. Fran J. Polek
(November 11, 1929-December 26, 2002)

and his creative writing class
at Gonzaga U. more than four decades ago;

and

For Mary,

who has given
so very much
of herself—

to my life
to this book
to everything.

CONTENTS

L'ENVOI

O for a voice like thunder, and a tongue
To drown the throat of war! When the senses
Are shaken, and the soul is driven to madness,
Who can stand? When the souls of the oppressed
Fight in the troubled air that rages, who can stand?
When the whirlwind of fury comes from the
Throne of God, when the frowns of his countenance
Drive the nations together, who can stand?
When Sin claps his broad wings over the battle,
And sails rejoicing in the flood of Death;
When souls are torn to everlasting fire,
And fiends of Hell rejoice upon the slain,
O who can stand? O who hath caused this?
O who can answer at the throne of God?
The Kings and Nobles of the Land have done it!
Hear it not, Heaven, thy Ministers have done it!

—William Blake

AUTHOR'S NOTE

For those of you who care about such things, this novel is an alternate history set in a Europe whose geographic features are similar or even identical to our own, with the major (but not sole) divergence from our timeline having occurred in the year 363 AD, when Roman Emperor Julian the Apostate, Constantine I's nephew, was *not* killed in battle against the Persians (as he was in our world), but lived on for another forty years.

For the geographic and personal names herein, I used mostly Slavic, Hungarian, German, and Greek models; there are no silent letters in such constructs. Forward accents are intended to provide guides to stress in Slavic words, such emphasis often appearing in locations unfamiliar to westerners; in Hungarian names, however, the accents merely indicate differences in vowel sounds. I've employed circumflexes in Greek words to distinguish between the letters epsilon and êta, and omicron and ômega. Umlauts can denote gutteral vowel sounds—or dress up otherwise pedestrian names. The letter "ß" stands for "ss."

In the end, of course, I have my own ideas about pronunciation, and each reader will undoubtedly have hers or his. Mangle them as ye will, folks, and no one will be the wiser, unless you actually hear me read a passage someday, and then you can tell me, with as haughty an air as possible, that I've got it all wrong!

I do try to have fun when creating these things; some of the names here have been invented from the flimsiest of constructs, bearing no discernible relationship to anything that anyone but I will ever be able to determine. Oh, well!

PROLOGUE

"SILENCE!"

Anno Domini 1166
Anno Juliani 806

The men came out of the night as a pack of wolves, running silently and low against the ground, taking advantage of every furrow and bush to erase any sign of their presence from the pale starlight. Anyone eying the scene would have spied no more than the occasional wavering of a shadow to betray their presence. They stopped just beyond the flickering aura of light cast by the torches surrounding the perimeter of the emir's camp, hidden from sight by a shallow declivity; and then the lycomorphs rose slowly from the ground, reconstituting themselves in human form, complete with dark gray mantles and hoods.

"Remember," hissed their leader, a tall, bearded man wrapt in a black desert *qaftan*, "no unnecessary killing. No noise."

He glanced around once to make certain everyone understood. Each nodded in turn, his head barely outlined against the horizon.

Then their leader raised his right fist, the ring on his smallest finger briefly glowing a dull crimson, and again the hunters rushed forward in a wave. The captain took the first sentry himself, surging swiftly into his mind, while simultaneously covering his mouth. He compelled the guard to walk out into the darkness to the nearest bush, there to sleep the night away. One by one the picket line was whelmed, until none remained. Then the wolves went searching for other prey.

The tent they were seeking was located on the south side of the encampment. It was set a little aside from the rest, large and looming, its canvas doorflap emblazoned with the crouching striped tiger of the House of Tighris, a creature that seemed to stalk back and forth as it flapped in the desert breeze. Tölgy spotted it first, and whistled the clear, piercing call of the desert nighthawk, immediately drawing the others nigh.

"*Csendes!*" whispered their captain in the common tongue, "*silence!*"

He then sent Páston to loose the emir's steeds, and ordered young Kyrik to guard the area just outside the tent. The rest would follow their captain inside.

The leader carefully slit the ties holding the tentflap shut, and led his cadre into the black interior, extending his senses throughout the space.

The servants sleeping on the floor of the outer chamber were taken by surprise, being placed into trances from which they would not waken for hours. The Psairothi bodyguard was muted by the onslaught of a dozen and one minds.

The hunters paused just outside the entrance to the inner sanctum. Their leader raised his arm once more, his hand self-illuminated with a rosy glow, and then folded his fingers over one by one. At the count of three, they rushed in, fanning out to either side to assume control of the chamber.

The woman was instantly awake in her bed, her defenses flaring in reaction, creating a brilliant blue aura around her body in response to the unauthorized intrusion. She was preparing to blast the invaders with all her might when the captain let his own flame re-emerge, just enough to show the two-year-old boychild dangling from under his right arm. An empty flock bed lay nearby, its covering still warm.

The soldier held up the lad to show his control of the situation. Then he nodded to either side, and his companions allowed their own auræ to illuminate their hands and bodies and gradually the entire room.

"What dost thou seek?" the woman hissed.

The covers fell away from her body as she sat up, but she paid them no mind. Her auburn hair tumbled loose around her full, bare breasts, gleaming dully in the dim light.

"You already know," he said softly, indicating the child.

She started to scream, but he cut her off by flexing his big fingers around the child's tiny neck.

"If you cry out," the captain said, "*he dies!* If you raise the alarum, *he dies!* If you fail to follow my lead, *he dies!* They told you that this day would come. You have two choices, madame, and two alone: you will let me take the boy away, or he will perish here. I give you my word that he will be protected, educated, and nourished. Open wide your heart, lady, and read the truth writ plain upon mine *espiritus.*"

"We see it," she said.

"You must choose now," the soldier demanded.

Then a mooring tore loose in her heart, as she silently screamed her soul out, unable to voice her despair and her sorrow, rocking back and forth on her haunches, her creamy breasts and dark hair bobbing in the cold light reflected from thirteen pairs of crystalline orbs. Finally, she found a place deep inside herself to hide, and would have remained locked away there for the rest of her days, had not the captain forced her back out.

"Lady," he prodded, his own heart grieving for her loss, "you *must* decide. *Now!*"

She raised a tear-streaked face to him.

"Have mercy!" she said. "Take us, if thou must, but let the boy go free."

"You know I mayn't," he said.

"Then damn thee to Hell!" she said, her voice cracking with the strain, "damn thee to Hell forever more!" The tent shook with the rocking of a small earthquake.

She began sobbing in earnest.

It was her son's frightened whimpers that finally opened a chink in her armor.

"He must not die!" she managed to gasp, choking out the words, coming to some resolution within herself. "He must live so that we may live. Pray allow us to kiss our precious babe one last time."

The soldier said nothing, but just nodded to her. The woman composed herself and rose from her pallet, carefully wrapping the bedclothes loosely 'round her body. Silently she padded over to the warrior on bare feet. She looked up at the man towering a head above her, and then bent to her son's squirming form, tenderly stroking his head to quiet him, and brushing his lips with hers, her tears wetting his forehead.

"Mamá!" the boy cried out, raising his arms to her.

"Yes, dearest one, Mamá is here," she murmured. "Mamá will always be there for thee, even when thou'rt far away. Thou must never forget our love for thee."

She again passed her hand over his head, murmuring a few words under her breath while she traced a symbol on his forehead.

"Never!" she said. "Now, be thou a good lad. Obey this man and he will protect thee from harm."

Her cold blue eyes again pierced the soldier's black ones, as she slid from her left wrist a slender gold bracelet endangled with a bronze torc inscribed incusely with the cuneiform script, and carefully unfastened the metal clasp of the collar. She placed it about her son's tiny neck, idly brushing aside the captain's giant hands, and squeezed the supple metal ring shut with a loud click.

"Remember us," she breathed, softly blowing the wind from her lungs into the child's open mouth. "Rememb'rest thou thy mother, and lovest thou no other. *Ánnash Vórlshar ran Mórlanndriyàzh.*"

Then she touched his heart, and just for a moment enveloped both boy and soldier with a vermilion glow.

"What have you done, mistress?" the captain wanted to know.

But the child just squirmed and giggled, thinking that she was playing with him, and she tried to smile back.

She let her right arm slowly drop to her side, seemingly in resignation, and then, with a sudden glint of light, quickly raised her hand and struck downward at the warrior, her small dirk glancing off the chain mail hidden under his robe. He abruptly transferred the child to the man on his right, and wrested the weapon easily away from her. She cried out in pain, and let the knife fall, her makeshift cloak slipping to the floor.

"*Disznó!*" she said, "*pig!*"

Raw hate flared in the azure sapphires of her eyes.

"Someday we will finish that stroke," she said, her naked body quivering with passion.

"Perhaps, madame," the man said, "but you will do nothing here until an hour has passed. Should the emir's men catch us, your son will be the first to die."

Then he motioned again to his men, and they silently withdrew, their lights going out one by one. Kölbas restored the boychild to his keeper. As the captain himself retreated, he turned again to the wretched woman, who had sunk to her knees in despair, tearing her hair and weeping most piteously.

"I swear unto you, lady," he said, "upon my sacred honor as an adept, that the child will receive every attendant care, every possible beneficence."

The lad cooed his acquiescence.

"Save for his mother's grace," she managed to choke out, "save only for that, captain."

Then she regained her composure and gazed up at him once more.

"Know this, sir," she said. "This damnable sacrilege, this blasphemy of *injusticia*, cannot and will not stand. Though it takes us a hundred years, though the pillars of Heaven itself be shaken into oblivion, he will be found. All of thy magics, all of thy brave men, will not rescue thee, will not save thee then."

Her bejeweled fingers were now ensheathed in a light blue flame that crawled up and down her hands and arms and alabaster shoulders, up and down and around, like aqua-tinted millipedes idly caressing her lambent limbs.

"You speak of sacrilege, lady," the captain said, deliberately spitting on the ground before her, "but you knew the limits under which you lived, and you knew the boy would be forfeit. You would disobey the orders of your master."

"We *have* no master," she said.

"So 'twould seem," he said, the disdain evident in his voice. "Then I leave to the One True God the elucidation of the future and the reconciliation of the past, whatever that might be. The game never ends, as well you know. Alas, madame, that I am rooted to *this* time and *this* place, and thus I must bid thee *adieu*."

The captain bowed his head slightly, placed himsefl before the lines that he'd opened in the æther, and stepped backward into his destiny.

The boychild traveled with him.

CHAPTER ONE
"NOTHING BUT SMOKE AND FIRE AND SHADOW"

Anno Domini 1177
Anno Juliani 817

Spring comes late to Zándrich.

For seven months out of the year, grim-visaged Boreas blows his breath down from the Baltískoye Mórye, chilling the Zaÿdar Steppe with his icy gale, and laughing at the poor mortals trying to scratch an impoverished living out of the red, clayey soil. Then gentle Zephyros and blustry Notos beat back their ancient foe, their brother, and a warm, mild breeze from the Blackish Sea restores the land to vibrant growth, so that men can smile once again at all of the good green things that Glorious God pulls forth from the emerald earth.

On the feastday of Saint Ktêsiphôn, a mounted man swathed in muddy olive robes paused before the gate of a well-kept monastery. With the sigh of a man who has finally reached jour-ney's end, he banged twice with an iron-tipped staff on the great bronze doors. The afternoon sun illuminated a small wooden hatch that popped open in the adjoining wall.

"Who seeks entrance to Holy Svyatosláv?" a high-pitched voice asked.

The traveler pulled the hood back from his face, revealing a shaved head and a well-trimmed beard streaked with premature gray. A single bushy brow slashed across his forehead, topping a crook'd nose that showed signs of an old break. His eyes were framed by lines that smiled when he squinted.

"Father Arik Rufímovich," he said, slapping a biting midge off his bare pate, "hieromonk and preceptor of the Order of Saint Mauros the Misplaced, *grammateus* [that is to say, secretary] to King Kyprianos III (may he live forever!), *diangelos* [or go-between] to Patriarch Kyriôn IV (may he bathe forever in Christ's Holy Light!), who seeks present audience with the venerable Archimandrite Jován Csigály, Abbot-Bishop of Saint Svyatosláv's Monastery."

"Father Arik? Is that really you?"

The traveler sat up straight on his saddle and stretched his back, groaning just once.

"Why, that sounds like Brother Philêmôn of the Holy Flame," Arik said.

"Why, bless my soul, I think I am!" came the response. "I mean, yes, of course I am! But, *but*, however did you know?"

"Just a lucky guess," the traveler said, audibly yawning. "I wonder if you could let me in, Brother Phil? I'm very tired."

"Oh my, oh my, of course, of course, *of course!* Wherever are my manners, where have they gone? Oh dear, oh let me see, just a moment, just a moment, if you please."

There was a rattle and a loud clang, followed by a distant thud and crash and bang and yell, echoing far into the distance.

The voyager dismounted, again stretching himself, but had to wait a bit longer before the massive entrance finally swung open. A little man in a dark brown robe was standing just inside.

"Welcome to our simple home, kind sir. Enter into this place of God in well-deserved peace," the monk said, rattling off the formula that he had memorized for the occasion. His hands were folded piously in front of him.

"My dear Brother Phil," Arik said, coming forward and embracing his host, kissing him on both bewhiskered cheeks. "You're certainly a welcome sight. I'd appreciate a meal and a clean robe, if that's possible. I must say, the roads have been particularly foul these past few weeks."

"Oh yes, oh yes indeedy, 'tis very true, very, *very* true," the monk said. "I just think, I *really* think the One True God was trying to make up in one season what He forgot to give us during these past years. Why, I've never seen so much rain in all my born days. Here, let me take your horse, Father: I'll make sure that he's properly tended to. Oh, *oh!* I almost forgot. You must tell me all the new stories you've heard along the way, and all of your new adventures, oh yes, pretty-please, with sugar and dumplings on it!"

"In good time, my old friend, in very good time," Arik said. "'Sufficient unto the day is the evil thereof,' as the philosopher Barlévin says. I pray that you and all of the community have all been well."

"Other than the troubles with the heathen-folk up north, we prosper very well, yes, we do," came the response.

"I'm so glad to hear it," the priest said. "Now, tell me how your plantings went last year. Weren't you crossbreeding several strains of gourds to increase their yield?"

"Well, *well*, of course, *of course*, but you know how *dry* it was back then, Father Arik," the monk said. "I mean, I guess I told you that, didn't I?, but still, it was just, just terrible. Much, *much* too little rain to grow much with, that is, much of anything, really and truly. Oh, but, *but*, come to think of it, I did manage to seed one small crop by scratching out a ditch down from the Yaroslávets, not far from where it flows into the lake. Ho, ho, *ho*, I can tell you, father, I got some *verrry* interesting results with my progressive postminimal program for propagating *les géants jolis verts*."

"The what?" the priest asked. "You mean, the *big* ones?"

"Yes, yes, *yes!* You see, Father Arik, they suddenly got, well, they suddenly grew remarkably *huge* in just a couple of generations; and after that, well, after I'd cleaned them out a bit—they made good eatings—I was able to cook up the husks during the winter doldrums, so to speak, and dry them out completely, oh, *very* completely, and then I fashioned a few of the larger ones into musical instruments."

"You did *what?*" asked the traveler, eying his friend most curiously.

"Yes, yes, *well!*" Brother Phil smiled, clearly pleased with his inventiveness. "You know that we don't have all that much to do during the long winter months, the days being so short and all, and the visitations, well, they're just so utterly lacking, and so we have to do our very, *very* best to keep ourselves entertained, in addition to our constantly puissant purification and prayerfulness, of course...."

"Of course," his friend said, shaking his head in wonderment.

"...'Idleness being the devil's woodbin,' as Brother Mendevíll is very fond of saying. So, we pluck the harps and blow the gourds, and make some music without dischords."

"Really?" the priest said.

"*Really and truly*, Father Arik. And, and, *mirabile dictu*, why, it's like a miracle, it's God's own hand at work, if I ever saw it, for I must tell you that several of our group of idle songsters and I are actually getting together later on this evening to practice our newest composition, a truly *truly* inspiring ode or hymn or paean to Saint Bogolén the Brewmeister, and I wanted to be the first of our company to invite you to join our *soirée petite* while you're still a resident here. Of course, many, many, *many* toasts will be offered in his memory, in addition to our celebratory music-making."

"Of course, Brother Phil. But alas, my dear old friend," Arik said, "oh, alas, that I have to see Abbot Jován urgently on business, and then just as quickly depart. If it weren't for that, well, you know that I'd join in."

"Oh, I do, I do, *I do!*" Brother Phil said, eyes perfectly downcast. "Oh my, oh my, oh my gourds and swords. Well, well, *well*, then, I guess we'll just have to get along without you, as hard as that may be. Oh my prayers and hairs! Let's get you taken care of, then, eh, father?"

He led his companion into the main compound, where

Arik was meticulously groomed and broomed in preparation for his presentation to the head of the Monastery of the Transubstantiation of the *Psychai Siôpêlai Agiou Sbiatoslabou*, which is to say, the Silent Souls of Saint Svyatosláv. The order had been founded nearly two hundred years earlier by a starving Saint Ézzard à Hagyma, who, having stumbled upon a sacred onion patch growing where none should have been found, just by the shore of the Työmny Lake, had acclaimed it a miracle of God Almighty that he should have been thus rescued from perishing at a time when all had seemed lost. Now, a dozen establishments of the order were scattered across northern Kórynthia, mostly in Zándrich, Trapézhia, Kúrskaya Kósa, Pustáya Boltoviyá, and Isaúria, with more planned for construction over the next two or three centuries—God willing!

Three hours after his arrival, Father Arik was fetched by Brother Milorád to the abbot's cozily appointed chamber overlooking the pebbly vistas of the great lake.

The Archimandrite Jován Csigály had been chosen abbot by the community some sixteen years earlier. A man of six-and-fifty years, he was thin and small, with neatly combed gray hair and a closely-cropped beard. Around his neck hung a pectoral cross studded with gems, and two gold-framed icons of Saint Gamaliêl and Iêsys the Christos. On the middle finger of his left hand he wore a curious ring of gold, cunningly wrought from five separate bands into a single intertwining unity, so that one could not tell how or why the pieces had been put together, or how they might be taken apart. His white woolen robe was fringed in red and emblazoned over the heart with the crimson Greek letter "psi" framed over a small black "sigma" nestled in its hollow. He sat in an old, weathered rocking chair before a large open fireplace, his feet and lower legs shrouded with rugs, a cup of spiced wine steaming on the small table by his side. He started to rise when Arik was announced.

"Sit down, old friend, please sit still," said the traveler. "I know how these cool spring evenings can pain your knees."

He deposited his large frame on a stool to the abbot's left, warming his hands before the flames.

"Might you have another cup of whatever that is?"

"Brother Mílo," the abbot called, "refreshments for our guest, please."

A few moments later the monk appeared at the doorway with a steaming drink and a plate of cakes dripping with honey. Arik murmured his thanks.

The two men sat sipping their cups for some time, listening to the popping of the logs and watching in silence the eternal dance of the flames. Finally the visiting hieromonk broke the peace.

"It's good to be home again, Father Abbot," he said. "I find in this place a tranquillity, a shuttered peace, that utterly eludes me at the Royal Palace or at the Cathedral of Saint Konstantín, or even in the *Megalê Scholê*."

"Which is why you return each and every spring, like one of our migrating lake fowl," the older man said.

"And every year," Arik said, "my beard grows lighter and my brow darker."

"Your visits," Jován said, "remind me of the happy days before the war when you studied here. Such a little troublemaker you were then! But very, very bright, almost too bright for your own good, I think. So tell me, Father Arik, what's troubling you these days?"

"Responsibilities," the traveler said, "cares and fears and rumors of war. Nothing you haven't heard, I imagine."

Arik sipped again from his cup before continuing: "You know that our young King Kipriyán, having recently come into his manhood, is determined to finish what his father began."

"So I'm led to believe," the abbot said. "I hear that he's begun assembling an army at Myláßgorod."

"Indeed," the priest said. "He and King Ezzö are determined to oust the House of Walküre, whatever the cost. But it's the king's new minister, one Doctor Melanthrix, who's actually been pushing him to take action."

"I've heard naught of this," Jován stated.

"It's a closely kept secret at court, although the word's gradually oozing out. But this Melanthrix character.... Despite my best efforts, abbot, I've been unable to determine who he is or where he's from. He just appeared from nowhere a few months ago, and drew the king into his hands like a spider enwebbing a fly.

"It happened like this. The king has been frustrated all winter in his attempts to organize a campaign against Pommerelia. He accused several of his generals of incompetence and abruptly replaced them, to no effect. Just a month ago, Kipriyán presided over a banquet celebrating the arrival of spring. This dinner was attended, of course, by all the notables in the land."

"Including yourself?"

"Including myself," Arik said. "He had rather too much to drink, a common fraility in his family, and started raging about his inability to promulgate the war, and how he would either proceed forthwith, or suffer heads to roll.

"Afterwards, during an impromptu audience, he had this, this *creature* dragged in, flapping and frumping in his multi-colored robes. It seems that Melanthrix had recently been caught practicing the astrological arts, and the church wanted him burned as an example."

The abbot snorted. "But this is very strange, Father. Of course, such laws do exist, but when has the church ever cared about their enforcement? Why, I can't recall the last time charges were actually brought against someone. Usually, they just run the offenders out of town."

"Well, Metropolitan Païsios encountered the man, they had words, and one thing led to another. He officially accused Melanthrix of paganism, and the good doctor then appealed to the throne, which was his right under the law, but which also took the matter out of the ecclesiastical courts."

"Very canny of him," the abbot said. "It almost seems to me that his actions were intended specifically to gain him a royal audience."

"Several of us have since thought so," the traveler said.

"When presented to the king, the astrologer called out in a loud voice, 'All hail Kipriyán the Conqueror,' and prostrated himself before the throne.

"'What do you mean?' came the royal response.

"'Those who have eyes can see what there is to see,' Melanthrix said. 'May this unworthy servant rise?'

"When Kipriyán nodded his consent, the mage drew a crimson square in the air with his right forefinger.

"'To those who understand *le plan astrologique*, my lord king,' Melanthrix said, 'the future hangs before us like the tapestry upon the wall.'

"The floating square suddenly began displaying images.

"'At the center of the weave,' the sorceror continued, 'is the mighty Kyprianos, king of kings, savior of his race, the greatest warrior of the Tighrishi line, veritably another Joshua laying low his enemies with the jawbone of an ass.'

"Now the image displayed the mounted form of Kipriyán himself, bloody sword on high, surrounded by the bodies of his enemies.

"'It is *you*, o mighty king, *you* who shall rescue Kórynthia from the heathen beasts, *you* whom men shall call Conqueror, *you* whom the Autokratôr at Julianople shall honor as his equal. Forgive us this great impertinence, great king, but you see before you only your humble servant, the lowly Doctor Melanthrix, who wishes only to serve you faithfully for the remainder of his days.'

"Then he pulled a pin from somewhere in his robes, and stuck it into the picture. The image vanished with a loud pop, leaving no trace."

"Incredible!" Jován said.

"Indeed," the priest said. "But this is the strangest part, my old friend. Neither I nor any other mage present could fathom how the thing was done, nor could we penetrate his mind, and those *psai* defenses were unlike anything we have ever encountered. I know of one assault that was made upon him a few days later; Melanthrix laughed at his attacker, and laughed again when that individual was executed by order of the king."

"Who was it?" the abbot asked.

"Lord Khaldán."

"Too bad," the older man said, "a good man, if a bit rough around the edges."

Arik drained his tea, then tossed another log on the fire. He sighed.

"Now the king will do nothing without consulting this charlatan, and neither his generals nor his ministers have been able to break his hold on Kipriyán's mind. And that, Father Abbot, is why I'm so dull these days."

"And I thought it was just your natural bloodymindedness," Jován said, grinning at his former pupil. "You say no one knows anything of his past?"

"Nothing," Arik said. "He was seen first in Myláßgorod a few days before his arrest. Some have speculated that he came up river from Susafön, but I can't confirm a sighting earlier than Myláß. He sports these strange, multi-hued robes, which may be a deliberate affectation to keep us from identifying his nationality. His accent seems stilted and formal, but indeterminate in origin; those scholars who specialize in such things have been unable to place it. He has an exceedingly odd physique: eyes the palest of blues, face and hair both stark white, beard nonexistent and brows very thin, limbs quite elongated, almost painfully so. He walks with a gait that reminds me of an old sailor I once met who had just returned from a long sea voyage. His age is unknown. He consumes no meat. He avoids the public baths. He eschews the company of other men, save for the king. He laughs strangely and at inappropriate times. He will not take the Body and Blood of Jesus Christ at Holy Mass. He cannot be probed. He cannot be forced. The 'sauce' does not affect him. And it is clear that nothing short of death will dislodge him from the affections of the king."

The abbot stroked his short beard, nodding to himself as he pondered the situation.

"Then, my dear friend, your course is very clear. You must

bide your time until he makes a mistake, which he surely will in due course. He is, after all, just a man. Shadow this individual and determine what you can of his origins and intentions. Protect the king always, and keep the kingdom from his influence."

"I'll try, Father Abbot," came the reply.

Then Arik cocked his head sideways, trying to hear a strange squealing and booming sound hovering just at the edge of his consciousness, somewhere in the distance.

"What's that awful noise?" he asked.

Jován sighed and moved his legs closer to the fire.

"Well, Father Arik," the abbot said, "that's my own personal cross to bear. 'Philêmôn and the Holy Flames,' they call themselves. It started last winter, and it has just never stopped, despite rather blatant hints from everyone who's not actually involved with the so-called music-makers. They say that they honor the Creator Himself with their sacred sounds, but it 'sounds' perfectly wretched to me, I must admit. Alas and alack, more and more of the brethren are joining in, saying that it's 'fun'; and so I cannot forbid the activity without causing, well, major difficulties."

The entire room was now resonating to a slow "boom, boom, boom" at the lower end of the scale, not quite loud enough to hear clearly, but just enough to penetrate the bone and irritate the soul.

Arik shook his head, as if to rid himself of the pesky drumming.

"I'm very sorry, Father Abbot," he said, "but that incessant noise would drive me wholly insane if I had to listen to it all the time."

"Oh, I just offer it up to the Christ," Jován said, "and I pray to God Almighty for a quick deliverance. Thus far, however, He has chosen in His ultimate wisdom neither to acknowledge me nor to listen Himself to the glorious gourdsmen.

"Howsomever, to return to our situation here, we've experienced similar unrest in the far northeast, as you may have heard.

Last year a man of the heathens called Dyggvi Bolkersson began agitating in Nörrland for a pogrom against the Christians. A few less sensitive members of our flock there had flogged a servant for refusing baptism. Dyggvi has attracted a following from those of the old elite who fear the prospect of change, and has been successful in getting the Nörrlander Thingë to expel the members of the true faith who are resident beyond our northeastern borders. Last month those who declined his invitation were abruptly slaughtered, God rest their martyred souls."

Both men crossed themselves from right to left, and kissed their hands.

"The remnants of those poor folk are still finding their way south by whatever way they can," the abbot continued. "Now I am told that 'Count' Dyggvi, as calls himself, is assembling an armed force in the woods north of Sevyerovínsk and Öldenburg. Most of the garrisons there were pulled to Myláßgorod earlier this year by Count Ygor, and the walls of both towns are in bad repair. There's been no threat from the heathens in several generations. Of course, I've put our community here on alert, and I'm having the country scoured for foodstuffs; but we could not long survive a siege, I think, particularly with the refugees starting to come in from all sides."

"Terrible news," Arik said, "terrible! Have you reported this?"

"Of course," the abbot said, "but the authorities just think I'm a foolish old man. Perhaps I am, but I truly believe that the north could explode into chaos; and if war does come, I don't think that it will end either quickly or well. For that reason, my good friend, as much as I enjoy your company, I must ask that you depart on the morrow. You can add nothing of significance to our defenses here, if the worse should happen. I would feel much more secure knowing that you were providing the appropriate counsel to the Royal Council."

"This is much more serious than anything I've heard in Paltyrrha," the priest said. "I can certainly help. I'll start with Melitón Count Zúmov at the ministry, and then try Metropolitan

Akakios at the chancellery of the patriarchate. However, before I go, I've still got my business to complete here, and the sooner we can get to it, the better."

He shook his large bare head and laughed, patting his mentor on the back.

"Now that we've managed to depress ourselves, old friend," he said, "whom do you have for me this year?"

"So now we don our practic hat, eh?" Jován said, with a wry grin of his own. "No more idle chatter for the ancient, decrepit abbot. Well, I do have a few prospects in mind, three of them, in fact: the acolytes Radó, Bayánik, and Yevstáfy, good lads all. If you'll extend your *psai*-ring, I'll give you the details concerning their backgrounds and suitability."

Arik touched the middle finger of his right hand to the bare arm of his mentor, and quickly re-established a long-familiar contact; the latter immediately began transferring images of the candidates and their accomplishments to the hieromonk.

"Hmm, Radó seems rather immature to me, even for his young age," Arik said. "I think I'll pass on him this time. Brother Bayánik is at least passable, although none of this group demonstrates particularly strong language skills. Yevstáfy looks presentable, but he's not quite adept yet, is he? He's young enough that I can wait another year for him, too. I'll test Bayánik tomorrow. But what about Afanásy, whom we discussed last year? He was a little green then, and we had such a good candidate in Görtenz that he was outclassed."

The abbot sighed deeply. "Ah yes, Brother Afanásy. Well, after some reflection, I do not think that friend Afanásy had a particularly good year, and I believe we should wait for him to mature a little more."

"You know as well as I that we must take these boys at just the right age if they're to be trained properly," Arik said. "How old is he? Twelve, thirteen at most? If he's going to be tested, it must be now."

Jován moved his left arm back and broke contact, rubbing his hands together to ease the strain.

"Sorry," he said, "but I can't recommend him."

Arik looked his friend in the eye. "Why? Whatever has he done?"

The older man rested his chin in his right hand, and idly began scratching his beard.

"It is not so much what he's done, father," he said, "as what he *hasn't* done. Afanásy handles all the chores assigned to him, *but he does no more*. He attends mass and prayers as required, *but he does no more*. He performs his mental exercises, *but he does no more*. He trains with the defensemen, subject to his physical limitations, *but he does no more*. Indeed, with such things he never seems to do *anything* more than he has to."

The abbot cleared his throat.

"And yet, his studies are exemplary. He reads better than most of the monks resident here. He loves to peruse obscure texts and scrolls. I found him one day pouring through the old chronicles of the abbey, and when I asked him what he could possibly find of interest there, he quite simply replied: 'Everything.'

"And I *believed* him,. I believed him, Arik! Afanásy has a great facility for language. From personal observation, I know that he reads some Greek and Latin, Slavonic and Magyar, perhaps even a touch of the Araby script, although no one has taught him that. He poses questions constantly to our resident masters, but some of his knowledge is self-taught. His Psairothi potential is unquestionably high: his lines are well-developed, and he has met every challenge our adepts can throw at him. Indeed, I suspect that he can do even more than he admits or knows.

"But that's precisely the problem that I have with this boy, Arik: what he knows and what he will admit to knowing. For some months I've had the distinct feeling that he's been holding back from me. I feel uncomfortable around him, and I know very well that it's *my* failing. I ask God for His guidance, remembering certain 'difficult' pupils that I've had in the past, and I do sense that he's trying to touch me in ways that I just don't understand and to which I can't respond.

"I'm also concerned that he seems to have few friends his own age, if any. God knows that I've tried my best to reach him, but there is very little response beyond the usual, the most respectful, 'Yes, Father Abbot.' He's quiet and agreeable at all times, almost to a fault, but I simply don't know what's going on in that little mind of his. I would rather see some passion there, some intensity, instead of the perfectly composed little gentleman. It's, well, it's unnatural."

The visiting hieromonk took a poker and stirred the unburnt portions of the wood in the fireplace, creating a cloud of sparks. He brushed one out of his beard before it took hold.

"You've given me much to consider, my friend," Arik said. "I had no idea that little Athy had changed so much. Do you remember his first day here? He didn't shed one tear, even though I'm sure he was scared beyond his wits. There was no whimpering, no mewling, even back then. I don't think I ever told you this, but only once on that long journey did he ever ask about his mother. He didn't especially want his mother, mind, he just wanted to know what had become of her. I couldn't tell him, of course, then or now."

"Oh yes," the older man said, "I remember him, all right, and what a well-behaved little lad he was, too. Brother Mílo gathered him up in his bear-like arms, and asked: 'Are you going to be a big boy now?' Athy looked him straight in the eye and said: 'Yes, sir. Yes, I am.' Everyone laughed. He did not like being laughed at, even at that young age. Those were the days, eh?"

Jován suddenly pushed his chair back and threw his hands out towards the fireplace.

"What's that?" he yelled, generating an orange flame of protection from his rings.

Arik came to his feet in one smooth motion, pulling a long dagger from its hidden sheath.

"Where?" he asked. He quickly scanned the room. "I see nothing but smoke and fire and shadow."

"I could have sworn...," the abbot said. He rubbed his brows and sighed. "I must be getting old, Arik. I thought I saw a pair of eyes staring at me out of the flames. Then I blinked and they were gone. This business with the Nörrlanders must be affecting me more than I'd thought."

Then he sat back and yawned widely.

"The bell for evening prayers will be tolling soon," the old man said. "We must go prepare ourselves. I give you permission to test the acolyte Athanasios on the morrow. Perhaps we should not deny him the same chance that we were given at his age, the same opportunity to succeed or fail on his own merits."

He awkwardly reached for the cane laying to one side of his chair, staggered to his feet, and then embraced the traveler.

"I'll see you at prayers, Father Arik. Peace be unto you, my old friend."

"And to you, Father Abbot," the hieromonk said. "And to you."

CHAPTER TWO
"I SHALL NAME HIM AFANÁSY"

On his cot in the dormitory for boys aged ten to thirteen, Afanásy jolted awake out of his trance, then just as quickly settled back down again. He'd nearly been caught by Jován, bless his interferring soul, but the boy's fear was quickly overwhelmed by the surge of excitement that he felt at having successfully penetrated the abbot's antechamber.

They know who I am! he thought to himself, *and they haven't told me. Why? I must find out.*

Earlier that week he had finally unearthed a cryptic entry in the old ledger books of the abbey, in a volume dated II Kyprianos III. On the second day of May in the Year of Our Lord 1166, the abbot had noted in his cramped Greek lettering:

> "**F[ea]st. [of] S[ain]t. Athanasios.** *AR* here with Child, after delay en route. Boy healthy. In honor of the Pillar of the Church, whose *celebratio* this is, I shall name him Afanásy."

This child was obviously he, but what did it mean? And who was the *mother* that the two men had discussed a few moments ago? What about his *father*? He would give *anything* to know the answers to these questions. He *would* know the answers, no matter the price.

He had carefully torn the ledger page from the book, folded it, and put it with his small cumulation of precious things, things that belonged to *him*, not the church. These included a minia-ture bronze torc inscribed on the inside with incuse cuneiform lettering, which he had owned (and had been trying to decipher) for as long as he could remember; a curious green crystal that someone had left in his room a year after his arrival; and a few other trinkets that he had kept for no reason that he could under-stand.

Manipulating the visiting hieromonk hadn't been all that difficult, although he still had to be *very* careful around Jován. The abbot somehow had notions about his abilities that weren't too far from the truth. It was time to move on before he was accidentally discovered. He'd outgrown this place anyway, had read all of the scrolls and volumes in the library, and even some hidden books in the monks' quarters, including one filled with writings of a salacious nature. The volumes that he *really* wanted to peruse, the ones referred to cryptically by various masters of the Psairothi arts, were just not here, but he would find them somewhere else, never mind. And then he would know *everything* that he wanted to learn.

Afanásy's musings were suddenly interrupted by a shower of water and a howl of laughter. He looked up to see a small cloud dissipating above his head, and just beyond his bed a crowd of his stupid *compagnons* headed by the acolyte Benedím.

"Nasty is a patsy," they chanted, "Nasty is a patsy."

"What's the matter, Nasty?" yelled Benedím, "did our naughty little boy wet his panties?"

Which again prompted catcalls and laughter from the boy's dozen accomplices.

Afanásy dug his fingers into his hands, drawing blood, then rubbed his palms together, smearing the sacrificial offering on his *ka*-ring, all the while muttering to himself in Greek, "*Mênin aeide, Thea.*" He took a deep breath, gently drawing all the moisture out from his clothes and bedding, and then carefully breathed out again through his slightly opened hands, blowing the vapor toward the boys. They would wake in the middle of the night, having wet their beds quite thoroughly. Benedím would find himself coming and going both ways, and wouldn't be able to stop until morning. Afanásy grinned to himself in satisfaction. When you came right down to it, the dumb ones were surprisingly easy to twist.

"Boys, boys, now stop this," the voice of Brother Nathanaêl boomed from across the room. "Enough! What's the matter with you, playing these kinds of pranks on each other? Enough, I say. Do you want me to report you to Father Abbot? Now, settle down on your cots before you go off to prayers. If you're not careful, the Dark-Haired Man will get you for sure!"

"Ah, everybody knows there ain't no Dark-Haired Man," Benedím said, drawing gasps from his accomplices, for no one had ever been foolish enough to challenge the dormitory monk directly.

"What did you say?" Brother Nathanaêl said, turning on Benedím.

He grabbed the boy by both arms and yanked him off the floor.

"What did you say?" the monk repeated.

"Friend Benedím," he said, "you will work garde-robe duty for the next ten days. By yourself. And if I do not find all of them spotless of piss and poop each and every day, your service will be extended until such time as they are. And, in your spare time, which you seem to have so much of these days, you will pray in the Chapel of Saint Abêl for God's forgiveness of your many detestable sins."

He then released the boy and turned his attention to the others.

"As for the rest of you, Brother Nate has a little word of advice: *do not doubt the power of evil.* Satan is as real as Almighty God Himself, and he's always eager to capture the souls of innocent little boys. And his chiefest ally, his greatest servant, is *The Dark-Haired Man.*"

Nathanaêl set his fists on his hips and proceeded to declaim with some evident relish.

"Now let me tell you something about The Dark-Haired

Man," he said. "He was once just like you and me, lads, just another young boy, unspoiled and true to the Holy Faith. They say that he lived in the Duchy of Pynchóv, being the younger son of a wealthy nobleman of that place, a century or more ago.

"Then one day, not very long after he reached his eighteenth birthday, he was riding in the woods and met a well-dressed man outfitted all in black, who saluted him and said: 'Aren't you Lord so-and-so? Why, I've heard such good things about you, such promising things. What a shame your brother will inherit your father's title and you'll get nothing. He's stupid and ugly, and you're handsome and smart.'

"'Yes,' said the boy, 'all this is true, but what can *I* do about it? The law is the law, and he is, after all, first-born.'

"'Ah,' the devil said, for that's who he was, my boys, the Evil One himself, 'Should he meet with a small accident before he marries, why, *you* would be first-born.' And so it happened. But the duke of that time, a powerful Psairothi, somehow discovered the crime and challenged the lad to the Code Duëllo. But he, being the coward that he was, refused the fight and ran away, vanishing before he could be caught.

"Today he roams the wilderness of the north, his dark hair tumbling loose down his back, looking for other young men to seduce into his evil ways. The devil gave him long life and the ability to change his shape at will, assuming the forms of beasts and men alike; but to sustain himself he must feed on the blood and souls of innocent boys. He has long yellow teeth"—he mimicked them with a quick downward slash of two fingers—"and glowing red eyes"—he used his hands to form two circles around his own sockets—"and a hideously crook'd nose, but he shuns the True Cross and can be seared with holy water. He fears the bright light of day.

"Do not scoff at his existence, my boys, for I have seen this foul fiend with mine own eyes, having narrowly escaped his clutches in my youth. Yea, I could even smell his rotten breath scorching my face. Thank the Holy God that I wore about my neck an icon of Mary the Mother of Jesus, or I would be dead,

dead, I say, or even worse, made one of his slobbering slaves! 'Ware The Dark-Haired Man!"

The monk drew his six-foot frame up to its fullest extent, raised his arms over his head, and yodled the low, moaning cry of the damned. His fingers cast a long, wavering shadow that ran up the cots to the far wall.

"Now go to prayers, the lot of ye!" Brother Nathanaêl shouted, and they all ran off squealing, like mice scurrying for their hidey-holes.

All, that is, save the acolyte Afanásy, still sitting on his dry bed, who quite patiently asked: "And what happened then, sir?"

CHAPTER THREE
"DO YOU KNOW WHO I AM?"

The next morning, the Feast of Saint Pêrêgrinos the Beknighted, dawned fair and warm, with a light breeze blowing from the south. After morning prayers the visiting hieromonk tested the acolyte Bayánik and found him wanting. He then broke bread with the abbot, and talked to him again for another hour, before the latter left to attend to the monastery defenses. As soon as he was alone, Arik summoned Afanásy to Jován's chambers.

"Do you know who I am?" he asked the boy.

Afanásy paused a moment before responding.

"You're the one who brought me here, aren't you, sir?"

Arik started.

"Who told you that, son?" the priest asked.

"No one, father," came the response.

The hieromonk ran his hand over the stubble of his bare head.

"Let's start over again, shall we, lad? I'm Father Arik Rufímovich, and I'm here to test you for possible training at the *Megalê tou Genous Scholê*, the Great School of the People, in Paltyrrha. Would you like that, friend Athanasios?"

"Yes, sir," the boy said.

"Good," Arik said. "I'm told that you know the Neustrian game, *les échecs*. Since you must relax before I can test your abilities properly, I propose that we play a match first. The abbot's pieces have been laid out for us before you. All you need to do is to pull up a stool. Which color would you like?"

"Black, sir," Afanásy said.

"Why black?" Arik said.

"It's easier to defend than attack," the boy said, "and I like black."

"Very well, then, since I'm white, I'll begin by moving my pawn two spaces forward, thus. Now, it's your turn," the hieromonk said.

But when Afanásy touched his black pawn to make the countermove, suddenly his left hand was riveted to the board, and his eyes rolled upward into their sockets as a surge of energy swept up his arm into his body, momentarily driving out his consciousness. When he could see again, he had been transited to another reality.

He was standing on a flat plain hatched with strange crossmarks. Surrounding him on either side were his comrades-in-arms, all dressed alike and ranged in two lines. His body was covered in black armor and his left hand gripped an upright sword. On the opposite side of the field was another group of warriors clothed from head to toe in white armor, also in two lines. Two of the soldiers, one of each color, had already faced off in the center of the plain.

Afanásy instinctively tensed, looking right and left for any danger to his king, then almost fled the field when he saw the long black hair writhing and moving as it hung behind his monarch's helmet. The king's head turned down and looked right at him, and Afanásy noticed two red spots where the eyes should have been.

"What's the matter, little boy?" the monarch hissed, a forked tongue flickering out from the opening in his armor. "S-snake got your tongue?"

And then Afanásy would have run, run as fast as his short legs could carry him, run anywhere but this awful place of death, except that he couldn't. He was nailed to his square, unable to leave it, because it wasn't his time. He was still looking at his terrible king when he noticed a movement out of the corner of his eye. A white knight had moved in front of the white pawns onto the field opposite him.

"Your turn, little boy," the black monarch said.

Afanásy found himself leaping over the soldier in front of him, moving sideways to offset the move of the white knight opposite. He could only move when it was his turn, and then only in ways prescribed by the rules; otherwise, he was stuck within the confines of his square. Pieces began to fall as the game progressed, but here, instead of cleanly being removed from the board, they were struck down by the awful weapons of war, with limbs and heads being hacked off and blood spurting everywhere, with men and horses groaning their death rattles and crying piteously for a succor which never came. But still the game remorselessly moved toward its end, as the number of players steadily diminished through deliberate murder and assassination.

A white metropolitan moved within range, and suddenly Afanásy attacked, wielding his sword with deadly accuracy, striking him down mercilessly. He stood there appalled while the churchman bled all over the square, crying out: "My brother, my brother, why hast thou forsaken me?"

He would have stopped and begged for forgiveness or at least tried to aid the archbishop, but there was nothing he could do: he could not cross the boundaries surrounding him on all sides. He seemed doomed to repeat what he now knew was an old, old game.

The white king was soon besieged within a protecting ring of his few remaining warriors. The boy could hear the black king gloating as he drew ever closer behind him.

"I have you this time, old friend, I have you now!" the fiend chortled.

But as the black monarch passed the boy on the square next to his, suddenly Afanásy swiveled with all of his strength, and somehow struck right through the wall of his square, cutting into the legs of the dark king, hamstringing him.

The face of the creature turned toward him, hissing, "S-strike the traitor down."

The remaining dark warriors began closing in on all sides, and the boy knew that he was doomed.

Then the hand of the white king elongated across the board and touched him lightly on the head.

"You'll do," he said, and the boy passed out.

* * * * * * *

When Afanásy awoke, he was still sitting on his stool in the abbot's antechamber, his left hand gripping the original pawn so tightly that he could feel the cold ridges of the piece digging into the cuts on his palm. He released it, and looked down at the brown, dried blood staining the insides of his rings. He then caught the hard eyes of the hieromonk staring directly into his soul.

"Never forget, son," Arik Rufímovich said, "that I know who you are. I am not the fool that you think I am. Neither are most people. Now let's go find the abbot."

Outside on the terrace, Jován was staring northward at a large, dark cloud that was billowing up on the distant horizon.

"When did that storm arise?" Arik asked.

"Sevyerovínsk is burning," the older man replied. "The Nörrlanders have come."

The hieromonk could see the tears staining the older man's cheeks.

"Time for you to go, friend Arik," the abbot said. "Use the *viridaurum* in my study to transit directly to Mylážgorod, and report to the king immediately. We need reinforcements and supplies as quickly as possible. Ah, I see that you will be traveling with a boon companion. Very well, I give you my blessing, but remember what I told you earlier.

"Come, there's no time to delay. The barbarians will be here within a few days, and I have much to do to prepare their especial welcome."

Half an hour later the two men embraced and gave each other the kiss of peace.

"Keep well, my brother in Christ," the hieromonk said. "Don't take any unnecessary chances, Jován."

"Nor you, my old friend," the abbot said. "You were always my best pupil, Arik, and watching you progress has been one of the great joys of my life. Never forget this place whence you sprang, when you walk amongst the tiled halls and titled nobles of Paltyrrha. I see great things yet to come for you, great sorrows and great joys. Keep true to Our Lord, and keep true to yourself, always."

Then he turned to the boy.

"As for you, Athanasios Hokhanêmsos, the Unvraveler of Fate, I know how much you like that name. You shall walk the path of the righteous man, and then you shall have nothing to fear when you come before the throne of God for His final judgment. I specifically charge you to serve, protect, and obey the hieromonk Arik Rufímovich as if he were your own father, for all of your days, for as long as you both shall live. Now, give me your pledge on this, and be gone, the lot of you."

"I do so swear, Father Abbot," said the boy, kneeling, crossing himself, and kissing his paired thumbs as they were both blessed by the primate. Then Afanásy entered the alcove with Arik, hand laced in hand.

As the travelers stepped through the *viridaurum* with a slight whoosh of air, Jován made the sign of the cross and whispered a quick prayer to the Holy Abbot Ézzard, asking him to watch over his two friends throughout their many journeys to come.

The cleric said out loud: "I shall not see you again in this world, my dear ones. May Almighty God bless you and care for you, forever and ever. Amen."

He turned his back on the great glowing greengold mirror and attended once more to his duties, but his last words echoed within the chamber for long after he was gone from this earth, until they too finally faded away with time.

For it is time, as Agnós Zélénÿ relates, it is Father Time who grinds down all men's thoughts into sand, sifting through the leftovers for a mere morsel of worth—but leaving unto history the human accounting of the whole, and to God the Adjudicator the final judgment of the soul.

CHAPTER FOUR
"I CAN DO AS I PLEASE"

Anno Domini 1205
Anno Juliani 845

The King of Pommerelia was drunk, drunk, *drunk!*, gloriously drunk and in love with himself and his destiny and his power!

This had been the happiest day of his thirty-eight years, and he was determined to relish every last moment of it. All about him the room glittered with promise, everything pointed to his great and glamorous and ever-grasping future. Four walls might restrain this hall, he thought to himself, but they surely did not constrain him or his ambitions one little bit, not at all. He would show them, *he would show them all*, exactly what he was capable of, now that he had come into his own.

He glanced to his right, and took note of his idiot father, demanding mother, silly brother, insipid sons, and uglier daughter. All were unworthy of this, his great night. To his left, he noticed, his scrawny little wife gabbled at her not-so-scrawny entourage, none of them making or having any more sense than a barnyard full of flighty fowl. *Squawk, squawk, squawk*, they jabbered, *cluck, cluck, cluck, blither, blather, bother*. Not worth a pail of warm horsepiss, any of them. And to think that *he*, His Royal Highness the Rightful King of Hinterpommern and Vorpommern and All the Pommerns in Between, actually derived from such miserable stock. Well, they'd soon be cackling to another chorus, if he had his way.

He peered straight across the great hall at another long-table crawling with the hairy beasts who called themselves the nobility of Kórynthia. *There*, just at the center, he could see the dreary old dog himself, balefully watching the proceedings with his all-seeing eye, and barking every so often at his pack of supercilious sons, who went running pall-mall to fetch his well-chewed bones. *Woof, woof, woof!* He had to lick their paws for now, oh, he understand that little fact all too well, but soon, yes, very soon, they would all be baying at the moon, would be howling a very different tune, and he would be the one leading the pack! A smile crossed his face as he contemplated exactly what he had in mind for the old king and his mangy hounds. A few leashes and lashes would do wonders for their dispositions, he knew.

A third longtable, ranging to his left, displayed to rather poor advantage Their Most Petit Sovereignties, the d-duke and d-d-duchess and d-d-d-daughters and all the d-d-d-d-dinky little lords of Mährenia the Minor-Pip-on-the-Map, a pimple of a state if there ever was one, whose "rulers" had presented themselves at this august gathering to set their seal on the "grand alliance" that would finally and forever finish the Walküre line. As if *they* could contribute anything worthwhile to the coming campaign, other than their toy soldiers and pipsqueak nobility.

Finally, there on the "right side" of the hall he could see the long, lazy line of the lords spiritual, all of them sitting up as straight on their seats as forbidden sins: the Thrice Holy Patriarch of Paltyrrha and All Kórynthia (ho hum, ho hum), together with his equally dreary metropolitans and archbishops and bishops and priestlings and protopresbyters and all that drivel, each of them damning this or prohibiting that, as if anyone ever listened to the old farts anyway. Gad, how stultifying that a man of *his* grace had to waste his valuable time bowing and praying and begging the help of these leeches upon the resources of the state. He'd like to put a few them out on the front lines and see how they'd fare when the Walküres started charging them with their lances leveled at their gullivers. He giggled at the thought of that fat little sissy, Archbishop Sisíny, writhing on the spit of an enemy spear.

He intermittently noticed (without really noticing) the retainers and lesser nobles flitting in and about and behind his table like burly bumblebees, waiting for a chance to cross-pollinate their many masters and mistresses, and thereby harvest, they hoped, a little honey; but only for a moment, because such passing moments were all he seemed to possess on this fine inaugural day. Suddenly the huge, flapping banners celebrating the arms of state and church caught his bloodshot eyes with their vibrant, beckoning hues.

Oh glorious day, he thought, *oh irreplaceable day, now slipping away!*

Then his attention was diverted by the macaronic performers scattered around the alternating black-and-white tile squares at center stage: jugglers juggling, clowns cackling, scantily-draped dancers dipping (ripe for the plucking they were!), fire-eaters tossing their brands high and high and higher into the air (one of them missed and set his own hair aflame!), gymnasts swinging and jumping hither and yon and in between, singers awarbling their warbles (whatever *they* were), and *oh!* so many others, far, far too many for him to count or even comprehend in this, his wretchedly glorified estate of grace. Every so often they would exchange places, and he tried to renumber and remember them again, but it was all too much, just too confusing for whatever it was that was in his mind. He really should stop them all, he thought, he really should order them to *cease and desist!*; but that would take too much energy now, just to levitate from his throne into the air, yes it would, and he didn't really have anything left, after all the contemplation of his gloriosities.

Then he perked up again and tried to catch the eye of the pretty Mährenian princess perched just to the right of her royal father, but she kept her face and lips most dutifully cast down.

"Lift up your bright ey'n, *ma petite karlina*," he muttered unto himself, "and I'll show you a few things about improving the relations between our houses."

A pity she was promised to that Kórynthi bratwurst, he mused.

That prompted an idea of such a lascivious nature that he laughed out loud, causing some of his family and retainers to eye him queerly.

"I can do as I please," he shouted back at them. "I'm the king now. I *am!*"

The newly-minted Queen Pulkhériya, perched immediately to his left, began honking like a goose in response to the mimes mimicking their meaningless, mindless routines.

God's breath! he thought. *She even eats like a fowl, pick-pick-picking at every little thing in front of her. No wonder her bosoms are so small.*

He belched quite loudly and wiped his mouth on his greasy sleeve.

"More wine!" he yelled at the morons serving him. "More food!"

More power! he shouted to himself.

None of them understood anything, but they would soon enough! A king had to rule or be ruled—he'd learned that by watching his father—and he was determined never, ever, *ever* to follow *that* particular example.

He raised up on his stool and farted a royal blast, and once again suffered the supreme enjoyment of seeing a look of disgust impress itself on his dear, dear wife's too-thin face. He turned to her, smiled, and deliberately stuck out his tongue, grinning even more when she turned her head away.

CHAPTER FIVE
"MIND YOUR MANNERS!"

Over at the Mährenian table Duchess Johanna caught King Humfried ogling her young daughter and shuddered, frowning in her distaste and disgust.

What boors these Forellës are, she thought. *Whatever was Ferdy thinking when he made an alliance with these uncouth easterners?*

She looked around the room, her mouth pursing with her displeasure.

And these furnishings: why, nothing matches anything else! In Zaragossa we could have taught these barbarians a few lessons. Now, if I were running things....

She suddenly spotted something out of the corner of her eye, abruptly thrust her husband back in his seat, and leaned her firm bosoms right across his chest.

"Rosanna!" she hissed, "straighten up, girl! You're a Kürbis! Start acting like one!"

To her left her other daughter started giggling over her elder's misfortune.

"Quiet!" their mother said, killing them both with thunderbolts from her eyes. "Mind your manners!"

Duchess Johanna then looked across the room at the Kórynthi clergy, and frowned again.

But the worst thing, she thought to herself, *is that we'll have to bow and scrape now before these heathen churchmen. They chant and coo all this Greekish lingo that none of us can understand, instead of good honest Romanish. Oh, dear Lord Almighty, how I wish that I was back again within the warm embrace of Andalusia, listening to the heated homilies of good Archquisitor Sylverio. Our Holy Roman Cæsar would know what to do with the* antipapistos. *He'd burn them all!*

A tear rolled down her right cheek. She daintily and taste-fully wiped it away with the linen nappy she always carried in her sleeve. Thank Jehovah that she had had it changed for a new one just before leaving on this arduous journey.

Directly across the hall from her, Timotheos Metropolitan of Örtenburg spotted Johanna looking at Humfried, and slyly canted his head to one side.

"Athy," he said softly over his shoulder, "who's that woman in blue near the center of the Mährenian table?"

Archpriest Athanasios, a man of some forty years, quickly stepped forward and squinted a little.

"I believe that's Duchess María Juana, called Johanna, consort to Duke Ferdinand," he whispered. "She hails originally from Zaragossa. Her father was Hereditary Prince Rómulo. If you recall, he's the one who was killed in that nasty jousting acci-dent at the Saint-Boeuf Fair in Austrasia. Of course, some folks don't really believe that it *was* an accident. After his younger brother Pelayo succeeded to the throne, ten or more years ago, he quickly packed Johanna off to Mährenia as Ferdinand's second wife. They say that the duke can't visit the garde-robe without her permission."

"She doesn't seem too happy about the proceedings," Timotheos said.

Athanasios laughed out loud.

"She has a reputation of not being happy about much of anything," he said. "Rumor hath it that she vigorously opposed the treaty of alliance between Mährenia and Kórynthia, mostly on religious grounds. She's a staunch cæsarist. Uncharacteristically, she failed to sway her husband's mind, despite several very loud and public attempts to do so; and thus she sits there pouting her displeasure out for anyone to see. I suspect that old Ferdy will pay a fearful price for his wayward willfulness."

Both men chuckled at the thought.

"What's your assessment of our new pretender?" Timotheos asked.

"Well, he's certainly a cheerful monarch, isn't he?" Athanasios said. "I'd say he's in particularly good spirits this evening."

"Indeed," the metropolitan agreed. "I wonder what our good King Kyprianos thinks of all this?"

But good King Kipriyán was troubled in his mind: everything was going well, rather too well, in fact. As he gazed around the room with his one good eye, he noticed Humfried guzzling another flagon of the Fontana brew and leering at the female guests.

Gad, he sighed to himself, *the man is incorrigible. The damned Forellës always were insensitive louts. We'll have to keep a tight rein on* that *one. Well, time to get the thing started.*

He caught his eldest son's eye, and said "come hither" with a quick sideways jerk of his bushy head.

Arkadios, Hereditary Prince of Kórynthia and Duke of Paltyrrha, was just thirty years of age, but seemed older. His frame was slight and his stature middling. His face was illuminated by a pair of crystalline blue eyes, shining intensely with a keen intelligence that missed nothing. His light brown hair had a curl to it that kept flopping forward onto his brow, but that was the only untidy thing about him. His reddish-brown beard was cropped close to the skin, and contoured along the jawline, giving him a rakish look.

Kipriyán nodded to himself: he liked the face, and he admired the man within. Here was a prince who knew exactly who and what he was, and who accepted the idea with great good grace.

I have done this one thing well, the king thought to himself. *If all else fails, I have at least sired a worthy heir.*

"Father?" Arkády whispered softly at the king's shoulder, startling the older man out of his reverie.

The prince shared his sire's distaste for the House of Forellë, but very carefully kept his opinions to himself. Humfried was, after all, his own first cousin, son of the Old Pretender Ezzö and Arkády's Aunt Teréza, and it was not the heir's place to challenge his king's policies. He lightly touched his father on the shoulder with his *psai*-ring, immediately establishing a practiced link.

We'd best begin the festivities, Kipriyán thought to his son, *before yon kingling finds his way into Slumberland.*

The king flashed his son an image of a braying ass with Humfried's face.

Arkády choked down a laugh.

On my way, lord father, he said psychically.

CHAPTER SIX
"TO SKIM WITH WINGS
THE PATH OF THE ÆTHER"

The prince carefully extricated himself from the group of servers and courtiers surrounding the monarch, and made his way down the left side of the longtable. Arkády was clothed in a striking white tunic enchequed with the crouching tiger from the Tighrishi coat of arms. 'Round his waist he sported a broad silver belt secured with an ornate buckle fashioned as a *tughra* swirl that, if held to the light, spelled with its shadow-cast the word "Tighris." The strap itself was embellished with incuse lettering in the Hellenic tongue, reproducing the motto first writ down by Iôv the Magôteros, mage and saint: *"Psairein pterois oimon aitheros,"* which is to say, "to skim with wings the path of the æther." These were the words, beyond "I believe," "I love," and "I serve," that had shaped the entire course of his character, and that he followed faithfully until the very end of his days.

After stopping briefly to pay his respects to the ancient patriarch, who gave the prince his blessing by kissing him on the forehead, Prince Arkadios entered into the realm of the Forellës. He heartily greeted the Old Pretender, former King Ezzö, a bearded man of some sixty years, and his consort, Countess Teréza, who had always treated Arkády with respect. He thought he caught some flicker of recognition in the old prince's eyes, but these days, one could never be too sure.

Their second son, the goateed Prince Adolphos, also embraced Arkády with genuine affection; for although poor

Dolph never seemed to understand much more than the chase and the hunt, he was kind-hearted to a fault, and well liked by everyone at court.

Prince Pankratz, the new monarch's heir apparent, coldly bowed his head without comment, while Norbert or "Junior," the second son, exuberantly saluted his cousin and kissed him on both cheeks.

Arkády noticed with amusement that "King" Humfried was much too absorbed in his own pleasure to recognize the presence of his relative. He reached out and touched the latter's arm, sending him the mental message, *Cousin, it's time to begin.*

The monarch started, pulling back his gaze from the crouching cat wavering on the opposite wall, which had been enchanting him by lunging back and forth at some mythical beast; and rather carefully pulled himself to his feet, adjusted his clothing, and brushed Arkády's hand loose from his shoulder.

"All right," Humfried declaimed quite loudly, "*all right!* I heard you the first time. You can go back to your kennel now, *Cousin.*"

Arkády bit his lip and bowed very formally, quickly withdrawing while pointedly wiping his hand on his tunic.

"*Részeg!*" he muttered under his breath, "*Drunk!*"

Humfried ignored him.

"A toast," shouted the new monarch over the racket. "A toast!"

As the multitudes began to quiet, he raised his goblet.

"I give you Kipriyán the Conqueror, Savior of Kórynthia, Destroyer of the Heathens, Barbarian-Killer, King of Kings, Overlord of Pommerelia, Mährenia, Morënë, and Nisyria."

"Kipriyán the Conqueror!" the throng resounded, as the ruler of that name rose from his seat, his right hand raised high, to receive the accolades of the assembled lords and ladies.

After bowing most graciously to the throngs, Kyprianos III raised his own cup in turn, and proposed a counter-toast to Humfried v, rightful King of Pommerelia, on this, his most noble day of investiture.

The great lords pounded their tables with fists and cups and whatever else they could lay a hand upon, creating a din that surely must have reached all the way to the gates of Heaven and Hell.

Further toasts were drunk to Avraäm IV, Thrice Holy Patriarch of Paltyrrha and All Kórynthia and Pommerelia; to Ferdinand VIII, Duke of Mährenia and Ptolemaïs and Lord of the Prüffenmark; to Ezzö VI, late King of Pommerelia and Count of Bolémia; and to many others besides, both present and absent, living and dead.

Then it was time for the real business of the day to commence.

Duke Ferdinand of Mährenia rose in his place and motioned with his arms for silence, even as the attendants continued to make their rounds, refilling all of the empty cups that they could find.

"I have the supreme honor," he said most sonorously, "to announce an affiliation of family between the Ducal House of Kürbis and the Royal House of Tighris.

"With the sanction of King Kipriyán, and the approval of the Royal Councils of Mährenia and Kórynthia, I do hereby declare the betrothal of my eldest daughter, the Hereditary Duchess Rosanna, to that most worthy Prince of Kórynthia, Nikolaí Kipriyánovich, Count of Arkádiya and second son to King Kipriyán. I further state that it is my intention that these two worthies shall eventually succeed me on the Amethyst Throne as King and Queen of Mährenia and Ptolemaïs."

"They are worthy!" shouted the assembled noblemen, again banging their tables so that the very rafters shook loose their years of accumulated dust.

"Secondly," said Ferdinand, continuing to wave his hands, motioning for silence, "secondly, it is my further intent that my next younger daughter, the Countess Rosalla, shall be betrothed this night to the exalted Prince of Pommerelia, Adolphos Count of Einwegflasche, second son to former King Ezzö Count of Bolémia. With the consent of King Humfried and King Kipriyán, I announce with the utmost pleasure that this noble couple shall be awarded the restored sovereign Duchy of Nisyria on their wedding day."

"*Axioi!*" the throng said. "They are worthy!"

Ferdinand said: "Let the newly betrothed come forward and be blessed by the Thrice Holy Patriarch."

From their respective places five individuals moved to center floor, the two couples linking arms and facing the Patriarch.

Then the octogenarian Avraäm raised his hands on high and said: "A man shall leave his father and mother and shall cleave unto his wife, and they shall be one flesh. He who finds a virtuous wife finds a good thing, sayeth the Lord. Her price is far above rubies. The heart of her husband does safely trust in her. Her husband is known in the gates, when he sits among the elders of the land. Strength and honor are her clothing. In her tongue is the law of kindness. She looks well to the ways of her household, and eats not the bread of idleness. Her children rise up and call her blessèd. Favor is deceitful and beauty is vain, but a woman who fears the Lord, she shall be praised. Give her the fruits of her hands, and let her own works praise her in the gates.

"Therefore do I sanctify the promises that are fearfully and wonderfully made here today. O Lord, seal these oaths upon the true hearts of Thy children. Make their love as strong as death itself. Let every day that they live give praise to Him that created us. Let the Three Lands rejoice in festivity. Amen."

"Amen," said the throng, clearly delighted with the spectacle, and the two sets of promised pairs and the Patriarch returned to their seats amid the cheers of their compatriots, shaking still more dust down from above.

CHAPTER SEVEN
"GUARDS! GUARDS!"

King Kipriyán then rose from his seat and motioned for silence.

"Let it be proclaimed before the world," he said, "that on this day the Kings of Kórynthia, Pommerelia, and Mährenia did pledge their joint honor to regain that which is theirs, and that to this end we shall proceed together against Barnim Duke of Walküre and all who support him, whatever the cost."

Prince Arkády handed his father a decorated vellum scroll dangling with official seals, which the monarch unfolded and read in his loud, commanding voice:

"Kyprianos III King of Kórynthia, Overlord of Pommerelia, Mährenia, Morënë, and Nisyria, unto Barnim III Duke of Walküre and Pretender of Pommerelia.

"Sirrah!

"It has come to our attention that you have failed to render proper homage unto your overlord in Kórynthia. Therefore do we charge you forthwith to proceed to our city of Paltyrrha no later than the first day of May next, and together with your sons and grandsons and noble fiefs make proper obeisance and submission to your lawful king; failing which, we shall take such steps as may be necessary to ensure your fealty, and shall...."

His words were cut short by a flash that seemed to come from nowhere. For a moment Kipriyán stood absolutely still, a look of great astonishment coming over his face. Then his hand dropped the parchment into the bowl of soup on the table before him, and he abruptly sat back into his chair, gazing down in wonderment at the crossbow bolt jutting straight out from his chest, a bright crimson stain spreading quickly across the front of his best tunic. One of the Mährenian princesses—the pretty one—suddenly screamed as if her world were ending, a long, high, tremulous falsetto that seemed never to end; and someone—one of the Forellës, perhaps—began shouting, "Guards! Guards!"

Prince Arkády cried out urgently for the king's physician, then placed his hand on his father's brow, trying to send him strength through their psychic link. Afterwards, everyone marveled at how fast the joy of celebration had turned to utter horror.

Fra Jánisar Cantárian, physician to the court of Kórynthály, came running to the longtable, his bag of implements flapping at his side. With the help of the king's sons, he brushed aside enough dinnerware to have fed a hundred men for ten years, letting the exquisite pieces smash into oblivion on the hard tiles beneath. They carefully lifted the wounded man onto the empty table.

"Quickly," Jánisar said, "cut away his tunic, here and here, and someone save these medals. My prince," he shouted at Arkády, "I need your help and that of your siblings. Call them and link their rings to yours immediately."

Even as he spoke, he was plunging his right hand into the entry wound, probing the damage with his mind to see what had to be done to save the king's life. The wreckage was appallingly severe, with the right lung deeply penetrated and one vein nearly severed. Somewhere a woman was sobbing inconsolably.

"Shut her up," he said, "or get her out of here."

The jingle of armor could be heard as the King's Guards poured into the room, searching for the instigator of the attack.

Fra Jánisar bumped into the ungainly figure of Doctor Melanthrix trying to see past him.

"Get back, you dog," he said. "Give us room to work."

Then to Arkády: "My lord, are you ready? Good! Link to me now and give me your power, so."

He showed the prince mentally what he wanted him to do.

Then Fra Jánisar breathed a prayer of supplication to Saint Panteleêmôn the Physician and tugged the bolt backwards, carefully sealing off the damaged sections with his *iatrodaktylios*, or healing ring. Bit by bit the arrow was retracted, and slowly but certainly the doctor used the energy of the princes to assist with the operation. The bolt was hot to the touch by the time it dropped loose upon the floor.

"Stay within the link," he said. "The king has leaked much of his fluid, and I must augment it with your young life force."

He again drew on the combined mental vigor of the royals to siphon some of their vitality into Kipriyán's depleted body, using his own mind as a conduit. They were strong, he knew, and they wouldn't miss what they had given.

"He will live," Jánisar finally announced to the relieved multitude, and a series of subdued cheers swept to the outer reaches of the crowd.

A moment later the king's eyelids fluttered and he regained consciousness. His voice was weak but alert.

"Did they catch him, Arkásha?" he gasped.

Prince Arkády roused himself from his stupor.

"Let me check, father," he said.

Sergeant Éfron Poliodór was already standing by with a report.

"No one has been found, Sire," he said. "But the search continues."

"Very well," the king said. "Order a council meeting for tomorrow morning, Arkásha, with all reports to be made by then. I'll attend if I can. In the meantime, let the festivities continue in my absence. You will preside. I can do no more."

He closed his eyes in weariness and slid into darkness, and for the first time in his life Arkády could picture his father as an old man. The thought shook his very soul to the core, but quickly faded. The prince ordered the servants to bear the monarch to his chambers. As they carted the king away, Arkády could hear Kipriyán thanking Jánisar for saving his life.

"Sergeant Poliodór!" the prince said.

When the man appeared, Arkády ordered: "You will search this room and its annexes again and again until something or someone is found. Do you understand?"

"Yes, Sire," was the guard's frightened response.

"All guests are to be screened by high-level Psairothi as they leave; any who refuse to submit will be stripped and searched manually, no matter their rank. See to it."

"At once, Highness," he said, and sped off, tossing orders left and right to his harried men.

Prince Arkády banged his fist on the table where his father had lain, and when every eye was upon him, said: "Honored guests of Tighrishály, noble princes and metropolitans. My beloved father and I deeply regret the insidious attack that has disrupted our festivities tonight. By the grace of God, good King Kipriyán has been spared. He wishes that these entertainments should continue. I therefore ask that you return to your places; and when you retire later this evening, that you graciously submit your persons to an examination, so that we may uncover this would-be assassin, if he should still be hiding among us. Now let us bow our heads for a moment and thank the good Saints Konstantín and Vasíly for saving the life of our noble king."

The crowd clasped their hands together, while Patriarch Avraäm led them in a prayer of thanksgiving. The prince then motioned to the tunesmiths crouching in one corner.

"Music!" he commanded, and soon the strains of "Redsleeves" were filling the hall. Servers again began making their rounds, refilling the empty goblets and cups with their prime vintages.

But the atmosphere had become strained, even when the jugglers and their compatriots began making their way again to the center of the cross-hatched floor. Not even a rousing rendition of "The Magic Tale of Harvanger and Yolande" could force more than an occasional smile from the celebrants. Instead, everyone was talking, talking, *talking* about the events of the evening, and what they might portend for the future; and they all agreed that the signs were not so good in that regard.

CHAPTER EIGHT
"MELANTHRIX *ASTROLOGOS*!"

For the newly-minted Humfried v, King of Pommerelia, Hinterpomerania, Schreckenhorn, Scopus, Graudenz, Zirrhose, Champerick, Nippsachen, Düngerbrötchen, *et cetera*, *et cetera*, *et cetera* (long may he reign!), who just that morning had been invested with spur and sword at Saint Konstantín's by the Patriarch and couped with the *colée* by King Kyprianos himself, the day that had begun with such promise, veritably the happiest of his life, had now ended in total disaster. As the midnight hour approached, he continued to empty goblet after goblet, and sank further and further into despair. Surrounding him he could only see bad feelings and evil prospects.

Ruined!, he shouted to himself, *ruined, ruined, ruined, the enterprise is ruined!*

He had to do something, he knew, he had to find *some* way to counter the downturned faces he saw peering back at him.

Then he spied the spidery form of Doctor Melanthrix out of the corner of his eye, and he remembered something he had heard once about how the old soothsayer had saved King Kipriyán from disaster near the beginning of his reign by prophesying that monarch's great deeds to come, and how everything that he had spoken then had actually come true. Could lightning indeed strike twice? In his besotted introspection and despair, it seemed to him the only possible solution to his problem.

So Humfried called out in his most noble, his most regal voice, "Melanthrix *Astrologos*! Stop!"

Doctor Melanthrix jumped when his name was called, swiveling almost in mid-stride.

"Whatever do you want?" the philosopher asked in his soft but penetrating voice.

When confronted with the soothsayer's piercing blue eyes, the pretender suddenly lost his train of thought. It was all he could do to avoid stumbling over his own tongue. He wanted to do nothing more at this point than run away, but he managed to concentrate very, very hard on performing this one task, not wishing to look the fool before the hordes of nobles crowding the great hall.

"Tell us of the year to come, good sirrah. Tell us of our future glories. Tell us of the great victories that we shall celebrate here in this very room a year hence."

"You do not know what you ask," the astrologer said. "'Tis the turning of the night. There are things abroad in the æther which must compel the truth. You do not want that truth."

But King Humfried would not be dissuaded.

"Good, good, good!" he cried out, grasping at any possibility to save face. "Tell us about everything that you see in *our* grand future...."

"This is the wine speaking," said the mage. "Go to bed and leave Doctor Melanthrix in peace."

But the king continued without interruption, as if he had heard nothing.

"...Tell us about how the Walküres have tried to murder King Kipriyán. Tell us how Barnim the Pretender shall finally be destroyed."

His loud remarks were now gathering the attention of others in the assemblage, who were watching the exchange and even urging him on, for most believed the Walküri monarch responsible for the unprovoked attack that they had just witnessed.

Melanthrix pointed one long alabaster finger at Humfried, freezing the king's heart.

"This is neither the time nor the place," he said.

"I, King Humfried, fifth of that name, I order you to give us your true prophecy," came the reply.

But Melanthrix deliberately turned his back on the pretender and strode away, only to be stopped by a guard.

"What?" the philosopher said.

"Very sorry, sir, king's orders, sir. You'll have to be searched, sir," the man said.

"Searched? *Melanthrix?* Melanthrix reports only to the king," he said.

But the crowd was growing angry at the mage's insolence, and began taking up the insistent cry of: "Prophecy, prophecy, *pro-phe-cy.*"

The soothsayer looked around the room, more than a little frightened now for his safety, and muttered to himself: "Fools. You are all fools."

Then he shook himself free, moved to center floor, drew up his robes with whatever dignity he yet retained, and abruptly swept his hand around his head in a grand circular gesture.

The princes and nobles quickly settled down to watch, as Melanthrix made a second sweep of his arm over his head. The hundreds of candles illuminating the hall began going out in the exact sequence of the movement of his right hand, as if a curtain was being drawn across the inside of the room, until the darkness was complete.

Everyone gasped as a cold green flame sprouted from the sorcerer's head, forming a sort of halo that bathed the multitude in a flickering, almost sickly, emerald hue. From his right index finger a bright red lance of light stabbed into the night, tracing the outline of a huge ruby triangle hanging high over center floor. Within that boundary vague images began to swirl and form, coalescing suddenly into a panoply of rolling green hills. Over them came running the images of three young women, their faces turned away from the audience, being hounded like wild foxes by a pack of dogs accompanied by the hunt of armed men on horseback.

Doctor Melanthrix then began speaking in a flat, emotionless monotone:

"Three demoiselles do I see
Up and down the hills they flee
Chased around the wedding tree—
Kings and knaves and Forellës three."

"What does he mean?" someone asked.

The crowds suddenly gasped as they heard the flutter of wings in the air, although they could see nothing until three great black birds emerged from the triangle and flew over their heads, sending gusts of wind everywhere.

"Three Forellës do I see
Caw, caw, cawing in a tree
All fly up, but none go free
Who can 'scape his destiny?"

Something dark and formless reached out from the triangle and grabbed the birds one by one, hauling them squawking back into the depths from whence they had come. Then the triangle cleared, so that it appeared as if one were looking at the southern approach of the Great Kings' Road to the city of Paltyrrha, flanked on either side by the large stone sculptures of the ancient Tighrishi kings.

"Three Tighrishi do I see
One is cloaked in infamy
One is crowned in great glory
One a king no more shall be."

But an earthquake seemed to strike the triangle, shaking the statues to the ground with an audible roar, toppling them one against another and shattering each and every one. The crowd cried out in collective dismay. A lone sculpture remained intact, and as it revolved on its axis, they suddenly saw displayed the image of Barnim King of Pommerelia.

"Three Walküri do I see
One is what he seems to be
Two shall find eternity
One shall stop the anarchy."

Barnim's mouth gaped wide, issuing a miniature angel that quickly grew in size. The heavenly messenger pulled from his robes a board for playing *les échecs*, and set upon it the stylized images of the Patriarch of Kórynthia and the Archquisitor of Pommerelia facing each other, one dressed in black and the other in white. Separating them was the small image of a monk clothed in dark green robes, a man with two faces who gazed in opposite directions simultaneously.

"Three archbishops do I see
Two struck down in agony
One shall perish peacefully
Checkmated eternally."

Then the triangle vanished, and the bright green flame rose straight up from Melanthrix's head to the rafters high above, illuminating everyone in the room, and his voice rose correspondingly to a high, excited pitch.

"'Ware the Knave who cannot see
'Ware the Queen who would be free
'Ware the King, uncrown'd is he
'Ware the Demoiselles, all three!
'Ware the Dark-Haired Man to be
'Ware the Dead Man's prophecy."

The magical torch was abruptly extinguished, leaving the crowd blinded by the dark, and when the candles were finally relit, Melanthrix was gone, nor could any trace be found of the man until the following day.

Prince Arkády then dismissed the banquet, and all went

off to their rooms, buzzing and whispering and seething over the visions that they had experienced so uncomfortably that night; nor could any of them, not a one, find the rest that they sought, but tossed and heaved and shook in their beds like a yacht buffeted by the rolling waves of some great storm, never to find safe anchorage in this world, never to sail home again unscathed.

CHAPTER NINE
"WHY HAVE YOU COME?"

Before the rosy-fingered Dawn could welcome the arrival of her brother, the Sun, Hereditary Prince Arkadios transited through the *viridaurum* mirror mounted in the Hall of a Hundred Kings to the chambers of the *Symboulion Magôn Christianôn*, which is to say, the Covenant of Christian Mages, being the very first member of that august association to arrive for the meeting that he himself had just called.

This was an organization which had been founded during the Millennium Year *celebratio* of the birth and ascension of Our Lord and Savior, Jesus of Nazareth, surnamed the Christ. For it had happened, *mirabile dictu*, that the Byzantine Julian Emperor of the time, Antiochos VII, had fortuitously encountered the Holy Roman Cæsar, Marcus Ætherius I, in the Basilica of the Risen God in Hierosolyma on midsummer's day, and despite the many centuries of antagonism resident between the two great powers, had forthrightly strode up to his counterpart and embraced him, kissing him on both cheeks; and turning widdershins, had proclaimed then unto the multitudes, "This is my brother, in whom I am well pleased." And, wonder of wonderments (for God doth work His magic in unfathomable ways), the Emperor of Rome then reciprocated, in the first overt display of good will between the emperors that the world had witnessed in some four hundred years.

Thereafter, these two great men had erected a council of protection, for their own safety and for that of their citizens, they said, consisting of an equal number of mages deriving from both spheres of influence, and presided over by a neutral individual, whose chore it was to arbitrate between the disputes that might cause either side to unleash the dogs of war, as had happened so often in the past. Thus, in the intervening years only one such conflict had broken out, some four decades earlier, but it had not escaped the confines of the Carpates Spinæ Mountains, thanks be given unto the Almighty, and also to those men and women who had worked so hard to prevent this war and others like it from spreading any further.

One of those individuals, Hereditary Prince Arkády, now collapsed wearily into a seat near the end of the great oaken roundtable, and considered for a moment suckling upon one of the *kokaphyllon* leaves he kept wrapt in a preservation skin within his purse, but finally thought better of the idea. He had another meeting to attend later in the morning, for which he would yet require both his wits and his wisdom to remain active; and his little restorative, while effective for as long as half a summer morn on occasion, tended to leave one with the same feeling that resulted from the overindulgence in *les esprits de la liqueur*. Thus it was that he just allowed himself to doze, counting on the others to rouse him whenever they chose to arrive.

As he drifted in and out of sleep, a dozen men and women silently filed into the room and seated themselves 'round the table. He abruptly stirred himself awake, prompted by an ache in the small of his back, and then realized that something was very wrong here, for he recognized none of the faces staring back at him, and the thirteenth seat of arbitration situate at the head of the table had been occupied by an elderly woman with green-gold eyes peering out from underneath her peasant's hood.

"Who *are* you?" he asked, sitting up straight. "What are you doing here?"

"You engaged the covenant, good sir, as the law doth provide in the canons laid down by Muravyóv and Bathyány," the lady replied, her voice a mere whisper of sound, "and so we have responded, each to our own, emerging from that place where we first found rest, as you yourself may have occasion to judge, o King-To-Be."

As he examined more closely the individuals seated around the great slab of polished ochre wood, it suddenly occurred to him that, despite their evident vitality, none of the mages facing him might actually dwell within the Land of Living Men.

"The just man requires neither judge nor jury to justify his actions," the prince finally replied. "So, why have you come?"

"Why?" she said in her soft voice, the merest shadow of an exhalation. "You ask why? The answer to that question would require a dissertation, princeling, a veritable treatise, an entire volume of words and ideas and notions, and still you would not understand.

"There is no covenant where the law reigns not supreme, over the kings and nobles of the land, over the servants of the state and those whom the state doth serve. We espy a Charybdis lurking within the body politic, a grand discontinuity in the æther which, if left unto its own devices, shall enswallow intact the lands of Nova Europa and all the realms sheltering therein. We feel the crisis come upon us. The men and women and entities inhabiting this vale shall soon be asked and soon be required to voice their 'yeas' and 'nays.' No one shall be exempt.

"And so we return to this place to offer our assistance for the struggle soon to come, knowing that the issue will be closely fought, that the stakes of the game inflate with each day and every hour that passes. A mere scattering of men and women stand now before the gate, guarding the exit and entrance into this place. Swing the aperture one way, and the world turns, perhaps just a nudge, towards God's grace; swivel the door else-wise, however, and thou venturest down that broad and easy way into strife, death, and destruction, where the darkness eats away the hearts of the decent folk who form the very center of our existence."

"But how can one man alter destiny's dictatorship?" Arkády

asked.

"Such answers are beyond our ability to provide," came the reply.

"Then what possible help can you be?" he said. "I didn't ask for this task, and I *surely* didn't request your assistance."

"Oh, but you *will!*" the old woman said, flashing a crooked smile. "You will, dear Arkásha...!"

CHAPTER TEN
"WHAT PROOF DO YOU HAVE?"

"...Arkásha! Arkásha!"

The prince heard the words as from a great distance, and struggled with some difficulty to bring himself back up to the world.

"Arkásha, awake!"

He found himself looking into the familiar, plump face of a woman in her mid-sixties. Her neatly dressed white hair was partially enshrouded with a black-and-gold striped shawl stitched with a *tughra* similar to that etched on his ornate buckle of silver. Hanging from a gold chain around her neck was a small globule of smoky green glass, within whose confines one could espy, if one looked very closely, a slow, swirling movement of smoke or perhaps vapor.

"Auntie!" he said with some evident relief. "Why, why I just had the strangest dream."

"Oh really?" she said. "Well, dearie, Homêros says that dreams are just the visions dispatched to us from God. Of course, I experience such revelations all the time, but nobody pays any attention to *my* visions, save for my little lovies. The dear sweetums, they *always* follow my lead."

Arkády quickly glanced at the ten council members (Mordekaí was missing, he noted) who had now taken their assigned seats at the table, and nodded his head when he recognized them all. Then he recovered himself.

"What did you say?" the prince asked, suddenly realizing

that he had missed part of the conversation.

Without waiting for her reply he turned to the entire council and said: "My father was almost killed tonight, shot with a crossbow bolt to his chest while attending a banquet in Paltyrrha."

Some of the attendees gasped in surprise, but others seemed unaffected by the news. Old Laössoös, slumped in the senior position at the other end of the table, just snored.

"My people blame the Walküri, of course. So my question, Count Zhertán"—he turned his eyes directly to the tall, bald septuagenarian sitting halfway down from him—"is simply this: did King Barnim or his government order this ill-advised assassination attempt?"

"Just one moment, sir," exclaimed Kulmann Graf von Einschlag, a burly, light-complected man in his thirties who represented Lothar King of Franconia.

He sat straight across from Arkády, constantly twirling his long, curled, blond mustachios.

"What proof do you have?" he asked. "What have you shown us? Why, nothing! Nothing at all! To accuse a Teutonic monarch of such crimes without any presentation of evidence whatsoever is certainly unacceptable to me, and also, I suspect, to the other august members of this body."

Zhertán, who represented the kingdom of Pommerelia, held up his right hand.

"It's quite all right, Kulmann," he said. "Prince Arkády has every reason to pose the question, and I invite all of you to test the truth of my reply. This *psairodaktylios* encircling my finger is my bond.

"King Barnim did *not* order an attack and neither did I, and I'm in a position to say that no one else in our government had anything to do with it, at least in an official capacity."

"I didn't really think your people were involved, but I had to ask," the prince said.

"But," Zhertán added, "I would certainly like to know the details, because whoever's responsible is obviously intent on driving us all towards war."

Arkády spent a few moments giving them an account of the attack.

"This entire business has a most curious feel about it," said Philodème Duc d'Albérique, the goateed younger brother of Tancrède II King of Neustria.

"Did you examine the weapon yourself, Arkády?" he asked.

"I did," the prince said. "It's an ordinary crossbow and quarrel. There's no indication of any magical apparatus involved, nor any curse, hex, jinx, or other device or taint that might have been applied."

"But who could have loosed it?" Zhertán said.

"Well, that's just the problem," Arkády said. "The weapon was mounted on one of the great wooden crossbeams over-looking the hall."

"But the ceiling must be, what, fifteen or twenty feet high, at the least?" Metropolitan Euphronios said. He stood in lieu of Autokratôr Dêmêtrios III in Julianople.

"At least," Arkády said. "I don't have an answer, Ephron. One of my soldiers spotted the thing after we'd removed the guests. He reported that the bow was tied to the rafter. There were no obvious footprints or handmarks left on the beam, just minor disturbances in the dust. We also don't know how the thing was aimed or fired. We thoroughly examined each of the guests as they departed, and none could be connected to the incident."

Philodème clucked his tongue. "I wonder, my friends, about the intent here. Surely the attacker knew that the king's physician would be standing by, that medical assistance would be available almost instantly. If they had really wanted to kill him, why not soak the bolt with poison? I think we're being played with."

"Why, indeed?" said Mösza, the *soi-disant* Countess of Rábassy, who represented Harûn Emir of Umm az-Zakkár.

Then she noticed Arkády's expression.

"There's more, isn't there, nephew?" she said.

"Yes, auntie," the prince said. "This is the sixth such attack against King Kyprianos during the last year, each one worse than the last. The first occurred in Faülniß: a cinch broke and the king slipped from his horse, severely bruising his thigh. He was very lucky the leg didn't break. We originally thought this an accident, but later found that the strap had been partially severed.

"This was followed by a series of similar incidents, including the collapse of a wall into the street just before the king arrived at a dedication ceremony in Daphnéa, the loosening of a brick in a stairway used only by the royal family, the toppling of a transit mirror just before the king was scheduled to use it, and so forth."

"I've heard nothing of these events," Zhertán said.

The prince sighed. "We've been able to keep them fairly quiet thus far, although this latest incident cannot be hidden. There's another problem, too. The king is convinced that the person responsible for these assaults is the Dark-Haired Man."

"What?" said Jerzy Count Waledynski of Polónia.

"Absurd," said Kulmann. "The Dark-Haired Man is a myth."

"Perhaps so," Arkády said, "but that's what he believes, and each subsequent attack has just strengthened his conviction. He's also come to identify the Dark-Haired Man with King Barnim, for no reason that anyone can discern. I and several others in the court have tried to move his mind, but nothing that we've said thus far seems to have had any effect. In the past few months, he has begun active preparations for a military campaign in the west. I now think that war is likely."

"If true, this is a misfortune of the highest order," said Zhertán. "Men have forgotten the devastation of the last conflict between Pommerelia and Kórynthia, although I recall it only too well, and how long it took for the Teutonmark to recover from the aftereffects. We simply cannot allow another such test."

"No one here would disagree with you, I think," said Arkády. "But the question remains: how do we stop what's already begun? I have no answers to offer at this wretched time of the night, alas."

CHAPTER ELEVEN
"WHAT DO WE REALLY KNOW ABOUT THE DARK-HAIRED MAN?"

Then he abruptly changed the subject. "What do we really know about the Dark-Haired Man?"

Ancient Laössoös, representing the Lakedaimônian Laconians, finally stirred himself at the other end of the table, slowly raising his eyes.

"*They say*," he said, "that Death snatches even the coward as he flees his every yesterday. *They say*...that man is but a breath and but a shadow, a phantom in time who quickly fades away. *They say*...that Kyprianos will cross the Carpathian Spine to keep his guilt at bay. *They say*...that He waits within us all to capture our souls when we look the other way."

Then he slid back into sleep.

Sayyíd Nur ad-Din ibn Shukr Alláh as-Saíf, a swarthy man of middle years who hailed from the Empty Quarter in southern Araby, but represented the Sharíf Quriyáqus of Libán, spoke up for the first time.

"I hesitate to offer my remarks, kindest of people, for fear of stirring your scorn," he said.

"Oh no, sayyídi," Countess Mösza said, "why of course you should lay bare your mind to us."

"I do thank you, most gracious lady," he said, bowing his head in acknowledgment. "This story that I now relate to you is both my life and my truth.

"During the far-distant years of my youth, such a very long

time ago, I was instructed in the lore by the elder members of my order, Les Gardiens du Saint-Maroún, deep within the Cedar Mountains, and became privy to certain details regarding the founding of our covenant by M. Zéléný, who sought to govern all Psairothi with his law, and, alas, failed in his quest."

He closed his hands together in front of him, as if praying, and bowed his head to the table three times.

"May Alláh give him peace and joy and contentment throughout all of his days. Amen."

"Amen," came the mumbled refrain from around the table.

"As I have said," he said, "I heard many tales of trials and triumphs and tribulations. There dwelt among us in those days an ancient one whom we called Yunús, now long translated unto his greater reward. He told me that after the establishment of the Covenant of Christian Mages, several hundred years ago, certain Psairothi living in the east came to resent what they saw as the interference of the west into *les affaires magiques*, even though that *is* not and *was* not the reason for which the convenant was established.

"These disaffected ones created, he said, an organization which sought in both name and practice to restore the traditions of their own ancestors, and specifically to offset the power and influence of this our council. The members of this group took a vow of secrecy and erected a cadre much like our own, but it was subverted, in his account, by a powerful changer-of-shapes who called himself the 'Dark-Haired Man,' amongst many other appellations. Those who opposed him in the organization were either killed or banished into the darkness.

"Now, how much of this is true and how much just another fancy fable from the *Biblos Moiras Atlantidos*, *The Book of the Fate of Atlantis*, I have no way of knowing; but I now believe that Yunús was himself a descendant of one of those exiled mages. The story made a great impression on me at the time, I must say."

"Just an old wives' tale," Mösza said. "I've heard it myself."

"Ah yes, my dear Mosie, perhaps it is so," said as-Saíf, "and

I should never try to contradict such a beautiful woman as thyself."

He bowed again in her direction.

"But...later I saw something that caused me to reshape my thoughts.

"I do not know how much of this tale I may tell you without violating a confidence," he went on, "and therefore I give it to you with no real names or dates, for you do not need to know them.

"As I progressed upward through the nine degrees of my order, I came increasingly to be trusted by my preceptor, and was sent on missions for the benefit and education of the Christian man. I would travel great distances throughout the eastern realms, carrying messages to and from the mighty potentates of the world and the catholicos-patriarch in Antukhia, or from the latter primate to our own bishops and clergy, leading the fight for Christ in the heathen villages of the Assyri and the Parsi.

"On one such occasion I came upon a member of my order lying near death's door in an oasis some leagues distant from Dabenégora. A cluster of palm trees surrounded a large pool of cool, pure springwater, quite potable although tasting vaguely of sulfur, and I saw ripe dates readily available, not to mention wildfowl clustered about the small lake. Yet my brother was perishing both from hunger and thirst.

"I said to him, 'My poor comrade, what illness is this that has overcome thee?'

"'Alas, effendi,' he said, 'I have bargained with the Dark-Haired Man, but he has wormed his way into my soul and I cannot remove him. Thus must I die unshriven by a priest and unlamented by my kinfolk.'

"'But where?' I asked, for the land was completely vacant to the eye, and I could see no one there.

"'In here,' he said, pointing to his own head."

Nur ad-Din shook his head in sorrow and disbelief.

"Just an hour later, he perished most horribly, his body wracked by convulsions that I could not stop, crying out for a succor that I could not give. And from his gaping mouth there abruptly issued the black body of a deadly scorpion that hissed at me and quickly began to grow in size and strength. And when it had reached the height of a man, it turned to me and said, "'Light of the Faith" you may indeed be named, but one day the Dark-Haired Man shall return to dim that glow.' I have never been more frightened, my friends.

"Then the creature turned from me and strode away rapidly across the desert, vanishing into the sunset. After burying the *corpus* of my brother, I left that place and never returned there again.

"I do not know whether that black thing was real in form, or just a vision rendered by the hot sun and the horror of my comrade's death, but I know that I dug a grave there and put a body into it and a makeshift cross over it, and I saw the tracks in the sand of an escorpion which cannot exist according to our law, and I believe now what it told me. The Dark-Haired Man lives, and we would do well to consider the notion seriously."

"But where lies your proof?" Lady Mösza asked. "And even if real, where dwells he now? We cannot take action, sayyídi, based upon such an account."

"I agree," said Aurora Lady Estavaye, scion of the ancient ruling house of Morënë and the youngest in age of the council members. "You've given us an extraordinary account, but I'm more concerned with the here and now. Pommerelia and Kórynthia may be heading towards war, and this newest attack on King Kipriyán will certainly not help matters. What can we do to slow the rush to arms?"

"More to the point, Rorie," said Mösza, "we have members on this council from both countries. If war does come, the council must surely be split, perhaps irrevocably."

"If there *is* a Dark-Haired Man," the Conde di Corovino said (he represented the Holy See in Ravenna), "and I for one am not yet convinced of his reality, then he and/or this other group may have instigated the attacks on King Kipriyán. Prince Arkády, who gave your father the idea that the Dark-Haired Man was behind all this?"

"I don't really know, Ariosto," said the prince, "although I suspect old Melanthrix, since he seems to be father's only real confidant these days, other than myself. He first appeared in court about the time I was born, but abruptly left after the great earthquake devastated the city two decades ago. I think there was a riot or something at about that time that frightened the man away. We thought him gone for good. Then, not long after the final campaign against the heathens, he returned to court, from God knows where. No one has ever been able to pinpoint his origin.

"You should have seen the stunt that he pulled last night after the attack on father. All sorts of wild prophecies about this and that and the other. Of course, that drunken fool Humfried egged him on."

"Melanthrix, eh?" Zhertán said. "We've discussed him before without reaching any definite conclusions."

Arkády glanced at Mösza.

"Auntie, were you still at court when Melanthrix first arrived?" he asked.

The old woman laughed and threw up her hands, her jowls shaking.

"My goodness, no," she said. "I left Paltyrrha long before that. My brother (your grandfather) and I, well, we just never got along, so finally I moved on. Never asked his permission, either, much to everyone's consternation."

She chuckled again, her big bosoms shaking up and down.

"Besides," she said, "as bizarre as he's been described, our dear old astrologer sounds very much like the figment of someone's imagination."

"I wish he were, auntie, but he has father completely under his spell," Arkády said.

Zhertán rubbed his bald pate and yawned.

"Arkády," he asked, "is Melanthrix close to anyone besides the king?"

The prince thought for a moment before replying.

"I think he's friendly with one of the monks attached to Metropolitan Timotheos and the *Megalê Scholê*," he said.

"Then might I suggest," said the count, "that you seek out this priest, whoever he is, and see if you can determine what Melanthrix knows about these events, or at least what he's been telling your father. You can report back to us at our next gathering, which will be soon, I hope.

"As far as this council is concerned," he said, "if war does come, I must remove myself from it, and I would suggest that Prince Arkadios do the same. You may choose to replace us with others or leave our seats temporarily vacant until the matter is settled. Agreed?"

They murmured their assent.

The chairman of the group, William Lord Eagleton of the Western Isles, glanced around the table, rose in his seat, and spoke for the first time.

"All of us will continue to work for peace in our time," he said. "Now, brethren, let us ponder these events on yet another day. *Pax vobiscum.*"

The prince rose from his seat and made his way to Zhertán's side, where he gave him the kiss of peace.

"And to you, my friend," Arkády said, then looked again at his comrades. "And to all of you."

He abruptly swiveled and left, and was followed in turn by each of his companions. But old Laössoös, waking to find himself abandoned and alone, merely chuckled and kissed his *ka*-ring.

"Oh yes, little one," he said, watching the *daktylios* flare its violet response, "yes and yes again! We shall!"

Then he mouthed an inaudible word, and drifted away into nothingness.

CHAPTER TWELVE
"IMPOSSIBLE!"

"As I was saying, Sire," said Sergeant Poliodór to the assembled members of the Royal Council of Kórynthia, "the bolt is definitely Pommerelian in origin. If you'll look at the way the leathers are attached, here and here"—he held out the quarrel and pointed to the appropriate spot—"you can see that they're notched twice right near the end. That's unique to the weapon shops of Ysherr."

"Bloody Walküres," Prince Kiríll said under his breath.

"What about the crossbow?" asked Prince Arkády, continuing his own examination from the previous evening.

He abruptly tried to stifle a yawn.

"Well, that's what's interesting," the guard said. "See, most crossbows are built so they can be quickly reloaded. The archer puts the weapon bow-down, uses his foot to engage the stirrup, and hooks the bowstring to his belt. Then he pushes down with his foot to cock the bow, which is caught by a trigger, here"—again he pointed—"and he's ready to shoot. In exchange for speed, you sacrifice some accuracy and range. But this piece is really unique. You have to have a special device to rewind it, which makes things go a whole lot slower. On the other hand, it packs much more of a wallop on the receiving end, so to speak, and it's deadly accurate to a far greater distance."

"Who made it?" Arkády asked, posing the question on everyone's mind.

The sergeant pulled the right side of his bushy mustachio into a curl, and shifted in his seat uncomfortably.

"Well, that's a bit of a problem, see? I once saw a bow like this in Érskeburg. Not *quite* the same, mind, but then, I've never come across anything that would match it exactly. Somewhere to the east, I'd say, but I could be wrong."

"The east?" Arkády said. "But I thought you just said that it was made at Ysherr."

"Well, like I said," Poliodór said, "it looks Ysherrian, but there are problems with the fashioning of the bow that point somewhere else. So, I guess I can't really say for sure."

He bowed his head in exasperation.

"How was it shot?" asked Prince Nikolaí, a large, muscular man in his late twenties.

"The bow was carefully secured with leather strips to one of the center rafters," Poliodór said. "The dust was disturbed a bit, but that's all we could see. I don't think the thing was triggered in the traditional way. It was set and cocked sometime before the banquet started, and then set off from a distance."

"Impossible!" everyone said together.

"But how'd he get up there?" Lord Feognóst asked.

Several others tried to interrupt.

King Kipriyán motioned for silence, and then posed a question himself: "What prompted your conclusion, sergeant?"

"Well, Sire," the guard said, "first of all, because we didn't catch anybody who shouldn't have been there. We closed down that hall within seconds of the alarum being given, and I don't see how even a mouse could have escaped from my men. We examined everyone as they left, even your physician.

"Second, well, because of how the bow was set. See, it was meant to be fired just once and once only, and it was aimed right at the place the killer knew you would be standing, Sire. All he had to do was wait until you were there. Why, any Psairothi in court could have released the trip."

"God's teeth!" Nikolaí said. "Then it must have been someone standing with us in the hall."

"There's something else, too, sire," said Poliodór. "We found a trace of some resin-like substance on the bolt. We pricked a few of the servants with it, including a Psairothi. It's not poisonous, and didn't seem to have any other effect that we could see. Maybe it's nothing, but I thought you ought to know."

"Thank you, sergeant," said Gorázd Lord Aboéty, who was chairing the meeting.

He looked around the table.

"Any more questions, gentlemen? Then you may leave, sergeant. Prince Arkády, do you have a report?"

"Thank you, grand vizier," said the prince, glancing down at his jottings. "As the king commanded, I questioned all of the guards present at the banquet last night, and gathered the results of their examinations of the departing guests.

"No weapons were found, the dignitaries having relinquished them before entering the hall. No unusual mental patterns were noted. No trace of the assassin was uncovered. I should also note that one person was not examined, because he could not be found after the festivities."

"Who?" asked the king. "Who dares question my authority?"

"Doctor Melanthrix," Arkády said.

"What!" said the king. "Arkásha, I won't have him accused of this, even by you. I've known the man for almost thirty years, and he's absolutely the last person in the world who would do me harm. In any case, he's certainly had opportunities before this, had he been so inclined."

"Father, I'm not charging him with anything," the prince said. "I'm just reporting the facts. Melanthrix vanished from the hall after his appearance there. He undoubtedly saw something of the events. Shouldn't we at least get his account of what happened at the banquet?"

"The request is reasonable, Sire," Gorázd said. "No man is above your law."

Arkády brushed back a lock of hair, and tried again, more diplomatically this time.

"Perhaps the king could ask Doctor Melanthrix to appear before this council as a personal favor to himself."

Kyprianos looked around the room, but found no support from his councilors for his own position. Finally he sighed.

"Very well. I'm tired, but I'll consent to having Melanthrix called as the final business of this meeting. See to it, Gorázd."

CHAPTER THIRTEEN
"CALL FOR DOCTOR MELANTHRIX!"

"Call for Doctor Melanthrix," said the grand vizier, turning to his assistant.

"Call for Doctor Melanthrix!" said Lord Feognóst, as he opened the council room door.

"Call for Doctor Melanthrix," echoed the refrain from guard to guard down the hall outside, carrying well into the distance.

The council then took a break from its deliberations, several of the older members departing to visit the garde-robes, while others just stretched, yawned, or moved about as they waited. Arkády gazed out through the glazed window at the courtyard, silently lost in contemplation.

They heard the creature before he actually appeared. In the distance, down the hall, came the jingling of chains and bells, a tramping of many feet, and the sound of a low voice chanting words which no one there understood.

"*Iluuu-Ashshuuur-etiluuu-ilaniii*," came the repeated refrain.

And suddenly he was *there!*, standing before them with his robes all aflutter, and they shrank back, every one. He towered well over six feet in height, taller than anyone in the room, but was slender as a reed, with skin preternaturally pale. His lips narrowed into nonexistence. He wore a small diamond embedded in one earlobe, and a silver ring in the shape of a small crescent moon dangling from between the nostrils of his nose. Winding around the middle finger of his right hand was a gold ring carved in the shape of an *ouroboros*, a pair of bright emeralds substituting for its eyes. His robes were aswirl with vivid colors running raucously together without pattern, but neither patched nor sewn together in any way evident to those present. Hanging from his neck were a dozen silver chains to which miniature bells and chimes had been attached; they made ersatz music as he swayed.

Then he stopped cold and became perfectly still; the quiet was almost worse than the racket he had made while in motion. He bowed most elegantly from the waist.

"You called, sire," he said, "and Doctor Melanthrix has appeared."

No one knew what to say. No one had the temerity to break the peace.

Finally, Prince Arkády bestirred himself.

"We thank you, sir, for your kind accomodation. Yesterday, the king my father was almost killed in the Great Hall of the Tighrishi. You were present. What are your impressions of the attack?"

The astrologer smiled or frowned, they were not sure which.

"Yes, my King-to-Be, Doctor Melanthrix was there, entranced by the entertainments which surrounded us."

He swept his long narrow hand in a semi-circle in front of him.

"There was a flash of light from above, and then King Kipriyán was lying on the table. A miracle it was that he survived, a gift from the Great Creator for which we must give our thanks. The king lives, and we are grateful that he lives. That is all that matters to us."

Timotheos Metropolitan of Örtenburg, a burly, bearded man of five-and-sixty years, sat in the patriarch's chair as his deputy.

"You speak to us of God and miracles, Doctor Melanthrix," the churchman said, "but I didn't see you at the thanksgiving mass held this morning in the cathedral, even though I would have expected *you*, of all people, to celebrate the feast of Saint Vasíly the Hierarch. Everyone else in this room was present.

You also weren't available for questioning by the guards last night. Everyone else in this room was willing to be searched. At the banquet you attacked both church and state with your scurrilous rhymes. Everyone else in this room heard them."

"Indeed," several of the councilors agreed.

"Just what is your question, *Sieur* Timofeí?" the astrologer asked.

The metropolitan drew his robes close around him, and put his right hand on the icons of Saint Svyatosláv and Saint Trankvillín which hung around his neck.

"Quite simply, sir, where did you go last night after the banquet?" he asked.

"Out," Melanthrix said, "out of that dark place past the ever-watchful guards. The atmosphere outside was more accomodating, for this warm weather will scarcely last us another day, as you well know. We should all find highly beneficial the inhalation of such air more frequently, and the exercise of one's limbs more regularly."

Timotheos snorted.

"We're not interested in your philosophies, doctor, unless they match those of the one true faith. Why do I never see you at our services?"

The astrologer swayed slightly, jingling his bells.

"Art thou so impoverished that thou canst admit no other ideas than thine own? Does Doctor Melanthrix ask thee to bend thy will to his? No, and not yet, and never. But thou wouldst have him bow and scrape before thee, when he owes allegiance to a higher authority. Let him worry about his immortal soul. Let him ponder his loyalty to his king, which has never been in question, even from such as thee. Let him pass."

"Pah," Timotheos said, "and what about your so-called prophecies? Last night you dared to attack the House of Tighris and the one true church. How can this council ignore your threats?"

Melanthrix started gurgling, but it was a moment before the rest of the councilors realized he was laughing.

"You will pardon me, Sire," he said, trying to catch his

breath, "for this breach of etiquette.

"Gentle *sieurs*, if a man reaches into the air and pulls forth a raven, so"—and a black bird appeared suddenly in his open hand—"this may be true magic or it may be a simple trick. But if he does not tell you how he did the trick, is it not still a form of magic?"

The bird flew up, circled around and 'round, and then darted through the open doorway as Feognóst quickly cracked it open.

"The future," the astrologer said, "is like a river full of water, constantly moving and flowing and changing, even as one watches. One may catch a glimpse of an instant in time, and have some sense of whether the river is flooding or slack, of whether the water is pure or clouded, of whether great trunks are being swept rapidly downstream or whether the flow is tranquil enough to row upriver for a bit. He who peers into the future does so at great peril, for he may step too close to the bank and be swept away himself.

"Now, as to whether these small prognostications are true or not," Melanthrix said, "let history judge, as it has always judged them before."

The mage cupped his hands and breathed into them, molding something hidden between, spitting on it and kneading it like a loaf of bread. He then released an iridescent bubble swirling with color that floated away above the council table.

"Look, then, *sieurs*, and see your own destinies, if you have the courage to do so."

As the oily, roiling sphere passed each person in turn, he could see the images flowing on the surface, pieces of the events in his life that might or might not come true. When the object approached the king sitting at the far end of the table, Kipriyán suddenly turned white and shrank back from the globus with a shriek, his hands raised to ward off whatever it was he saw there.

"Enough of that," said the Archpriest Athanasios, the council scribe, abruptly puncturing the bubble with his quill.

With an audible "pop," the sphere disappeared.

But when the council members turned their attention back towards the door, Doctor Melanthrix was gone, leaving no sign that he had ever been present. Lord Feognóst questioned the two men standing guard outside in the hall, but they reported no one leaving the room. Prince Arkády proposed that a warrant of arrest for the soothsayer be issued at once by the High Council, but King Kipriyán immediately objected.

"I have to know," he kept saying, "I have to know."

Finally the prince adjourned the proceedings on behalf of his father.

"Arkásha," they heard the monarch mumble as he was being led out of chambers, "Arkásha, I'm so tired, I'm so very tired, boy."

CHAPTER FOURTEEN
"A SPARROW ALONE
UPON THE HOUSE TOP"

That same afternoon the Archpriest Athanasios went to the Hanging Garden of Queen Landizábel to read his breviary, as was often his wont. The garden sprawled across the roof of the residential part of the Royal Palace, rising in slow, gentle tiers from its lowest point in the west to the place where the wing attached itself to the multi-storied central core.

The roof had been covered with soil, irrigated, and then planted some four centuries earlier by King Tarás I to assuage the homesickness of his eighth wife, who had been accustomed to a climate in which the vegetation remained verdant all year 'round. Plants had been brought from her native Tuscania and many other lands, and the small patch kept warm and fertile with a localized weather spell that was renewed weekly.

Athanasios found a tranquility here that he had known in just one other place in his life. There was something to be said for warm breezes, the smell of freshly-cut flowers, and the presence of growing things. He thought back upon the garden of his youth, that refuge that had given him so much pleasure, and he sighed. All of those whom he had known there were gone now, save only for two, including he who had been like a father to him.

Of all the places within the Hanging Garden, that which pleased him most was the small maze situate at its center. It was not truly a maze, if one understood the thing, for it followed the shape of the Tighris *tughra*, winding 'round and 'round itself until reaching its own conclusion at the middle of the muddle. There, surrounded by hedges, was a small grotto, called by some "Land's End," after the queen who had designed it, complete with stone benches protected from the sunlight by the overhanging shrubbery, and a statue of the monarch herself reading from a book of her own poems. She was not an especially pretty woman, but the sculptor had captured in her face a sensitivity, a gentleness, that moved one even at several centuries' distance.

Here the words of God made sense, here the world was an ordered place where every man knew who and what and where he was, here one could think and reason with the dæmons of the world.

Of all the scripture, he loved the *Psalms* the best.

"He that dwelleth in the secret place of the most High shall abide under the shadow of the Almighty.... Thou shalt not be afraid for the terror by night; nor for the arrow that flieth by day."

And again: "I watch, and am as a sparrow alone upon the house top."

There were always things like that, little pithy sayings, that a man of wisdom, of deliberation, could apply to his own life, or use to help others.

"I am fearfully and wonderfully made," he read aloud.

But who *made me?* he thought, *other than God, of course*, he added, quickly crossing himself out of respect. *And why am I so consumed by this quest? I must find some measure of peace.*

He returned to his book. His reveries were interrupted by a trod of a foot along the pathway to the interior.

"Arik Rufímovich!" he said with affection.

"Afanásy Ivánovich. *Pax tecum*," the older man said, embracing his friend and kissing him on both cheeks. "I thought I might find you here."

"I was just thinking about the old days," the archpriest said, "of the challenges we faced together, of the joys and sorrows, of the abbey and the *Scholê*. They've been good years, for the most part."

"And for me as well," Arik said. "I think you've been more of a son to me than any child I might have sired during the great war."

The archpriest looked up quickly.

"A child?" he said. "Is there any possibility that one actually exists?"

The older man smiled.

"Well, friend Afanásy, before I became a priest, before I had professed any vows, I was a very ordinary person with ordinary desires, I'm afraid."

The cleric sat down heavily on the bench near Athanasios.

Afanásy put down his book.

"I'm always interested in hearing about the old times from someone who was actually there," he said. "Please, tell me again about your adventures then."

CHAPTER FIFTEEN
"WHAT BECAME OF MY MOTHER?"

Arik Rufímovich gazed into the eyes of the Queen's statue and reflected upon the past.

"My father, Rufím Katúnovich," he said, "belonged to the landed gentry. He had a small estate and orchard in lower Nördmark, all of which my elder brother Armén eventually inherited, although that's another story. So it was either the church for me, or the soldier's life.

"In the twenty-first year of King Makáry I I took the hundred gold staters that my father gave me as my due, and bought myself a commission in the King's Own Guards. Thus I became *Lieutenant* Arik Rufímovich."

The older man smiled.

"Now I suppose that you would think me a very foolish boy indeed in those far-off days, but I had ambitions then. I saw my commission as a pathway to fame, riches, status, lands, even a title. All I had to do was to please my superiors and learn how to kill most efficiently, and I found within myself the ability to do both. So I rose very quickly in the ranks when war actually broke out. I managed to attach myself to Hereditary Prince Néstor's personal squad, *Les Gardes Élites*, as it was known in society, and I thought I had found the perfect spot.

"You see, we got the best of everything," Arik said, "the finest mounts, the newest weapons, the shiniest armor, and, of course, the prettiest women, who followed us around like puppies looking for a new home. Soon I came to regard this special treatment as no more than appropriate to one of my exalted status.

"In those days I was callow and ever willing to seek pleasure in the most superficial ways, and I cut a very handsome profile back then, with a full head of curly hair and my smart military uniform."

His face clouded.

"Then the war began in earnest. Prince Ezzö the Elder and Kazimir his heir were determined to take back Pommerelia, and together with Prince Néstor, they persuaded King Makáry to support them. That was a black day in the history of Kórynthia, let me tell you.

"Oh, things went well enough at first. King Michael of Pommerelia was killed outright, and we thought in our arrogance that we'd won it all. I think we would have, too, if God hadn't laughed at our complacency. As we gamboled madly south towards Balíxira, suddenly the winter storms came rushing in, a month too early, and near froze us all to death."

He paused to wipe a tear away on his sleeve.

"Many a good man perished on that plain, and not from fighting any battle, either. The following spring King Makáry resupplied the Forellës with arms and mercenaries, and so we tried again. Then came Dürkheim, where King Barnim, Michael's successor, fooled us all, and killed Makáry and Néstor and Kazimir too.

"Somehow we managed to retreat to Borgösha, where we were determined to revenge our friends' deaths. The following summer our enterprise failed when Count Vandorf, Ezzö's new commanding general, perished at the Battle of Audergrimm, and most of his army with him. Afterwards, Ezzö took his own life rather than be captured. Borgösha promptly capitulated, and we survivors were taken hostage. A few months later I was paroled to my family's estate, where I found my father dead and my brother less than hospitable. I was sick to death of all the killing, so I resigned my commission and joined the Silent Souls."

"Did you ever meet my father?" the younger man asked.

Arik smiled fondly and shook his head.

"We've been over that ground before, Afanásy. Even if I hadn't given my most solemn oath to keep silent, a *geas* was placed on my soul that keeps me ever from responding. All that I *can* say, all that I'm *allowed* to say, is that your father died fighting bravely in the war, before you were born, and that your mother, as much as she loved you, was prevented by circumstance from keeping you herself, and so placed you lovingly with the church."

"What became of my mother?"

"Well, that one I *can* answer," Arik said. "I honestly don't know. I have not seen her or heard tell of her in a very long time."

"Then she could still be alive. Why were *you* chosen to bring me to Saint Svyatosláv's?" Afanásy asked.

A shadow appeared on Arik's face.

"Why pursue this now? These people have all passed into the dustbin of history, friend Afanásy."

"It's hard to explain, Father," the younger man said. "You have a family. Knowing what you know about yourself, you can choose to embrace or reject your past. My parents are unknown to me. I don't know why they left me without an identity, or what they were like, or how or why I came to be. Without a name—my *real* name—without a beginning point to my life, I drift like a boat without oars upon a sea of uncertainty. What's old history to you is my entire life to me."

"You must place your trust in Almighty God," Arik said. "*He* should be the central axis of your life. *He* must be the identity that you give yourself. You already have a name. It was lent to you by God's agent here on earth."

The older man rested his hand on the archpriest's shoulder, and then said: "Athy, there are questions that should not be asked, and answers that should not be heard. Trust me when I tell you that this is one of them."

"I *do* trust you, Father," Afanásy said, "and I pray for His guidance constantly. But I have a hollowness within that demands a response, Arik. Try as I might, I can't let this issue go. I'm truly sorry."

The metropolitan sighed and rose from his seat.

"Then you must do what you must, my son," Arik said.

He traced the sign of the cross over his pupil.

"May God grant you the wisdom to go with whatever knowledge you find. Now, my limbs grow stiff, Athy, and I must walk a bit before suppertime. I'll see you, I trust, at evening prayers."

And he left Afanásy wondering, not for the first time, if Arik Rufímovich had been his biological father as well as his spiritual one.

CHAPTER SIXTEEN
"YOU SAID THE KING WAS SICK?"

The Archpriest Athanasios had returned again to his breviary when he heard a child's voice nearby. It sounded as if she were talking to someone. He looked up and abruptly shut his book with a small clap of thunder.

"La-ti-dah, la-ti-day," he heard, "let's all go run away."

She suddenly came skipping around the corner of the maze, and when he saw who it was, he immediately jumped to his feet.

"Princess Grigorÿna," he said, bowing to the seven-year-old firstborn child of Prince Arkády.

"Oh!" she said. "Oh, my! I didn't know anyone was here."

Her head darted back and forth 'round the grotto.

"I'm not supposed to be here, you know. Papá says I shouldn't play in the maze, 'cuz I get lost easy, but I didn't get lost today, did I?"

Then she noticed the archpriest was still standing.

"Oh, you can sit, now, sir, if you please. You haven't introduced yourself very properly, you know."

"I'm the hieromonk Archpriest Athanasios Hokhanêmsos apo Sbiatoslabou," he said. "I teach at the *Megalê Scholê* and I also work as grammateus for your grandfather, the king."

"Papá says Grandpapá is sick," she said, plopping down on the bench opposite, next to the image of the queen, "and I can't play with him today, 'cuz he needs his rest, and I'm not to disturb him, neither, so I have to go outside to play."

She cuddled a rag doll to her chest.

"This is my friend, Milady Louisa. She says that Grandpapá is very mad about something, and that makes everyone else mad, too. Mamá always says we have a 'wery trézhik fämlyi,' but I don't know what that means, and Ouisa doesn't, either. Do you, Athy...Athynaysus?"

The archpriest smiled broadly.

"I think so, Princess Grigorÿna, but I don't think it's anything that you need to worry about. You can call me Athy, if you'd like, since you're a princess."

"And you can call me Rÿna, at least when we're alone."

She abruptly jumped up.

"Of course, in company you must still call me 'Princess....'"

"Of course," Athanasios said.

"...'Cuz that's the proper thing to do, and I have to learn how to do everything 'proper,' that's what Mamá says, even when I don't want to. Someday I'll marry and have children, and then I'll have to go away, just like she did from *her* Mamá and Papá. Sooomedaaay...."

She started to leak tears down her ruby red cheeks.

"There, now, we mustn't cry," said Athy, brushing the moisture away. "That's such a long, long time from now. Where are all your friends?"

She suddenly brightened up again.

"Oh, they're just boys. They don't know anything. 'Sides, Ari is sick all the time, so he can't play very much, and Siggy's just a little brat, and I don't like him. My sister Mellie is too little, she's only two. No one else wants to play with me."

"I'll play with you, Rÿna, or just sit and talk, if that's what you'd like," said the archpriest.

"I'd like that, Athy," the princess said.

She sat back down again, and smoothed her dress.

"Now, what shall we talk about?" she asked.

Athanasios put his book down on the bench.

"You said the king was sick?"

The princess nodded her head, her reddish-golden curls dangling across her brow.

"Well, that's what Papá said. He said Grandpapá's hyu-some-thing were out of place, that he just wasn't making any 'cents.' I didn't understand what they were saying. Then old Melánty came in and made him feel good again."

"You mean Doctor Melanthrix?" the archpriest asked.

"That's what I said," she said. "He's always around, but I don't mind, 'cuz he gives me sweets, and then he tells me things. If he's not talking to Grandpapá, he's helping Arión with his pains. Ari tries not to cry, he tries real hard, Athy, but his joints hurt so much, I know, 'cuz he tells me. He does try to be 'a proper little prince' just like Papá wants. Siggy just laughs. He's mean."

"You said Melánty tells you things?" Athanasios said.

She hunched down and put on her serious face.

"Oh yes, he tells me *lots* of things, just me, even though no one believes me. He said Papá has to go away soon to fight in a war, but he'll be OK. He said Ari and Siggy and Mellie will all have to go away some day, and then I'll be all by myself again, until Nesty is born, whoever he is. He told my fortune, and said I was a lucky little girl, but he wouldn't tell me anything else except that the lines on my hand were kinda short, so I guess that's pretty good. He said I'll be happy most of the time. I know Papá doesn't like him, but he's always real nice to me. I don't think he has many friends to talk to."

"I like him, too," said Athy.

She sat up as an idea came into her head.

"He even talked 'bout you once, Athy," she said. "I 'member now. He said you were a good man, 'better than he was,' and he said you were better than he de...deserfèd, I think. He said you would be what, what he couldn't be. I don't know what he means."

"I don't know, either," the archpriest said with a grin.

"But he said you had been real good to him, and you and me were 'the only two friends he had.'"

She beamed.

"So I guess you must be my friend, too."

Then they heard someone calling in the distance, "Rÿna, Rÿna."

"That's Papá," she said, jumping up. "I've got to go now. Bye."

She ran over and kissed Athy on the cheek, smiled, and said, "Friends?" before running off down the path.

Athanasios sat there bemused, wondering what sprite had been sent by the angels to brighten his day, before returning to his breviary.

CHAPTER SEVENTEEN
"I THINK IT WAS
QUEEN LANDIZÁBEL"

The archpriest was contemplating another passage—"We have left undone those things which we ought to have done; and we have done those things which we ought not to have done"—when he became aware that someone else was approaching through the maze. He rose to his feet immediately when he saw who it was.

"Your highness," he said, bowing deeply.

Prince Arkády smiled, and quickly motioned the priest back to his seat.

"I just wanted to thank you, father, for watching out for my little girl," he said. "Sometimes she gets lost in this maze, but she likes the adventure, so I thought I might find her here."

Athanasios smiled in turn.

"I actually think it's Queen Landizábel," he said, pointing to her image, "who watches over us all. And Almighty God, of course, always Him. I am just His humble servant."

"Do you mind if I sit?" asked the prince, taking his place on a nearby bench. "So much has been going on these last two days that I've scarcely had a moment to catch my breath. What did you think of our council meeting today?

"I think our friend Melanthrix was having his fun again," the archpriest said, putting down his book, "even though nobody seemed to appreciate the joke. They mostly just fear him."

"But not you," Arkády said.

Athanasios grinned again in acknowledgment.

"No, not me, but then, I've seen a side of him that few people seem to know. He's really quite harmless, once you understand how he thinks."

The prince arched and stretched his back, passing his hand over his head in evident weariness.

"Do you mind if I ask you a personal question?" he said.

The priest hesitated for a moment before replying.

"That would depend, Highness, on the question," Athanasios said.

"Of course," Arkády said. "I hope you don't find this too intrusive, but I'd really like to know how you and Melanthrix first met."

"That's easily answered, sir," the cleric said. "I was about twelve when I was brought to court, or actually to the *Scholê*, to be educated for the church and later for the king's service. When I was presented to King Kyprianos for the first time, Doctor Melanthrix was already on hand, although but recently come, as I later understood. He looked much the same then as he does today.

"My master, Arik Rufímovich, traveled widely on the king's business during the early years of the war with the northerners, and he sometimes left me at Saint Theophanês's Abbey in Paltyrrha. During that time, I deliberately made the acquaintance of Doctor Melanthrix, thinking that I might learn something useful from him.

"When I was about seventeen, the doctor was almost killed in a riot near Kórynthály, and he left court, returning thereafter only when the king was present in Paltyrrha, which was not much during those years. He saved my life during the great earthquake, when I was trapped by falling *débris* in the cathedral. Somehow, although he had then been long absent from the capital, he suddenly appeared and lifted the wreckage off my legs. I still don't know how he knew of my distress, but I believe that I would have been crippled or worse if he hadn't found me in time."

The prince's attention was caught by a beetle trying to pull itself through the tall grass near his feet.

"I'm a little concerned, Father Athanasios, about the effect that Doctor Melanthrix is having on the king. He now listens to no one else. And these attacks...."

The insect reached the pathway, and began walking more rapidly toward its destination. Suddenly a large spider popped out of the ground, grabbed it from behind, and began wrapping it in silk.

By this time the archpriest had also noticed the drama being enacted before them.

"Surely you don't think Melanthrix had anything to do with them?"

"Of course not," Arkády said, still watching the beetle, "but you'll admit that he's very strange, not at all Psairothi. And because of this, there are those at court who would very much like to see him gone. Very permanently gone. He doesn't help matters any by his attitude."

The arachnid daintily began her feast.

Athanasios nodded his agreement.

"I know. I've tried to talk to the man, but he won't listen to me. Even after the mob came for him, when he barely escaped with his life, he wouldn't pay attention.

"'Be careful,' I'd say, 'be more politic,' and he'd just laugh and quote from the classics, saying that 'the longest-lived and the shortest-lived man, when they come to die, lose one and the same thing.' He has no fear for his own life."

"Why does he persist in pushing people to their limits?" asked the prince.

"I wish I could answer that," the archpriest said. "At times he seems so wise to me, so knowledgeable about past and future, so immersed in things not of this world, that he scarcely has time for the present, and certainly no patience for anyone who doesn't share his vision. I know that something drives him, possesses him almost, but I don't know what it is. All I know is that he has ever treated me kindly and with great affection."

"*My* concern," said Arkády, leaning forward on his bench, "must be the well-being of king and country. When the king sneezes, the country catches cold. Much is happening now, as you may have noticed, not all of it good. We can't afford to have the æther disturbed while these actions are underway. The enterprise itself could be jeopardized. Do you understand?"

"Oh yes, Highness," the priest said.

"Then I hope you'll convey that message to him," Arkády said. "I have just one other question, father. If Melanthrix isn't Psairothi, what is he?"

Athanasios paused a few moments before responding. He was growing weary of this game.

"I think you would have to ask Doctor Melanthrix that question himself, Highness. The only answer that I can give is the obvious one: he's a man like you and me, with the same feelings, desires, and yes, failings as the rest of us. He deserves neither your pity nor your fear, but your respect."

"Thank you for your candor, archpriest," said the prince, "and for your service to the state. Might I have your blessing before I go?"

Then he suddenly dropped to his knees before the priest of God.

The startled cleric was taken aback by the gesture, but his ingrained training quickly took over, and he gave his benediction willingly, suddenly adding at the end: "May God grant you the wisdom of Solomon, for there will come a time when you will need it."

CHAPTER EIGHTEEN
"THE ÆTHER IS STIRRING"

After the prince had departed, Athanasios returned to his breviary, wondering why he had uttered precisely those words. It was near the dinner hour before he closed his book for good, and stretched his arms. He was rising to leave "Land's End" when a rustling of the leaves behind him made him jump, and he turned to find the stooped form of Doctor Melanthrix emerging from the shadows. He slowly grew to his full height right before him.

"Friend Melánty," the priest said, "you gave me quite a start. What brings you here?"

The astrologer took his place on the bench beneath the queen's statue, inadvertently crushing the spider and her dinner with his heel.

"Melanthrix's name was taken in vain, so he thought to join the game. You've had quite a busy afternoon, my boy."

Only Melanthrix still called the forty-year-old archpriest a boy.

"I thought to find some peace here," Athanasios said, "but every time I discover a new and interesting verse, someone else wanders by."

"And you don't find that significant, Athy?" asked the philosopher.

He then pulled a ripe apple from inside his cloak, quite out of season at this time of year, twisted it into halves between his long alabaster fingers, and gave one piece to the priest.

"Everything is connected, you know," he said, gesticulating with his arms to emphasize the point. "Sometimes those bindings are obvious, sometimes they're not. It's rather like this fruit"—he displayed the core and black pips quivering in his palm—"By the simple sharing of this apple, we strengthen the bonds between us, we build connections to the tree that bore it, we touch the earth that nurtured it, we pay homage to the orchardmen who tended it, we bow our heads to the bees which polinated the glorious flower which became, yes, the ripened fruit."

The philosopher suddenly scattered the seeds to the wind, then began rubbing his hands together, muttering a few words to himself, and smiling as several of the pips abruptly sent green, wavering shoots right up through the earth. Athanasios was pleased with the trick.

"Perhaps a hundred years from now, when the king of Kórynthia is just a boy, he'll pick an apple from the tree we've made together, and be nourished by it. There are no accidents, Athy. At this time and in this place, *you* are the nexus around which the world is revolving. Don't look for 'why' so much as 'who.'"

A cool breeze began ruffling the rapidly increasing sprouts.

"The æther is stirring. Listen to it, feel it, open your mind to it. If you try, you can sense all of the great things rushing in upon us. Give us the right fulcrum, my boy, and we can leverage even the world. Do you see?"

Athanasios shook his head in weariness.

"I don't understand, Melánty. Sometimes it seems to me as if I'm about to grasp whatever it is you're saying, and then it just slips away. Why can't you speak more plainly? Why me?"

The philosopher laughed.

"Firstly, my boy, because that's not the role of old Melanthrix in the grand design. He's growing a bit ancient, you know, and his course is nearly run.

"Secondly, because you are who you are. A year ago, a year from now, you might not have been part of this working.

"Thirdly, because you must learn at your own pace. You can only apply the lessons of life when you're ready to face who and what you are.

"Do you remember," the astrologer said, "when you tried to teach us the game of *les échecs*? You showed us the relative values of each piece and how they moved, and when we pointed out that 'La Reine' seemed a far more powerful piece than 'Le Roi,' who was very weak, you made what we thought then, and still think now, was a most potent observation. Do you recall what it was?"

"I confess not," the archpriest said.

Melanthrix pointed a wavering ivory finger right between his eyes.

"You said, my dear child, that without the king, there *was* no chess, for the whole object of the game was to *kill him*. Melanthrix has never forgotten that lesson, and he learnt it from you. He knew then that you would one day cut a slice of wisdom to go with the bread of your life, and that you might just survive the experience with a modicum of understanding of what was happening around you.

"Most people are pawns in the game of life, Athy. They'll follow their leader anywhere, even when that individual hasn't the faintest idea of where in the world he's going. They'd follow him to perdition's edge if he took them there. Doctor Melanthrix decided early that he didn't want to be someone else's pawn, to be moved around the board at another's whim, and he made his choices accordingly.

"These 'great men' and their 'great councils,' *pshaw!*, they look upon us like so many sheep ready for the slaughter, if they regard us at all. They make their gestures like those *maîtres grands des échecs*, scarcely giving a thought to the feelings of their pieces. And if a few of their subjects should be injured or killed, or even more than a few, well, so what! They're just so many odd tokens to be removed from the board, to be cast away with no other thought than the grand design. And then it's on to another game. These games must end, Athy, before our grandmasters destroy their very boards, and us along with them."

Athanasios shook himself.

"I still don't understand what you mean. Who *are* you, Melánty? One of my visitors asked me that question, and I didn't know how to reply."

Doctor Melanthrix smiled broadly, and pierced the archpriest with his piercing blue eyes.

"Your true friend, Athy, at least that. And also your teacher, if you allow us that honor. And perhaps, should God or fate grant us this one last boon, your protector as well. The game has truly begun. We don't think that many of the pieces will be left standing on the board when the king has finally been checked and mated."

The emerald eyestones in the astrologer's signet ring suddenly reflected a ray from the declining sun, flashing its green light directly into Athy's eyes and temporarily blinding him. When he looked up again, Doctor Melanthrix was gone, vanished as mysteriously as he had arrived.

All that echoed of his presence in the garden was the encrushed, intermingled carcasses of beetle and spider, intertwined now into an unrecognizable mass. Already the ants were beginning to feast on the delicious remains.

CHAPTER NINETEEN

"THE AMBASSADOR PLENIPOTENTIARY OF POMMERELIA AND THE COURT OF SAINT WARTISLAV"

In the latter part of January, on the Feast of Saint Sávva of the East, an emissary from the Court of Rabestadt in Pommerelia was formally received in Paltyrrha. During the previous week he had been pulled up the Paltyrrh River from the Blackish Sea with the king's permission, disembarking on the day previous at the *Quai de Saint-Basile*, and spending the night there on his own ship, the *Lorette*. In mid-morning he rode in the king's carriage of state up the *Avenue du Saint-Constantine*, flanked by an escort of the Royal Guard, bared *kiliçs* held up smartly in their right hands in formal salute. He was presented at court by the Hankyárar of Konyály, Tivadar Zsitvay, who sonorously recited the ancient formula:

"My Lord King, there cometh before you the Ambassador Plenipotentiary of Pommerelia and the Court of Saint Wartislav, Widdekin von Lorestan, Hereditary Count Körvö, Graf von Elsevarr, Baron du Haut-Repère and Chanutierre, Conservateur of the Duchy of Morënë, Lord High Admiral and Guardian of the Three Rivers, Master of Ünterziebött, who craveth present audience. What say you, milord?"

"We will entertain the Ambassador from Pommerelia," Kyprianos said.

He looked rested and fit, sitting upright on his obsidian throne in the Great Hall of Tighrishály Palace. On his head sat the plain beaten gold crown of his ancestors, unadorned by jewels. His long gray beard was curled, and his hair plaited to either side of his face, hanging in locks down past his ears, one of which was nicked along the upper edge from an old war wound. The years of home life had added gravity to his middle, but he still sported massive muscles in his arms, the result of daily workouts with sword, spear, shield, and bow-and-arrow. He was covered in a simple white mantle trimmed in purple; his tunic, where it showed in front, was emblazoned with the image of the crouched tiger symbolizing his house. In his right hand he held the long ivory staff of his office, carved with intricate cuneiform designs winding up the shaft.

Widdekin, the eldest surviving son and heir of Zhertán Count Körvö, was an imposing man of some forty years of age. Tall and slim, he bore the unmistakable aura of authority wrapt about him like a cloak, as he strode boldly up the center aisle, looking neither left nor right, a rolled piece of parchment tucked in a leather case under his left arm. On his right side marched his eldest son and heir, Lord Ákos, nineteen years of age, and immediately to his left Lord Tibor, eighteen months junior to his brother; and behind him trailed his entourage, a dozen courtiers, advisors, and guards.

Ten yards in front of the king he bowed, successively, to King Kipriyán, Queen Polyxena, Hereditary Prince Arkády, Patriarch Avraäm, and to the Great Sword of State mounted on the wall behind the throne. Then he pulled out his message, and began reading in a loud, penetrating voice that carried unto the farthest reaches of the hall:

"Barnim III, King of Pommerelia, Overlord of Morënë, Nisyria, Ptolemaïs, and Mährenia, Lord of the Prüffenmark, sends greetings unto his brother, Kyprianos III King of Kórynthia.

"*Cher Cousin*:

"We were dismayed to receive your *communiqué* of Marymass, in which you did threaten us and our kingdom with force if we did not accede to your unlawful demands. We have also been apprised of your alliance with the Duke of Mährenia, a union that threatens the longstanding peace between the three realms.

"Sirrah, we must tell you that this proposed affiliation of family between your son and the Kürbisci heir cannot stand, seeing that it would forever alter in your favor the balance of force in the Teutonmark.

"Excepting that one issue, however, we are willing to meet with you on neutral territory, at a time of your own choosing, to seek some middle place on which our grievances can be settled without war. Let us not go hastily onto the battlefield.

"I call upon you to heed the words of our ancestor, the great King Tighris of revered memory, who on his deathbed reminded his heirs of the scripture, saying: 'Blessèd are the peacemakers, for they shall be called the children of God.' He spoke wisely, my brother, and we would both do well do honor his words.

"But if you cannot find a place within your heart that cries out for peace, be advised that we will defend our lands, our peoples, and our rights, even unto the last valley and farm, as we have done so rigorously in the past, to the great and enduring distress of the nobles and the people of Kórynthia. Do not allow the lies of the Forellës to lead you down this unholy path.

"We entrust this message to our beloved cousin, the Hereditary Count Körvö, another scion of the great House of Tighris, who speaks with our voice, and to whom you may entrust your response.

"We have spoken.

"By our hand and under our seal, on the Feastday of Saint Lorenz the Abbot, in this, the XLIIIrd year of our reign.

Barnimus Tertius Rex."

Widdekin rolled up the parchment, put it back in its case with a flourish, and stepped forward with his sons to hand it to the king, who graciously bent down to receive it.

Suddenly there was a loud shout of "Stop!" and a man rushed forward from the group of courtiers and princes clustered to the left of the throne, brandishing a naked sword.

Widdekin instinctively jumped back, pulling his son Åkos with him and throwing him to safety off to one side, as the weapon cleaved the spot where they both had just been standing. Chips scattered from the black-and-white tile squares as they were struck by the sword's tip. The defenseless ambassador tried to retreat once more, but tripped over one of his own aides, falling heavily to the floor.

Lord Tibor pulled a stiletto from his belt and stepped forward to defend his father, waving it in front of him over his sire's outstretched body.

"Noooo!" shouted Widdekin, as the heavier blade hewed through the boy's limb like a branch being trimmed from a tree. The knife went rattling and spinning across the floor, coming to rest against the elegantly encased foot of Antónia Lady Vydór. Tibor's hand and arm fell to the floor as he collapsed sideways across his father, his blood spurting like a fountain over Widdekin's disbelieving face.

As the assailant raised his arm to strike a final fatal blow against the ambassador and his son, Prince Arkády grabbed a spear from the left hand of a nearby guard, and in one smooth motion, and without any conscious attempt to aim the weapon, launched it down the aisle at the broad back of the attacker. There was a noticeable thud that echoed dully throughout the hall. Time seemed to stop as the bloody greatsword remained poised at its highest arc for one long moment. Then it clattered noisily to the tile, bouncing several times, and the killer dropped wordlessly across the tumbled bodies of his victims, dead as he hit the floor, his heavy weight driving the protruding spearhead deep into Lord Tibor's back. Lady Vydór daintily bent down, retrieved the stiletto, wrapped it in a napkin, and tucked it up her sleeve.

Arkády immediately took charge.

"Nicky!" he shouted, "remove the king and queen to their chambers, and take some guards with you.

"Captain Fösse! Seal the hall: no one may leave without being searched.

"Zack! Find the king's physician. We need him right now."

Then the prince ran to the bloody mess piled in front of him, but was stopped by the outstretched swords and knives of the Hereditary Count's retainers.

"Let him be," came the faint voice of Widdekin from underneath the pile, and the guards backed off.

Arkády and his brother Prince Kiríll mentally probed the bodies, quickly determining that both the assailant and the boy were already dead. They lifted the heavy body of the assassin to one side, gently disengaging it from the younger man's lifeless corpse.

"My God," said Kiríll, "it's Dolph!"

Little echoes of horror skipped their way from person to person down the hall, like pale moths fluttering futilely against a windowpane.

"I felt their spirits being welcomed into Heaven," said Widdekin. "The man didn't know what he was doing. In his mind's eye he saw me holding a poisoned blade and thought he was protecting his king. Oh dear God! My boy, my poor luckless boy. Whatever shall I tell his mother?"

Tears began furrowing down his cheeks as he gathered the body to his bosom, and rocked back and forth in his grief.

"Whatever shall I tell my dear Ivana?"

A scream added to the chaos as a woman pushed her way

through the milling crowd. Arkády saw his Aunt Teréza crying and tearing at her garments as she ran forward, and stepped to intercept her.

"Dolphie!" she wailed. "My son, my little son, what have they done to you? Arkásha, why have you taken my boy from me? Ezzö! Oh God, I think he's dead. *Ezzzööö!*" she screamed again, and collapsed unconscious into Arkády's arms.

When a pale King Humfried came rushing up, Arkády had him take his mother to her rooms.

Metropolitan Timotheos offered to administer the last rites, his aide hovering at his side. To the Hereditary Count, he merely asked, "May I?" and when Widdekin nodded his head, quietly and reverently began his office. He motioned Athanasios to do the same with Prince Adolphos.

There was a moment when the stark horror of the scene threatened to overwhelm Arkády's tightly-guarded emotions. He realized suddenly that he had just murdered his first cousin, that that same cousin had just violated the holy sanctity of the embassy. Had the world gone utterly mad? The prince walled such notions away in one corner of his mind, willing himself to continue functioning in spite of what had just happened. He would deal with the consequences later.

Arkadios took Fra Jánisar Cantárian aside when he finally arrived.

"There's nothing more you can do for these two," he said, "but there's something you can do for *me*. I want to know why Dolph acted as he did. Find a Psairothi who's experienced in necroprobing, and have him search through the count's mind, looking for anything out of the ordinary. This is wholly unlike the man. He had no imagination, indeed, scarcely any wits at all. He was harmless. What happened to make him a murderer and violator of truces? I want some answers. Preferably by this afternoon," he added.

"Highness, I don't think it can be accomplished that quickly," said the doctor.

"*Try!*" the prince thundered.

"Yes, sir. I'll have a report ready for this afternoon's council meeting," Jánisar said.

As soon as Athanasios had finished annointing the dead assassin's lifeless body, the physician corralled several guards, who took the *corpus* away.

Ambassador Widdekin had finally staggered to his feet, being helped by his eldest son, Count Åkos. The Hereditary Count's green-and-silver tunic was covered with rusty brown blotches. He had aged ten years in an hour.

"He'd just turned eighteen," Widdekin said, gazing down at the body of his younger son. "He attained his majority three weeks ago, and begged me to take him along. Whyever did I listen?"

He struggled to regain his composure, and then said to the prince: "We will return to the *Lorette* and await your response there. We sail in the morning, whether or not we receive one."

Then he turned away.

"Ambassador...," said Arkády.

"Enough!" spat the emissary, his rings flaring in reaction. "Enough, please! You have all done *enough*! We take our leave, o King-to-Be. Would that we had never come."

He led his small group of retainers down the hall, carrying the body of the lad with them, daring anyone to interfere with their right to depart. Across the boy's chest flopped the severed arm that his father had retrieved. On either side the crowds of courtiers shrank back from the bloody ensemble as it passed by.

There was nothing more to be done but to order a mass said for the repose of the souls of the recently deceased, and to make way for the washerwomen to clean the sticky mess off the floor before it had a chance thoroughly to dry.

The Archpriest Athanasios watched in shocked silence as the laborers began their rough, dirty work, dropping to their knees next to large wooden buckets filled with cold water, and scrub, scrub, scrubbing at the tiles with their stiffly-bristled brushes to remove the deeply-embedded stains, assuming almost a prayerful posture in their work, backs bent far forward, faces close to the floor, never complaining, never ceasing, until the task was finally completed. One of them crossed herself as she moved to a new patch of blood.

Why, this is God's work, he suddenly realized. *These women are closer to salvation than I. They reach for Heaven's Gate through their uncomplaining labor. They do what must be done in God's Holy Name.*

The revelation stunned him even more than the horrifying events of the past hour.

What am I doing that even comes close to this? he wondered. *Why am I...?*

"Athanasios!" came the command, "I need you."

The priest shivered himself free of his thoughts, sighed once, and then straightened his back.

"Yes, Metropolitan," he responded. "I'm coming, Your Grace."

CHAPTER TWENTY
"WILL IT BE WAR?
WILL IT BE PEACE?"

"God's breath, what in the seven circles of Hell happened here!" raged the king in council, which had been expanded with this meeting to include the Forellës. Even the guards in the corridor could hear him through the walls.

"Whatever possessed Dolph to do something like this? Arkásha?"

The prince stood up, motioning the rest of the room to silence.

"Sire, I'll have a detailed report for you later this afternoon, before this council ends. I ordered an immediate death-probe of Prince Adolphos, and I hope we'll find it instructive.

"However, before we proceed further," he said, "we need to draft a response to King Barnim's letter. That's why this session was originally called, and despite the tragedy that occurred this morning, we still must frame a reply. Ambassador Widdekin sails at the third hour of the morrow."

Lord Gorázd agreed.

"Sire," he said, "we need your guidance on this issue. Say the word. Will it be war? Will it be peace?"

Ezzö, Count of Bolémia and late King of Pommerelia, then asked to be heard.

"Sire," he said with a catch in his voice, blinking back the tears streaming from his hollow eyes, "I have lost a good son today. Your dear sister Teréza bore me five sweet children, three boys and two girls, and now all are gone but one. Adolphos was never the smartest of my children, but he was the dearest of them to me. Never once did he harm a soul until today."

He turned to the hereditary prince.

"I can't blame you, Prince Arkády, for what you had to do. No one must violate the sanctity of the embassy, and my poor Dolph, well, he had to be stopped."

He breathed deeply to regain his composure.

"Oh, he must have gone mad. He was possessed by Shaitán, or, more to the point, swayed by the devil's agents, those papal-loving Walküri. The Cæsarists continue to persecute our people in Vorpommern, denying them the right to have their masses sung in Greek and forbidding them their own clergy, and sending their Romanish priests and agents eastward into Kórynthia itself. All of you know this. The Holy Roman Cæsar was once content with the lands south of the German River in the west, and the Ister in the East. Now he wants it all.

"*Cousin*, I demand my vengeance! I demand a restoration of the old faith! I call for *jihad!*"

Murmers of approval trickled 'round the room. These men of action were sick of the senseless attacks that had been nibbling away at the realm, were tired of the Latinist incursions into the east, and were determined to do something about them. King Kipriyán's eyes darted quickly back and forth across the table, measuring this lord's mind or that.

Finally, the king looked at his eldest son.

"What say you, Arkásha?"

The prince rubbed his short beard, trying to find some way to slow the rush of events.

"We have no proof, sire," he said, "absolutely none, concerning the origin of these crimes against your person. We don't know who caused them, or why. We should first determine something definite about the attacks before taking action. And you lose nothing, father, by agreeing to meet with King Barnim."

Prince Nikolaí stood up, his cheeks flushed.

"For once I must disagree with you, brother," he said. "Whether or not the Walküri are responsible for this particular outrage, they've certainly given us more than their share of evil over the years. Maybe they're these Dark-Haired Men we keep hearing about."

The councilors laughed.

"I say it's time we put an end to the sons of Walküre, once and for all. Let's clear out the lot of them, and install some responsible orthodox kings in their place.

"I too call for *jihad*," Nikolaí said.

"And the rest of you?" asked the king.

Metropolitan Timotheos, sitting in the place of Patriarch Avraäm, lifted his hand.

"I'm afraid, gentlemen, that I must raise my voice in support of Prince Arkády."

There were groans from around the table.

"Hear me, my lords. I bear no love for the House of Walküre or their Romanish ways. I know the crimes of which they've been accused, and I agree that they've overstepped the bounds on too many occasions, persecuting, torturing, and killing thousands of innocent people whose only crime was their orthodox faith.

"But I too urge caution. Unlike the rest of you, I served in the last war with Pommerelia, fighting alongside King Makáry, Hereditary Prince Néstor, King Karlomán, King Ezzö the Elder, and Prince Kazimir, and participating in every major battle of that conflict. I was *there*, which is something no one else in this room can claim. And I saw all of those men, and many others besides, die horrible deaths.

"Even after we had killed King Michael of Pommerelia, even after it seemed that we had won it all, the enemy rallied behind this very same King Barnim and drove us back. Do not think for a moment that this will be a romp in the countryside. Our forces are very closely matched. We could still be fighting there a decade from now. We should wait."

Comments were also heard from others in the room, all of them supporting war.

"Very well, I think I've heard enough," the king said, cutting off further debate. "This is my judgment, *sieurs.* For their crimes against God and the true faith, for their crimes against Kórynthia, for their crimes against my house, we call the *jihad* against the Walküre. Let the word go forth to every town and dale, that the fighting men of the kingdom shall gather together at each castle and fortified place by the middle of April in this our XLIst year of reign, thence to gather at our fortress of Mylášgorod no later than the middle of the month following.

"Let the metropolitans bless our soldiers, let the patriarch bless the king and court, and may God smile upon our great enterprise.

"This is the word of Kyprianos III King of Kórynthia. Let it be recorded."

Thirty-five fists beat as one upon the council table, shaking the panes of glass in their frames, as Athanasios marked the words down in the Great Register.

"Jihad!" they shouted.

"Jihad!" echoed the king.

"Jihad!" confirmed Metropolitan Timotheos, acting for the ailing patriarch.

Lord Gorázd motioned for silence.

"I will draft the proclamation this afternoon for the royal seal, which will be presented to Ambassador Widdekin before he departs tomorrow, and a second document will be dispatched to all of the meeting places of the kingdom. Now, let us adjourn briefly before taking up the matter of this morning's attack."

CHAPTER TWENTY-ONE
"*HOW* WAS IT DONE?"

Arkády promptly left the room to check on Fra Jánisar's investigations. He returned a few moments later with Alexis Andrássy Count of Görgoszák, an accomplished Psairothi master.

Andrássy was a short, plump man in his forties, clothed in a rich maroon robe striped thrice in black across each sleeve to indicate the level of his proficiency. He frowned as he sat himself to the right of Arkády, and rubbed his beringed hands across the front edge of his receding hairline, wiping away the sweat. He then pulled a sheaf of notes from his sleeve.

When the others had returned to the Council table, Gorázd Lord Aboéty motioned for order.

"Prince Arkády," he asked, "are you ready?"

"Yes, grand vizier," the prince said. "We all saw the unprovoked assault made this morning on Ambassador Widdekin and his son by the late Prince Adolphos Count of Einwegflasche. After questioning the participants, I have concluded that the count believed that an attack was being pressed against the king, and responded accordingly. When the ambassador advanced towards King Kipriyán, Adolphos somehow saw a poisoned knife or sword in Widdekin's hand, instead of the parchment, and when no one else came to my father's aid, bravely stepped forward himself. He is innocent of any crime, and I believe that God will judge him accordingly.

"The question is 'why?' What prompted this assault? I asked

the king's physician, Fra Jánisar, to examine the count's body, and to arrange for a necroprobe of his latent memories.

"The doctor found nothing wrong physically with Prince Adolphos, other than the wound which was the immediate cause of his death. There were no malformations of the brain or other irregularities which could have fostered delusions in the man. His humours were in good balance. Therefore, I propose that we must look to the psychic plane for the cause of Adolphos's actions, since the mildness of his character was well known to all of us here."

Arkády cleared his throat before continuing.

"Count Alexis of Görgoszák, an instructor in necroprobing at the *Scholê*, will now report on his findings."

"I thank you, Prince Arkády," Görgoszák said. "I wish that you should understand that I was unable to perform a completely thorough examination of the subject, due to the short amount of time that was available to me. Normally, the elucidation of a death-probe of this complexity requires several days at a minimum, and preferably a week to assimilate all of the victim's subtleties, and to understand their devious interactions. However, such as that...that is, with all appropriate caveats having now been expressed here, I can proceed with an account of my discoveries, such as they may be."

The count pulled an oval-shaped piece of glass from his pocket, and examined his notes more closely.

"Ahem, yes, this is most, *most* interesting. Beneath the surface level of the victim's thoughts, that is to say, his ordinary personality, there was an underlayer, a substratum of interference from some outside agency. Several triggers were introduced into the subject's brain, so that certain events would inevitably proceed if they matched the appropriate visual and auditory stimuli.

"Specifically," he said, "when the ambassador from Pommerelia was announced at court, one of these triggers was thereby enabled, and when the ambassador stepped forward toward the king with his hand outstretched, a second switch closed in the count's mind, the additional compulsion then forcing the victim into his attack mode. He firmly believed at all times throughout this process that he was taking the only right and necessary action to defend both king and country."

He smiled his pedant's smile of supercilious triumph.

"It was most cleverly accomplished," Görgoszák said.

"Count Alexis," Metropolitan Timotheos asked, "specifically *how* was it done?"

"Well, as to that," the adept hemmed and hawed, "well, I am not really certain. You see, it takes time to assimilate all the years of a man's life, and this was a most sophisticated working, very unusual in many respects. There are layers upon layers of interference embedded in the count's mind, some locked behind the green door, at least one of which I have thus far been unable even to crack. One must proceed very cautiously, because there are certain unscrupulous mages who will place traps in their workings, twistings that can destroy an investigator's mind if he does not unravel the thread in just a certain way. There is much..."

"Stop!" interrupted the metropolitan. "Just tell us this. Did a Psairothi fashion the spell?"

"I, uh, that is to say, I really do not know," said Alexis, "at least not yet. There are t'ings about this, uh, this event that are very strange. Certain sins, that is, signs, that only an accomplished researcher such as myself would even recognize. Like, uh, for example, the frontal lobe being affected by the hyperthalmoidus. Which is to say, I see another's hand at work here. One who has made some weary, that is, very good stuff. I think."

Prince Arkády tried to steer the proceedings back to some semblance of normality.

"Is there anything you can tell us about the level of training that would be required to place such a compulsion in a Psairothi, even one not especially accomplished?"

Alexis was sweating very heavily now, and he wiped his brow with his sleeve.

"Ahem, well, I do t'ink ve have to go with the flow in an investigation of this type. There are intrinsicacies of the nature that can be seen in the lodes of Prince Dolphin's mine. Like here," he said, pointing to his own head and then rubbing the top vigorously. "In here we find much the same. I, uh, I can feel the nature of this coming through wery well, and hope you will do the same. I can feel them little fangers trying to work their way out of my skoal. Even so, princy, uh, princely, we see much in common between the work of Bózard de Guardrobus and, shall we say, Ludolf von Gegendreck. Or was it Rudolf. No, Waddolf, I fink. Anywho, you can see there sorta what I'm talkin' about. Jesu Christu, they're crawling all over my head. I, I find more t'ings to investiture..."—he started beating the top of his head with his right hand—"ah, got t'em suckers. Yes, now, as I was saying, they have to be wery good to do this. T'ey, uh, t'ey t'ink t'ey got me, but I knows better. T'ey comin' t'rough my eyes now. I most stup t'em. Most stop, must, must pop."

Suddenly the count plunged his fingers into his sockets, scooping the eyes out with his fingernails, and popping them one at a time into his mouth.

"Ah," he said, biting down and smiling his crocodile smile, "T'at's gut. Ha! Ahhh-ha!"

Then Alexis started screaming, and he couldn't be quieted, even when the guards dragged him away down the hall, kicking and biting and fighting.

"I sees you," they heard him yell one last time, "I sees *you*, Kyp. Kyp, Kyp, Kyp-ri-yan-os the Brief, chief!"

"Someone clean up this mess," Arkády managed to choke out, before running hurriedly to the garde-robe to void his lunch.

The king just sat stunned in his place, his face as pallid as that of the absent Doctor Melanthrix.

When the prince returned, he asked the question on everyone's mind.

"Do any of you know what just happened here?"

Metropolitan Timotheos rubbed the new lines etched in his brow.

"I would venture a guess, Highness, that whatever 'claw' was planted in Prince Adolphos was assimilated by Count Alexis during his probe, and suddenly erupted in his mind, eating away his sanity from the inside out. Whatever it was, I would not want to encounter it myself. The Count of Görgoszák, in spite of his pedantry, was superbly trained, and certainly as proficient as anyone at this table. If this menace can whelm him, who was expecting it, then none of us is safe."

All nodded soberly.

King Kipriyán suddenly gasped out, "Then, then, what do you expect us to *do?*

"What!"

He pounded the table with his right hand.

"What!!"

He pounded again and screamed.

"What!!!"

Suddenly realizing what he was doing, he looked around at the faces staring at him, blushed, and abruptly said in a weak voice, "This meeting is adjourned," before rushing out of the room without even waiting for his guards to catch up with him.

"God in Heaven," said Prince Arkády, "the enterprise has begun. The Great Lord help us all."

CHAPTER TWENTY-TWO
"MAY GOD HAVE
MERCY ON HIS SOUL"

For Arkády, the next several hours passed quickly. His immediate concern was the safety of the royal family. He dispatched trusted members of his own elite guard to oversee the security arrangements at the personal apartments of his parents, his brothers, and the Forellës. Messages were sent to Patriarch Avraäm and the chief officials of state to take all appropriate steps to protect themselves. When the prince was satisfied that he had done all that could be done for the moment, he summoned Archpriest Athanasios from the nearby *Scholê*.

When the cleric arrived, Arkády asked him to take a seat opposite.

"I know you've served as occasional private secretary for my father the king," the prince said, "although I myself haven't used you in this capacity before. However, I now have need of your services."

The prince gestured to his office table, awash in piles of documents.

"I must have someone whom I can trust to help sift through the dozens of reports I'm been receiving about these outrages, and choose those important enough to bring to my further attention. I also require someone to handle confidential *communiqués*."

Athanasios bent to the canvas satchel at his side, and took out several sheets of parchment, a sharpened quill, and a small pot of ink. These he placed in front of him on the desk, and took pen in hand.

"I'm ready to begin now, Highness," he said.

"Good."

First Arkády dictated a short, formal letter of sympathy on behalf of king and country to Ambassador Widdekin and his family, also expressing his own regret for the grief they were experiencing. The priest's nimble fingers flew quickly across the page, finishing the document within moments of Arkády's dictation. Then Athanasios sanded the ink, scanned the page briefly, and handed it to the prince for his approval and signature.

Arkády read the sheet carefully, and nodded in appreciation. He noted a few places where the priest had corrected a word, or had made a subtle change in the phrasing to more closely approximate his master's meaning.

"Excellent. Truly excellent," he said.

The prince inked the letter with a flourish, and set it to one side.

"Now," he sighed, "an even more difficult note...."

He rose and walked to the nearby window. Gazing out at a gray sky which threatened snow, he began dictating to King Ezzö and Queen Teréza a heartfelt expression of the mutual grief their families were sharing in the death of his cousin Dolph.

"...I would give anything if the events which transpired this morning had not happened...," he added. "Please believe me when I tell you that I would have gladly offered my own life for his if I could have saved him. I shall always regret the fact that I could not...."

Arkády paused to regain his composure, cleared his throat, and continued.

"...With the king's permission, I have dispatched my own guards to supplement those protecting you and your family. A state funeral for the soul of Prince Adolphos will be held four days hence at Saint Konstantín's Cathedral. May God have mercy on his soul...."

He stopped.

"Please finish it, Athanasios," he said. "I can do no more."

The priest continued writing for a moment or two more, sanded the missive, and passed it along.

Arkády sat silently, reading both letters over several times. Finally he signed the second one and laid it aside to dry.

"Thank you, Archpriest. You've done me a great service today, one which I will not soon forget. Now, you may go. Please send in Tyrvón as you leave."

"Yes, Highness." Athanasios bowed. "Call me should you have further need."

Then he left the room, quietly closing the door behind him.

Shortly thereafter, Arkády's chief aide, Tyrvón Baëthy, entered. Arkády asked him to prepare the two letters for transmittal. As the prince affixed his seal to each, pressing his *sphragis*-ring deeply into the bright red wax, he thought of the blood which had oozed from the bodies of the two young men who had met their premature ends this day.

He handed the first document to his aide.

"Send this by fast courier to Ambassador Widdekin's boat."

He picked up the second letter.

"Deliver this note personally to Prince Ezzö's quarters. Now!," he said, more forcefully than he had intended.

"Wait," he added, as Tyrvón opened the door. "What I meant to say was, 'Thank you.'"

"Of course, sir," came the reply.

"I'll be in my quarters the rest of the day. Please don't disturb me."

"Yes, Highness," Tyrvón said respectfully, bowing deeply.

The aide carefully took the documents entrusted to him, and paused, as if he wanted to say something, but finally just shook his head.

CHAPTER TWENTY-THREE
"YOU CAN LEAD AN ORT TO WATER..."

Day was now easing into early evening. Surrounded by his heavily-armed personal bodyguard, Prince Arkády wearily made his way back to his apartments within the palace. Leaving the gendarmes stationed at his door, with instructions to summon him if they noticed anything out of the ordinary, he entered his quarters with a sigh of relief.

A short, slightly plump, dark-haired woman was giving instructions to some servants at the rear of the room, but she turned quickly as he entered.

"Kásha!" the Princess Dúra cried out, running to him. "I heard.... Are *you* all right?"

"Physically, I'm fine," he said, "thanks to God's good grace. As for the rest...."

He gathered her into his arms, and just rocked for a moment, holding her warmth tight against him.

"Do you want to talk?" his wife said, stroking his brow, smoothing away the lines of care etched in his forehead, brushing back the undisciplined lock of hair she so loved.

Arkády shook his head "no."

"Maybe later," he said. "For now, though, I should eat something."

He shuddered.

"Gad, even the thought of food absolutely sickens me. But I must eat...and rest. And then, I'm afraid, I'll have to leave again for a few hours."

He clenched her even tighter.

"What do ordinary people do, Drúsha?" he said quietly into the mass of her hair. "How do they cope? I spend my days running from crisis to crisis, trying to shore up the walls of state here and there, but all the time seeing them crumbling everywhere I look. And father! God save us all."

"Shhh," she said, "shhh, my love. Relax for a time. Let your cares slip away just now. I'm here. Lay back on this couch. Put your head down and close your eyes. Katrina will prepare something light for supper. There'll be plenty of time to talk later."

She motioned with one hand to the hovering servant, who rushed off into another room.

"How're the children?" he said, half asleep already.

"Ari misses you, of course," Dúra said, "and so does Rÿna. She's made friends with that hieromonk from the *Scholê*, the one whose name I can never recall...."

"Father Athanasios," Arkády said.

"...Yes, Athanasios. He told me yesterday that she had great *psai* potential. He wants to test her power. I said you would have to decide."

"Hmmm," was all Arkády could manage.

She paused.

"There's something else, too, Kásha. Please don't be angry with me, but I had to call Doctor Melanthrix again today. I know you don't like him, but he's the only one who really seems to help Ari when he has one of his spells."

Tears filled her dark, luminous eyes.

"I just can't stand seeing him in so much pain, dearest."

Arkády reached over and took her hand, rubbing the fingers.

"And did he help?" he asked quietly.

"Oh, yes." Dúra smiled though her tears. "Oh, it was a gift from God! The doctor just sat there, very patiently, holding Ari's hand and telling him stories, and slowly, ever so slowly, the pain began to subside.

"Sometimes, if it gets too bad, he uses those needles. It makes me shudder to see those awful things sticking in my poor Ari's body. And if they don't work, he'll give him a little fluid from an odd-shaped bottle. But afterwards Ari seems so much better. I apologize, husband, for not consulting you first."

Arkády put her hands together and brought them to his face, kissing them.

"How could I possibly chide you for easing our son's pain?" he asked. "Dúra, I was forced to kill cousin Dolph today. Nothing..."—his eyes turned cold—"nothing that I'll ever do again will make me feel quite this way again. I can still see Aunt Teréza, crying her heart out, blaming me with her tears."

"The world may fall around us, dearest," his wife said, sitting next to him and pulling his head to her breast, "but as long as we have each other and our children, we'll survive somehow."

"Now I must eat," Arkády said, sitting up straight, as Katrina entered the room with a small platter and placed it on his lap.

He looked down at the hodge-podge piled before him.

"What *is* this stuff?" he asked, aghast at the jumble of dried-out bread and multi-hued meat and cheese.

"Well, you did say you were in a hurry, madame," the servant said, "at least I thought you did, and so I had to throw everything together, whatever I could find, this and that and the other, and make it somehow all fit. I usually have more time, sir, but I didn't have time this time, I did the best I could, really, sir, but there wasn't enough time to do it all right, and they're, they're, they're *orts*, sir! *Orts, orts, orts, orts!*"

She suddenly screamed again, "Not enough time to get it done right." And then she just ran off, shouting, "orts! Morsels of orts! Orsels of morts!"

"Did, did I say something wrong?" Arkády asked, laughing to himself while pushing the food around with his finger, trying to find something, anything edible in the greasy mess.

"Well, dearest," his wife said, "you learn very soon that just can't pressure old Katrina into finishing something quickly."

Then they both laughed out loud.

"You can lead an ort to water...," he said.

"...but you can't make it sink!" she finished.

They chuckled together again.

"Poor Katrina," Dúra said. "She'll be complaining all next week about her orts."

There was a knock at the door, and the prince went immediately to open it, even before his servants could respond.

"Yes, Tyrvón?" he asked, when he saw who it was.

"Highness," said the servant, bowing, "terribly sorry, but I thought you'd like to know. Count Alexis couldn't be revived. His son, Lord Gorténz, was at his side, and will make the arrangements. Do you want the body sequestered?"

Arkády thought for a moment.

"Order it done," he said, "and have a stasis placed on the corpse. I'll give them further instructions in the morning. Now leave me in peace."

But there was no peace to be found that evening, not for any price, not for the trumpeters of war, who spent their dreams dashing in triumph upon the enemy, again and again, killing them all, only to find them resurrected just a few moments later; nor for the peacemakers, who knew that the Rubicon had been crossed once more that day, and that Cæsar would not now be turned back by reason or love or by anything else short of victory or defeat.

In later years Arkády would come to regard this day as the worst of his life, and vowed to spend an entire week of each year thereafter clothed only in black, doing penance on his knees before the cold, stony shrine of Saint Sávva in Bizerte. But no matter what he did, no matter what he said, it was never enough to erase the memories or ease the pain. Never.

CHAPTER TWENTY-FOUR
"HE DIDN'T KNOW WHAT HE WAS DOING"

An hour later Arkády transited to a meeting of the Covenant of Christian Mages. Several members had already arrived, among them Count Zhertán, and the prince motioned him aside, where they could talk privily.

"I have terrible news," Arkády said, "and I didn't want to tell you in council. Your grandson Tibor was killed this morning in Paltyrrha."

The old man sagged and almost fell, his face going completely white.

"Give me the details," he said.

"Touch your *psai*-ring to mine," the prince said.

When the Count complied, Arkády showed him the attack exactly as it had happened.

"God rest his innocent soul," was all that Zhertán could say.

His face had gone a pasty gray.

"I have no doubt, sir," Arkády said, "that your grandson is in Heaven. Poor Dolph, he was under a compulsion. He didn't know what he was doing. And it was my spear that killed them both...."

"No!" the count said, rousing himself. "That road is a path to self-destruction. You did what you had to do, what I would have done in your place. Poor Tibor was in the wrong place at the wrong time. This was someone else's game, that of an evildoer who pushes us ever closer to war.

"Great God in Heaven, Arkásha! I think, finally, that I've lived too long."

Then Zhertán straightened his back, and wiped away the tears dripping from his eyes.

"I...I must return home immediately," he said. "Give my regrets to the council, and tell them, please, that I'm withdrawing from their deliberations until this business is concluded. I would expect you to do the same."

The count strode rapidly towards the *viridaurum*, then abruptly stopped and looked back.

"We must find a way to end this madness, Arkády," he said. "If it costs us our lives, we must stop this."

Then he was gone.

When the council began its proceedings, the prince gave an account of the day's sad occurrences, before also resigning his seat.

"You may replace me if you choose," he said, "but I can't in good conscience remain here. I'll be happy to send appropriate updates of a non-military nature through Mösza, if you approve."

He glanced over at the familiar figure of his great-aunt seated in her usual place across the table.

"Oh, Arkásha," Mösza said, pursing her lips in sympathy, "my poor, poor boy. Of course I agree."

"However, I must express my concern over these events," said Ariosto Count of Corovino, a potbellied man in his seventies, and official representative of the Holy Roman Cæsar, Marcus Ætherius III. "If war does break out between Kórynthia and Pommerelia, we will want some assurance that our Latinate clerics and churches in the latter country will not be molested."

"We would insist on the same promise from the other side, respecting our clergy and facilities in Kórynthia," Metropolitan Euphronios said.

"Gentlemen, gentlemen," William Lord Eagleton said. "Let us not immediately make assumptions about this little disagreement. Even should a conflict develop, we have months to make arrangements concerning noncombatants, and I have no doubt that we will. We can do things in a civilized way or in an uncivilized way, and civilized is always best, wouldn't you agree?"

The two antagonists just glared at each other, without speaking another word.

"See!" the chairman said. "See! We can all just get along if we try really, really hard. Of course, Prince Arkády, you can certainly pass along information to our group through Countess Mösza, provided that it contains no military data and makes no attempt to sway emotions one way or the other. Agreed?"

"Very well," the prince said. "Then please join me afterwards, Auntie. Meanwhile, I urge all of you to be careful these next few months. There's a rogue rampaging through our community, someone who's trying to destroy everything we've built. He's very good at hiding himself, and very, *very* accomplished at subverting others. If he can destroy Count Alexis so easily, he can get to any of us. Guard yourselves with great care."

"What about Melanthrix?" Mösza asked.

"Sorry, I just forgot with all the other business," Arkády said. "Well, I did make a few inquiries, but I discovered very little new. He appeared about thirty years ago, ingratiated himself with my father, and then left, coming back to court at odd intervals. He's friends with Father Athanasios, *grammateus* to the High Council and aide to Metropolitan Timotheos, and not with anyone else except my daughter. I suggest that the matter be postponed until our present difficulties are settled."

Arkády rose in his seat.

"I hope that we can meet again in peace when this is over. Fare thee well, my friends."

He formally saluted them.

The council then adjourned, each member going his or her separate way, although at least one of them had another rendezvous planned for later that evening. Finally, only Arkády and Mösza remained.

"Auntie," he said, "if you'll give me a quick mental image of your *viridaurum* mirror, I'll be on my way."

"Well," she said shyly, a pink glow slowly suffusing her full cheeks, "well, perhaps we can find some other place to meet. You know how much I value my privacy, nephew."

She hesitated a moment, fiddling with a stray tendril of snowy white hair that had escaped from her hood and drifted over her forehead.

"Ever since I was...well, that is, ever since I *left* court many years ago, I've just been more comfortable just keeping to myself. Someone once abused the privilege, and I've never forgotten or forgiven. You understand, I'm sure."

She shook her head to clear it of such disagreeable thoughts.

"But I do know of a few other places that no one ever visits today, sites where mirrors yet remain active, I believe. Let me think about the problem a bit, and I'll contact you again soon."

"Whatever you say, Auntie," the prince said, rubbing his neck to alleviate his weariness.

"My dear Arkásha, this has absolutely nothing to do with you. It's just another silly rule I made up for myself many years ago."

She laughed, her whole body shaking.

"And oh, and I'm such a firm believer in following the rules, right down to the very letter. You see, whenever someone breaks the law, whatever that law might be, he cuts a little piece out of the fabric of society, and that's a terrible, terrible thing to do, my boy. You see the result coming upon us in this crisis. The transgressors, well, they all have to be punished, you know, every last one of them. If we Tighrishi had been as careful about following our *own* rules as we've been about condemning someone else's, why, *we'd* be ruling the world by now.

"At any rate," she added, "I know you think I'm just a fuss-budget, and you're probably right, too. I'm an old lady, after all. What do I know, anyway?"

Suddenly she turned deadly serious.

"But you remember what I tell you, Arkásha, when the time comes. You remember *that*, dear nephew. Now I must go."

And then Mösza left the chamber more quickly than Prince

Arkády would have ever believed possible, had he not seen it himself. As tired as he was, he lingered in the old gray chamber of the Covenant of Christian Mages another few moments, pondering the day's events, and wondering, not for the first time, about the curious and convoluted history of the ancient House of Tighris; and whether the tigers to be most feared were those already set loose upon the world, or those still locked tightly in their captivating cages.

CHAPTER TWENTY-FIVE
"THE SITUATION IS FAR MORE SERIOUS THAN I THOUGHT"

The one known as Alpha stood on the cliffs of the island of Loryùppa, gazing out to sea. In the distance he could barely make out the dim shapes of the other islets of the chain, most of them bare rocks thrusting several hundreds or thousands of feet above the surface of the sea, outlined by the churning white surf at their base. The archipelago was all that remained of the lost continent of Atlantis, which had sunk beneath the waves a thousand or more years earlier. Of the eighty or one hundred islets that remained, only Loryùppa, the largest, was habitable, and it was completely inaccessible, being surrounded by sheer cliffs on all sides. Where he perched, at the mouth of a lush valley that ran almost the entire length of the land, the rocks dropped some three hundred feet to the surf below; elsewhere, the cliffs swelled to a thousand sheer feet or more.

To his left he could hear the gurgling of the stream that drained the valley before dying in a spectacular waterfall not far from where he stood. As he turned widdershins, the moonlight revealed the eerie remains of the temples which had once dotted this place, their fallen stone columns littering the landscape like the bleached bones of some elden giant. Of all the ornate buildings which had once adorned the valley, monuments erected by a long-dead people to their equally dead gods, only one now survived, and that because it had been cut from the living rock of the mountain that rose to his left. What had become of those gods, no one could really say. That they had abandoned their people in the face of the One True God was obvious to some, if not to him, for he knew of places on Loryùppa that still held something of their presence, and which he would not dare challenge or even visit.

The Brotherhood had found this place several hundred years ago, from an account left by Mikhaêl Phôstêridês the Grand Mage in his *Historia Nisyrias*, which, despite its title, was actually more of a grimoire and travelogue than a history. There he had described the nine great temples of the Vale of Loryùppa, which he himself had visited, listing their purposes, attributes, and transit points. They had lost several volunteers before finding the lone surviving mirror in the sole surviving temple. He wondered idly where those acolytes had gone.

A movement to the right caught his eye, as one of the huts discharged a figure.

"Are you ready?" Alpha asked.

"Yes, master," came the muffled reply.

"Then let us proceed," Alpha said.

He led the way down a path through the woods on their left. Around a bend they abruptly came upon a door that entered directly into the mountain face. The acolyte had the impression of great stone pillars carved from the rock on either side of the opening, but the muted moonlight provided very little detail.

"Please cover your features," Alpha said, fastening his own cloth mask in place with leather ties. He then flipped up his hood, checked his associate's dress, and without further ado led the way inside.

The first room they entered was small and austere. Perhaps it had once been used as a guard or cloak room, or possibly for something else. There was simply no way to tell. Now its furniture consisted entirely of two benches and a table. Alpha motioned to his associate to seat himself at one of them.

"Wait here," he said. "I'll ring a bell when we're ready for you."

Then he exited through the only other door.

Alpha passed down a long corridor that had been cut cleanly through the rock. The walls glowed faintly with their own light, sufficient for him to find his way to the end. There were no side passages. He eventually came to a metal door, which he unlocked with a key he carried hanging 'round his neck, and entered, closing the entrance after him.

He found himself in a large chamber called the Enneaphon, or "Nine Tones," which had nine sides, one representing each of the old gods and bearing his or her image graven high on the wall, just below a small opening. The temple had been constructed in such a way that the air vents built into the top of the chamber would produce notes randomly throughout the day, making music whenever the breezes began blowing in from the sea, particularly at dawn and dusk. At times these created a horrendous racket, but there were other occasions when one could imagine Pan and the other elder beings sitting up there playing their pipes, and still other moments, much rarer, when one could almost hear them singing arcane words just beyond the grasp of one's understanding.

Nine thrones were carved into the naked stone, seven of them now filled by hooded, masked individuals. Alpha sat himself in the largest and most ornate position.

He said: "I call the Brotherhood of Tighris into session. With one spirit we meet, into one spirit our voices mingle, our souls are uplifted by becoming one.

"Brothers and sisters, I bring you good news and bad. One of our own has passed into that great adventure beyond life itself. His name can now be mentioned in this assembly. Count Alexis of Görgoszák, who sat among us as 'Xi,' was foully murdered this afternoon. Let his *nomen* be inscribed among the immortals, let his fame be etched upon these hallowed walls."

He stretched out his right index finger, and from his ring sent forth a narrow beam of red light. Using it like a stylus, he began pressing a name into a blank space on the bottom part of the wall, just above the vacant chair, joining a short list of others already noted there. The other seven raised their hands in turn, and simultaneously bathed the name of Alexis with their incandescent light, sealing it forever into the stone.

"We shall remember him always," Alpha said, "for his wisdom, for his valor, for his companionship. So mote it be."

"So mote it be," came the combined response.

"But with each death comes a new birth," Alpha said, "and with each ending a new beginning."

He rose from his seat of primacy, went to the door, opened it, and struck a silver bell that echoed down the corridor. A moment later the acolyte had joined him.

Alpha turned back to face the seven: "I present for your consideration 'Thêta,' who desires to take the seat left vacant by Xi's untimely passing."

He led the candidate to a stool placed in the depressed circle at the center of the chamber.

"You must judge," he said, "is he worthy?"

The seat on which Thêta sat rose from the floor and began to revolve. Each of the seven turned their full psychic concentration on the man, trying to break down his will and his ringshield.

For he who would become Thêta, it seemed as if he encountered each of them individually on a different plane. In one instance he sat across *les échecs* board from a masked player, in another he rode a destrier in a tournament against an anonymous armored opponent, in another he was paired in a contest of thespians with a tragedian wearing a downturned face mask, in another his masked rival met him face-to-face in the wrestling ring, in another he was a tamer of beasts surrounded by a pride of hungry tigers, in another he faced judgment from a court for a crime he had not yet committed, in another he played a lyre for a king who could not be satisfied.

"Is he worthy?" Alpha asked again.

"*Axios!*" said Tau. "He is worthy."

"*Axios!*" came the response in turn from Gamma, Rhô, Mu, Epsilon, and Kappa. Only Lambda was silent.

"*Is he worthy?*" Alpha asked of Lambda.

"*Axios*," the latter finally said, with obvious reluctance.

"Then let Thêta be seated amongst our company," Alpha solemnly said. "We welcome him to our Brotherhood, from which there is no parting but death. *Evoê!*"

"*Evoê!*" they repeated.

Theta rose from his stool, and took the empty place of Xi.

"Brothers and sisters of the Nine," Alpha said, "we face a crisis of confidence. One of our own has been killed by magic dark and foul. See now his passing."

And he created for them an image floating above the center of the floor, one that gave each a perfect picture of the afternoon's event and how it had unfolded.

"What say you?" he said.

"I have seen this done before," said Mu, "in distant Asshyria, where they practice a magic both weird and unnatural. This is not dissimilar, I think, to something I once experienced there, but neither is it precisely the same."

"Indeed," Tau said, "yet whatever hybrid of magical traditions this working might represent, there is no question in my mind that whoever promulgated such an abomination will do so again."

"This person," said Kappa, "will go to any lengths to attain his goals. I smell a vendetta at work, brethren. Consider the crimes: each required direct contact with the victim and a close and exact knowledge of the Kórynthi court and its principals. All contain an particle of humiliation. Who would do this, and to what purpose? I see a spider lurking at the center of this web, pulling the strings and gloating over his triumphs, and chuckling at his victims' discomfiture. I suggest that we are equally in danger."

Lambda raised a hand.

"More to the point," he said, "these actions violate the very tenets by which this organization was established. We exist with the sufferance of the higher Psairothi community in Kórynthia to regulate and control the unauthorized use of the lines, and secondarily to further the study of our heritage and knowledge, and thirdly to counter the influence of the Covenant of Christian Mages and other such groups. We provide a neutral arbitration of disputes. This individual seeks the destruction of such norms. Only one of our own could have penetrated so deeply into our midst without being detected. Ergo, we have a rogue among us. He will destroy anyone or anything who gets in his way. Such a person would risk all, for in his own mind he loses nothing except by failure."

Rhô finally spoke.

"Then we must bend all of our efforts towards finding and destroying this individual immediately, no matter the cost."

"What about the Dark-Haired Man?" Epsilon asked.

"I don't believe in fairy tales," Rhô said, "nor should any of you. This is a *real* man. He has a *real* goal in mind. He is using magical techniques that may be partially unknown to us, but that are based on *real* principles. If we can discover his goal, if we understand *why* he is attacking these individuals, we may be able to stop him before he can cause more damage. But stop him we must."

"It's not that I *believe* in the Dark-Haired Man," Epsilon said, clearly piqued, "but to name him is to know him, and this person, whoever he might be, possesses a nature that's black to its very core. It's also important to state what we can reasonably infer: that this is one individual, not a group of conspirators, who most certainly would have tripped over themselves by now, and thus stand revealed."

"Agreed," the one called Gamma said, "but I think we're missing something vital here, although I'm damned if I remember what it is. It hovers just beyond my ability to retrieve. I do recall having heard or read about a similar situation once...."

Above them a few notes tentatively began, softly at first, and then with more vigor. Suddenly all nine were craning their necks to see the tops of the walls, from which a whisper had begun hissing through the vents:

"Alpha bêta gamma delta epsilon,
When shall I begin to set upon?
Zêta êta thêta iôta kappa,
When shall you all come to papá?
Lambda mu nu xi omicron,
You'll all die, one by one,
Pi rhô sigma tau upsilon,
Till all the nine but mine are gone,
Chi phi psi ômega,
Wizard, witch, and strega,
Alpha bet a game at Delphi."

The words metamorphosed into the raucous squawking of a cacophony of crows, quickly growing in amplitude, until all were covering their ears in pain.

"Enough!" roared Alpha, raising his hands in a spell. *"Theos avertat!"*

The awful racket ceased, but now they could clearly hear the sound of someone breathing, someone who would have had to have been very large indeed to be so noticeable.

"The situation is far more serious than I thought," Alpha said. "This place has never before been violated by an outsider. It needs cleansing immediately. You must leave, all of you, right now, while I set the evacuator in motion."

Hurriedly they began moving towards an antechamber whose entrance opened to the right of the corridor door.

"We'll meet again in four weeks," Alpha said, "and then I want answers from each of you. Until that time, take all appropriate steps to protect yourselves. We stand adjourned."

Then he walked to the center of the room, crossed his arms against his chest, and began chanting something in a language that none of them recognized. As his body began to rotate in place, out from his hands and rings streamed rays of red and gold, washing up the walls from their base, scraping away the residue of the evil. The last of the eight looked back over his shoulder as he entered the portal, but could no longer distinguish any semblance of a man in the rapidly spinning figure of their leader.

CHAPTER TWENTY-SIX
"RECEIVE THIS LANCE"

The king's eldest daughter came to court on the snowy feastday of Saint Katoulina in February. For the past seven years the Princess Arrhiána had served as Regent-Countess of Arrhénë for her underaged stepson, Valentín, since that day when the old Count Rufín had finally succumbed to his many ailments. She had been married at age sixteen to Rufín's eldest son, the Hereditary Count Avrelián, who had coughed out his life from the consumptive complaint just six months after their union, leaving a son and heir from his first marriage to Lady Marionílla of Kazincbarcika.

The County of Arrhénë, although not the largest in Kórynthia, was the key to the kingdom's eastern defenses, guarding it from invasion by the Åvarsmen in the north, and the Golden Horde of Szátmár to the east. Many a potential conqueror had pounded his army to pieces trying to take the massive fortified city of Aszkán.

Arrhiána's son had now reached his majority, and she was preparing to relinquish her stewardship of the county. Together with Gorténz Hereditary Count of Görgoszák, Philoróm Hereditary Lord of Szent-Péter, and Levónty Hereditary Lord of Vélents, the Hereditary Count Valentín would be presented before King Kyprianos this morning in formal court, there to receive the tokens of their high offices, and to pledge their loyalty to their sovereign and master. There was no more solemn occasion in the state than this endless procession of lord and liege before the Great Sword of Tighris and the throne of Kórynthia.

The Hankyárar of Konyály, Tivadar Zsitvay, made the formal announcement to court.

"Sire," he said, "my lords and ladies, I present to you Her Serene Highness, the Princess Arrhiána, Regent and Dowager Hereditary Countess of Arrhéně, and her stepson, Valentín Hereditary Count of Arrhéně, who crave present audience. What say you, milord?"

King Kipriyán responded with the customary formula.

"We will entertain the Princess-Regent and Hereditary Count of Arrhéně."

The Princess Arrhiána proceeded slowly and carefully down the main aisle of the hall, her long black gown of mourning trailing in her wake. Valentín marched two steps behind her, immediately to her right, clothed in a somber gray tunic striped in black. His foster mother had refused all other accompaniment, despite the entreaties of her courtiers, saying, "Should I die today, it's God will and nothing can stop it. And if I live, I don't need any of you holding my hand."

"Sire," she said, "I bring you tidings of great joy. The Hereditary Count Valentín has attained his majority on this day. Therefore, I petition the Court of Kórynthia to release me from my service, and to take back the regency which it gave me seven years ago."

The king sat up straight on his throne, and slowly looked around the room.

"Who objects to this petition?" he asked.

No one responded.

"Hearing no objection," he said in a loud voice, "I do declare that the regency of Arrhiána Dowager Hereditary Countess of Arrhéně is terminated, and order this action to be so recorded in the *Annales*.

"Valentín Hereditary Count of Arrhéně," he said, gazing down at the young man's head, "dost thou desire to become our vassal?"

"I do most earnestly, Sire," he said.

"Then approach us," Kipriyán said, coming down from the obsidian throne.

Valentín knelt before his king, raised his hands together in supplication, and bowed his head. Kipriyán reached behind him for something, then took the count's outstretched hands, opened them, and placed within the cupped palms a clod of raw earth.

"Receive this soil as a token of the land thou shalt ever nurture and protect," the king said.

"I do accept it," the vassal said.

An aide to the king quickly moved to Valentín's right, to take each token from him when the young man relinquished it.

Then a stalk of grain was placed in Valentín's open hands.

"Receive this as a token of the crops thou shalt ever provide thy people, in good times and bad," Kipriyán said.

"I do accept it."

"Receive this lance," the king said, "as a sign of the protection thou shalt ever provide thy people, from all disturbers of the peace, internal and external.

"I do accept it."

"Receive this ensign," the monarch said, as he placed a staff topped by a white flag into the young man's hands, "as a token of the loyalty thou shalt ever show thy king and lord."

"I do accept it, and I hereby pledge thee my unswerving fealty, forever and ever. Amen."

Kipriyán raised the lad to his feet, kissed him on both cheeks, and then turned him around, formally presenting him to the assembled nobles and courtiers.

"My lords and ladies," he said, "I give you Valentín Count of Arrhénë!"

Spontaneously, they erupted in shouts of joy and thumpings of hands upon breasts. The new nobleman beamed with pleasure as his stepmother became the first to acknowledge his suzerainty, curtseying before him.

Then Arrhiána turned to the king.

"Sire," she said, "I crave a boon from thee."

"What is it, my daughter?" he asked.

"I would return to court," she said. "My stepson must make his own way into the world, learning from his mistakes and receiving credit for his own triumphs. The art of governance is largely self-taught. Should he have need, he can easily reach me. I've been gone from Paltyrrha for far too long."

"How could I ever deny you, my daughter?"

The king grinned broadly.

"The Princess Arrhiána is returned to court," he said, "with her father's blessing."

This provoked another outburst in the hall, for the countess had ever been a favorite of the crowd.

Arrhiána kissed her father in gratitude, bowing low in respect, and then withdrew while the other candidates were being brought forward. More than one lord and more than one lady in that hall, watching her fair form depart, wondered who her next husband might be.

CHAPTER TWENTY-SEVEN
"A NATURAL CHILD"

The Archpriest Athanasios, meanwhile, was engrossed in his favorite pastime, searching for himself. After his discussion with Metropolitan Timotheos the previous month, he had pulled out the mass of documents and papers that he had compiled over the years, and had meticulously reexamined them one by one, discarding many, and putting aside just a handful of sheets that might yet have significance. He then considered his past history thoroughly for the first time in a great many years.

Clearly, he had missed the obvious. There was a reason that he had been taken to Saint Svyatosláv's Monastery, and it must have had something to do with the laws of inheritance and bastardy. A few hours ago he had researched the relevant legislation himself. In XXII Arsenios I was recorded a particularly interesting decree:

> "Arsény I King of Kórynthia, in order to combat the plague of bastards now besetting the kingdom, doth hereby promulgate and enact the following statute:
>
> I. A natural child who can prove the parental ties to his father shall be entitled to a portion of his father's estate equivalent to one-half of the share allotted to each of his father's legitimate children, provided that the bloodline can be demonstrated conclusively by the mother and verified by a Psairothi judge. In the

absence of any surviving legitimate children or grand-children of his father's flesh, the natural child shall be entitled to the two-thirds portion of his father's estate that would have gone to the latter's legitimate children; and in such an instance he shall also be eligible to succeed to any title which his father might have held or been heir to at the time of his death, even when the parent has full brothers surviving of his own blood.

II. An exception shall be made if the father of the child shall, prior to his death, accept the child as his own, declaring such before a magistrate of the state or a priest of the church, and thereupon make appropriate provisions for the livelihood of that child, through endowing an apprenticeship, providing a marriage settlement, or ensuring some other emolument during the parent's natural life, or by providing similar legacies in his will. Having made such provisions, the father may declare, at his sole option, that any natural child who is his legal ward be disinherited from any additional title or estate that otherwise might accrue to him.

He had ignored any supplementary clauses that did not apply directly to the situation at hand.

During the great conflict with Pommerelia, the number of natural-born children had greatly increased in the kingdom, due to the vagaries of war, and many of their fathers had never had a chance to acknowledge or adopt them. At the same time, some of the young men who would eventually have inherited titles and estates had been cut off abruptly in their prime, causing disruption in the normal pattern of succession. Some of these titles had become extinct, while others had passed to distant cousins who had never given a thought to the possibility that they might someday have the opportunity to sit as peers of the

Kórynthi kingdom.

Yes, Athanasios thought, *this might well be the answer, or at least the beginnings of one.*

And the priest was certain that Arik Rufímovich had known, or perhaps even had served, with his father. Whoever had arranged the boy's exile had gone to a great deal of trouble indeed. This implied that the stakes had been very high in this particular case, and that the child might have been heir to an estate that was quite substantial, potentially from either side of his family.

Arik would likely have been captured at the fall of Borgösha in the year 1165, and then, according to his own testimony, have been paroled just a few months later. By spring of the following year he had already joined the Silent Souls of Saint Svyatosláv, and had retrieved the infant child Afanásy from wherever he had been birthed and weaned, after an apparently long and difficult journey.

Somewhere there would be records of these events. Even if the state and religious archives had been thoroughly purged, there would be items that had been missed, records whose significance would not be obvious except to the seeker-after-truth. Those were the documents that he would now attempt to find.

And that was why the Archpriest Athanasios was spending his free morning at Saint Ptolemy's House, the official State Archives of the Kingdom of Kórynthia, plowing through old documents and ledger books dealing with the war years, and looking for any clue to his origins. No one had questioned his presence, for his association with king and Council was well known at court. He had only to wave his hand, state "king's business," and all doors were opened to him. Besides, who would suspect a churchman of deviousness?

The first thing he had to do was to confirm Arik's movements during that crucial period from 1163-1166. To this end he retrieved a set of ledgers marked *Military Rosters, 1160-1169,* which provided annual lists of the officers of all the standing regiments in the army of Kórynthia, as well as complete lists of some of the select units. *Les Gardes Élites* were recorded at the end of each book. On May 1st of the year 1163, which was also the xxi[st] year of the reign of King Makáry, the *Gardes* mustered 166 lancers. He would start with the assumption that his father was one of these men.

Athanasios recognized some of the names, including the then hereditary prince and his brother, plus some twenty or thirty scions of the noble houses of Kórynthia, among them Susafön, Mylåßgorod, Scribónia, Braëntha, Isaúria, Pedanión, Láris, Tléshna, Brócchos, Zikhárra, Lickkaíra, Mattírëa, Zörzö, Iadirénna, Migginsch, Anaráxia, Assaël, Márö, Kranzhkör, Bórkiqvant, Linósz, Ubick, and others, but the rest were unknown to him. He assumed that they were either the offspring of the landed gentry, or younger sons of foreign nobility serving from states then allied with Kórynthia.

Ah, there it was!

Halfway down the list was an "Arikhos o Rouphinidês," noted as having enlisted as a Lieutenant on the 5th day of April in xviii Makarios i, three years earlier.

To this list the archpriest added several other names: King Makáry himself, the Pretender-King Ezzö the Elder, Ezzö's heir, Prince Kazimir, and other male members of both royal families.

Then he began excising those names that he either had known personally or could verify had actually survived the war. This reduced the number of possibilities by perhaps one-third. Of the 111 individuals remaining, another twenty-six were noted in other sources as having lived until at least 1165. Fifteen were confirmed as land-poor foreigners whose deaths meant nothing to their family's fortunes. Twenty-two were identified as having had similar situations in Kórynthia. That left forty-eight men who would have to be investigated further. He checked the roster book for 1165, but the page recording the *Gardes* had been torn from the volume; he could see several small pieces of the sheet still stuck in the gutter of the binding. The unit appeared to have been dissolved in the following year. Clearly, he was on the right trail!

He finally decided to scratch King Makáry, the pretender, King Ezzö, and Hereditary Prince Kazimir from his list, because any natural son born to these men, although he might have been entitled to inherit part of their material estates, yet would have had no legal claim to their thrones or pretensions except after those of any elder legitimate brothers, seniority still being a factor in such cases.

Further investigation in the peerage books cut another eleven individuals from his list, reducing it to just thirty-seven. These had been younger sons of the nobility whose elder brothers or their children had survived the war. He could probably trim the list a bit further with a trip down the street to the Church Archives. He would leave such research for another day, however.

Now for the second problem.

Arik had stated that he was taken prisoner by Pommerelian forces at the fall of Borgösha in 1165. As one of the landed gentry, he would have been ransomed. Athanasios found a volume from that year recording *Exchanges of Prisoners, I Kyprianos III.* On page after tedious page were noted the names of hundreds of detainees and their dates of parole. On the 6th day of September was an entry, about a third of the way down the page recording the men exchanged at the Skopélosz Pass between Borgösha and Myláßgorod, one "Erich Rufím, *ætat.* xxv." Fifteen staters had been paid for his release by "Harmon Rufím, *dominus.*"

So *that* much at least was confirmed. Arik had also mentioned returning home and subsequently resigning his commission. The question was: where had the resignation taken place, and had a report been filed at military headquarters outside Paltyrrha? But his efforts here came to naught, for he could find no volumes that specifically recorded terminations of service. Such notations seemed to be scattered throughout the voluminous military *Annales*, with no easy way of locating a specific record.

The archpriest then thought to check Arik's original enlistment papers, and he did find a series of annual volumes providing such information. However, they were arranged geographically, and it took an hour's difficult searching finally to locate what he was seeking. Under the heading of "Örtenburg," the capital of Nördmark, one "Erik son of Rufím" had enlisted there as a sublieutenant on the 15th (not the 5th!) day of April in the year 1160, aged twenty years.

It was obvious that some effort had been made to keep these volumes current until the onset of the war in 1163 had overwhelmed the clerks. A number of enlistees, about a third, did have entries marked with "dec.," "res.," or "dism.," plus an accompanying date in most instances. The rest of the records, unfortunately, among them Arik's, displayed no evidence of the soldier's ultimate fate, other than a set of abbreviations scribbled onto the final column of the page with some (but not all) of the entries. For Arik Rufímovich, the clerks had noted in several different hands the following groups of letters: "SL, NG, FL, KG, CP, DD."

Athanasios studied the volume very carefully, but could make no sense of the code. He hesitated to ask one of the librarians, for fear of drawing unwarranted attention to his quest. He determined to locate the information in some other way.

He would be unable to discover when Arik joined the Silent Souls of Saint Svyatosláv until he visited Saint Alexios's House, the church archives. However, he might be able to verify Arik's statement that he had returned home after being paroled. The personal property tax rolls were arranged by county or barony and then by year, and further subdivided within each book into localities. Athanasios had to look long and hard, but he jumped up and clapped his hands when he spotted the item he was seeking. In the book for Nördmark, in the region called Oberpfitzner, on the 16th day of January in the year 1166, was recorded, with other names:

"Harmanos Rufímobich, 2 st.
"Harikos Rufímobich, 25 ob."

So Arik had indeed made it home from his two-year ordeal. Just what had prompted him to leave the cozy confines of his family's estate in the middle of winter? What was so important about the child whom he had brought to Saint Svyatosláv's?

These questions and others would have to wait for another day. Now, alas, the archpriest must return to the *Scholê* for his afternoon class on "The Scrying of Entrails." Lord, how he hoped that that dunderhead Pókazh would restrain himself. Last time the room had reeked of vomit for hours thereafter.

Oh well, he thought, *sufficient unto the day are the entrails thereof.*

He gathered together his notes, carefully filed the volumes back where he had found them, and quietly departed, brushing the dust from his cassock. None of the clerks noticed that he had left.

CHAPTER TWENTY-EIGHT
"YOU'LL DO JUST FINE"

That evening the Princess Arrhiána and her stepson dined with her brother, Prince Arkády, and his family in his luxurious, well-appointed apartments in the palace. The adults ate on the enclosed balcony that overlooked the lights of the city, while the children were fed separately in a small alcove near the main dining room, and then packed off to bed, protesting sleepily.

"But I want to stay up and talk to the grownups!" wailed Rÿna to her governess. "Especially Auntie Rhie. She's my favorite! I never get to see her and cousin Val!"

"Hush, little princess," said Márissa, tucking a stray lock back under her white lace caplet, and wiping her hands on the snowy apron covering her plain gray frock. She was the middle-aged widow of a former soldier from the provinces. Impoverished and reduced near to beggary after her husband's premature death, she had been brought to court through the offices of the hereditary prince. Her partial predecessor, the overworked and overwrought Katrina, had, after the incident with the orts, "taken the vapors" and departed for Grüninsel, where, so she said, there were far better orts to be had than those available in the palace.

"Don't want no one touchin' mine orts," she said loudly to Princess Dúra. "*Mine* orts! *Mine, mine, mine!* You can't share any of them!"

"Whatever is she talking about?" Arkády asked.

"I have no idea," his wife said.

But they both agreed that Márissa was an excellent replacement, and a better disciplinarian than Katrina had ever been.

"Don't encourage your brother," the governess told Princess Grigorÿna, hoping to appeal to her charge's better nature. "You know how he hurts the next day when he plays too much."

"Oh, all right, Márissa," said Rÿna grumpily. "But I do want to see Auntie soon."

And with that she flounced off to her bedchamber, eyes flashing, curls bouncing, and Louisa clutched tightly to her chest. Once Rÿna had capitulated, Márissa had no problem in getting the other children off to bed. Ari went almost eagerly, for he was already beginning to feel the cost of his day of excitement.

Márissa shook her head sadly as she watched him hobble away.

Poor young master, she thought. *Such a terrible affliction.*

Meanwhile, the adults were enjoying a sumptuous meal, the winter evening providing a pleasant backdrop to the tantalizing aromas rising from the varied dishes put before them: tender peppered lamb, juicy game hens, and crisp vegetables, all delicately seasoned and cooked to perfection, plus sweet, candied fruits and honeyed pastries loaded with dates and raisins, all washed down with flagons of Fontana's best, followed by tiny delicate cups of the thick, dark, sirrupy beverage known as *café* in Araby.

Arkády had requested Valentín's presence at the "adult" table on this night of nights, since the young man had reached his majority earlier that day; but for the same reason, he intended to keep the conversation light and insubstantial.

The view of Paltyrrha from the overhang was stunning. By the reddish glow of the setting sun they could see Saint-Basile's Quai interrupting the broad, slow-moving expanse of the great waterway. The Paltyrrh River was filled with ships and barges coming and going in both directions. In the distance the River Argus, which branched from the main stream just south of the city, snaked its way east towards the county of Arrhénë.

"It's good to be back," said Arrhiána, after the last empty dish had been cleared from the table, and Arkády's servants had retired to a position where they could see and anticipate their master's wishes, but not overhear any private conversation.

"It's one thing to visit now and then," she went on, leaning back on the comfortable, padded *banquette*, sipping her *café*, "but it's quite another to settle back into my old haunts. I've missed you so. Aszkán is pleasant enough, I suppose, but it's still the provinces, and we feel terribly isolated during the winter months, portal or no."

Dúra laughed. "Yes, Rhie, you *have* been stuck out in the netherlands, haven't you? As soon as we can shed our mourning clothes, I'll have my seamstress measure us for completely new wardrobes, including court dresses and gowns!"

"Kásha!" Dúra suddenly said, as an idea occurred to her.

She turned to her husband, who had been yawning his boredom while gazing thoughtfully out over the city.

"Couldn't we organize a court ball to welcome Rhie back to Paltyrrha? These past few years, with the king at home...."

She chattered on, not giving Arkády a chance to answer.

"...It's *much* more lively now!"

"How *is* Papá?" Arrhiána asked, lines of concern etched on her normally smooth face. "He looked a little worn today, not at all the way that I remember him."

Dúra started to reply, but Arkády shook his head "no."

"Later," he said, at the same time sending a silent message to his sister: *I'll discuss this with you privately.*

Changing the subject, he turned to his young cousin, who had been politely but somewhat impatiently listening to the conversation of his elders.

"Count Valentín," the prince said, "tell us of your plans for the next year. What changes will you be making now that you're in charge?"

"Well, sir," the young man said, eager to talk about himself for a change. "The War Council has asked me to call up the

Arrhënë levies by April, and that's going to be my priority for a while. We have a long march to the west before we can join your expeditionary force. Our hilly terrain and numerous rivers will make it difficult for us to assemble our troops very quickly after the snows melt. We'll do what we can to speed things up, but as you know, things just can't be moved very fast."

He paused to finish the dregs of his wine, and belched slightly.

"I'll need to hold some reserves back to deal with any problems on our own borders. The king was *most* insistent that I remain in Aszkán as Commander of the Eastern Marches. So I guess I'm going to miss all the fun out west," he said wistfully. "I really wanted to go along, too, but Uncle Sándor will be commanding the Arrhéni Lancers and the Guards."

"You'll do just fine, Val," Arkády said, clapping the lad on his shoulder. "Never forget, it's only been a few years since the barbarian threat was crushed. They could always return, especially if they hear we're at war somewhere else; and if they arrive while we're in Pommerelia, you'll have the only forces capable of stopping them. You're our first line of defense, and that's a very important task."

"Yes, I know, but...," Valentín said, clearly disappointed.

"Arkásha," Arrhiána interrupted her foster son, "I wonder if I could ask a favor of you. It's been a year or more since I've seen our sister, and even longer since I've visited Granny Brisquayne. I'd like to arrange a meeting with them both in Kórynthály tomorrow, and it would please me so very much to have you as my escort, if you can arrange the time, of course."

She simultaneously signaled the message: *I also need to talk with you!*

The prince paused a moment.

"I have a staff meeting in the morning," he said, "but I would be honored to accompany you in the afternoon, if that suits your schedule."

"It does," she said, "very well indeed. Let's go by way of the river, Kásha. We haven't done that for such a long time. I think the weather will hold, don't you? And now, even though I could enjoy the splendid view and the good company all evening, it's been a very long day for everyone. I still have much to do to get settled in my old apartments, and Val must transit to Aszkán this evening. Will you excuse us?"

After Arrhiána and Valentín had been sent on their separate ways, and the servants dismissed, Dúra turned to her husband.

"I wonder if she'll ever remarry?" she said.

"I don't know," Arkády said, wholly uninterested in his sister's personal life. "If she does, I hope it'll be for love this time."

"*We* haven't done so badly," his wife said, twirling a lock of his light brown hair 'round her finger.

"We were lucky," Arkády said, embracing her soundly. "Or at least *I* was!"

Her response was smothered by his kisses, and gradually degenerated into a short series of giggles, which very quickly became a set of long and short sighs.

"Out here?!" she finally managed to gasp.

"Ah, madame, we take our joy wherever we can find it," he said. "And we probably shouldn't delay overmuch."

"I hear thee and obey, oh prince."

"Oh Drúsha!"

"Oh Kásha! Oh my!"

CHAPTER TWENTY-NINE
"A HUNDRED-WEIGHT LIFTED FROM MY SHOULDERS"

On the following afternoon, Prince Arkády and his sister took sail for Kórynthály. Despite the chill of the day, the sun was bright and the sky a brilliant, robin's-egg blue. Warmly cloaked against the breeze, they embarked at Saint-Basile's Quai on the royal *caïque*, a large, white barge decorated in silver and green and black, and topped by a raised canopy of scarlet velvet embroidered with Tighrishi tigers and fringed with golden tassels as their tails.

Princess Arrhiána sat back on the puffy cushions, her fine blonde tresses flowing free and glinting in the sun. She was eight-and-twenty years of age, with fair skin and a creamy complexion. The angles of her high cheekbones could have been sculpted from the palest shade of pink Carollan marble. In her blue eyes was the faintest hint of amusement as she regarded her eldest brother.

"I feel as if a hundred-weight had been lifted from my shoulders," she said, stretching luxuriously, like a satisfied cat who has just finished licking its cream.

The constant sweep of the massive oars and the light beat of the master's drum provided a hypnotic backdrop to the barge's sensuous glide upriver. The brown waters of the River Paltyrrh flowed by in slow counterpoint, occasionally rippling and whitening in the breeze. Nearby, a large, silver fish splashed as it leapt for a rare winter fly.

"That lazy, eh?" Arkády said, smiling. "Perhaps I should suggest to Papá that you be married off to some fat eastern potentate with a big belly and fifteen other wives. You could spend the rest of your days in a place like Umm az-Zakkár, consorting with the camels. Dúra is already wondering about the possibilities."

She poked him goodnaturedly in the ribs.

"Don't even joke about it, Kásha," she said. "Remember what happened last time?" She paused, then added a little sadly, "I was young, far too young. And poor Avrelián was always sick."

"You know that people are already talking," the prince said. "You don't have anyone in mind, do you?"

Arrhiána turned a pale pink, or perhaps her fair skin had taken on its raw glow from the rays of bright sun glancing off the bow of the *caïque*.

"Let them talk," she said, to Arkády's amusement. "I'll choose my own husband next time, thank you, and with no help from you, if I choose any at all!"

Her brother looked her up and down very deliberately.

"Hmm. Not so sure anyone would want you," he quipped. "Too plump here"—he touched her waist—"too short there"— he pointed to her head, which barely met his chin—"and entirely too independent to suit any man."

She smiled wickedly.

"At least I don't sport all those lines around my eyes like you," she said. "Honestly, Arkády, I think you were born old."

He raised his hands in surrender.

"*Touché*. I give up," he said. "You know I'm no match for you verbally."

"Then tell me this, brother." She turned suddenly serious. "What's wrong with Papá these days? He looks terribly tired, and the entire court acts like it's walking on stilts, very precariously balanced over a pit of poison-tipped stakes. I know I've been away for a while, but not that long."

Arkády got up and went to the rail, where he watched an erne diving for fish, perhaps even the fish that had just snagged the fly. He wondered idly if the bird ever gave a thought about the life it was taking for its own sustenance.

He turned back to Arrhiána, his eyes mirroring her concern.

"You're right, of course: the mood at court has declined markedly since the new year. And father's ability to rule seems to be falling at even a faster rate, Rhie.

"I think...no, I *believe* that someone or some group is trying to destroy our house, and possibly even our state. I don't know why and I don't know who, but in my own mind I have no doubt that we're being deliberately manipulated by an unseen and very clever hand or hands. Alas, though, that there are just too many questions still unanswered, and not enough answers to make any determinations. If I only knew a little bit more, perhaps....

"Thus, I'm now forced into my most difficult role, sister, of waiting for developments, of playing the patient, deliberate statesman, when in my heart I just want to take action, *any* action, to solve this crisis. But I can't do much else at this juncture, not if I'm going to save Kórynthia and its king."

"I look at Papá," Arrhiána said, "and I see a man eaten away by his cares. I'm very concerned for him, Kásha, and for you too. And what on earth is that horrid old specter, Melanthrix, doing here? I spotted him lurking at the back of the hall today. I thought he'd left for good years ago. He follows Papá around like his pet lapdog, licking his hand and waiting for the crumbs to drop. He gives me the shudders."

"Me too, Rhie," her brother said. "Unfortunately, I can't seem to pry him away from father, or even from my own wife. I truly think that if Dúra had to choose between the pair of us, well, let's just say it would be a close decision."

"And how *is* my little namesake doing?" she asked.

"Not good, sister, not good at all. I watch him struggle each morning and wonder why God has cursed him with such pain. What did that innocent little boy ever do to deserve this? Sometimes, Rhie, Doctor Melanthrix seems to be the only one who can help him. If *I* had to choose, I'm not at all certain what choice I'd make these days. Ari tries so hard not to let anything show."

She reached out a small, pale hand to cover his larger tanned one, and they sat in silence until they reached the *Quai de l'Amirauté* at Kórynthály. The rowers neatly folded their oars into an upright position as the *caïque* glided to a smooth halt. On the dock a small contingent of soldiers awaited them.

CHAPTER THIRTY
"I GET SO LONELY HERE"

"Attention!" the squad commander said as they debarked.

Arkády acknowledged Captain Kérés with a curt nod of his head, declining the two-seated carriage standing nearby. He and Arrhiána walked the half mile to Saint Exouperantia's Convent, tailed respectfully by their guard. Although the ground was still damp from melted snow and the air brisk, the sun was shining brightly. The light sparkled around them off the wet points on the well-kept trees and shrubbery, glittering like tiny diamonds. Occasionally they heard the "klink" of icicles as they broke and fell from the northernmost eaves of the nearby buildings. Waiting for them at the entrance to the monastery was their youngest brother, Prince Andruin, a hieromonk of the Order of Saint Stylianos.

"Dru!" Arrhiána said in pleasure. "Why, I had no idea you were in town."

"Dearest sister," he said, embracing them both together in an exuberant bear hug, his student robes fluttering. "Mamá said that you were visiting here, so I came up immediately."

"How are you coming with your studies?" his sister asked.

"They're going well," the nineteen-year-old student said. "I should make my intermediate vows this fall, and my permanent ones in about three years. I've already decided to take the name Stephanos."

"I'm so very excited for you," she said, "and so pleased that you've settled on a vocation. Will you visit Sachette with us?"

"That's exactly why I came," Andruin said. "That, and to see the both of you, of course. With you in Aszkán, dear Arrhiána, until just recently, and with Arkády so busy most of the time in court, I sometimes feel like I have to make an appointment just to say hello. Not that I'm complaining, mind."

He laughed at the expressions on their faces.

"I wouldn't trade places with either one of you. No, give me the peace and serenity of the cloister anytime. It suits my nature so much better."

Andruin ushered them ahead of him into the dim anteroom of the convent. The nun in charge scurried about, anxious to be of service to the hereditary prince and his family.

"Wait here," she said, "and I'll see if Sister Vibiana is ready for you." She bowed out of the room.

In a few moments she returned and silently motioned them to follow her down a series of corridors and into a darkened cell. In the corner they could barely discern a pale, thin girl sitting quietly with her head bowed. The acolyte was wearing a robe of some nondescript fabric, a knitted shawl wrapped loosely around her shoulders.

"Oh, Sachette!" Arrhiána cried out, in spite of herself.

"Is that really you, Rhie?" came the querulous reply.

"And Kásha and Dru. We've all come to see you."

Arrhiána choked back her tears, and resolutely moved forward as her brothers hovered awkwardly in the background.

The girl rose unsteadily from her seat and stumbled toward the sound of their voices with trembling, outstretched arms. Arrhiána had to touch one of Sachette's hands before she could run forward into her sister's embrace. Rhie folded the girl's slight frame against her.

"I get so lonely here," Sachette quietly said. "I have no one to talk to and nothing I can really do. Sometimes the nuns will read to me. They tried to teach me to sew, but I can't see what I'm doing, and I'm not really very good at it anyway, and I get soooo...impatient. And I have such terrible, terrible dreams."

"Oh, my poor dear," said Arrhiána, trying to calm her sister's sobs. "My poor, sad love. What kind of dreams?"

"I s-s-see Papá in such terrible danger," Sachette said, "and I s-see this, this thing, all hairy and dark and menacing, and I s-see Arkásha almost being killed by an ax thrown by a big man covered in armor, and I s-see cousin Dolph singing with the angels up in Heaven, and I, I..."

"It's all right, my dear."

Arrhiána looked pointedly at her brothers and raised her eyebrows.

Arkády nodded and moved forward to grasp his young sister's hands in his.

"Chette," he said, kissing her forehead gently, "would you mind terribly if we looked at those dreams together? You could share Rhie's eyes for a few moments."

"Oh, may I? I'd love that, Kásha. Oh, please, please!" the girl pleaded.

The prince motioned to Andruin and his sister. Each of the men took hold of one of Sachette's hands, while Arrhiána placed her *psai*-ring on the girl's cool, pale brow. Quietly and expertly the siblings settled into a long-familiar bond, one that they had practiced frequently as children.

"The colors," squealed Sachette. "I can see colors again! Oh, thank you, thank you, thank you!"

Tears streamed down her face anew, this time in gratitude.

After some moments had passed, Arkády began to break the bond.

"Sister!," he said, "sister, it's time. We mustn't overstrain you."

"No, Arkády, no!" Sachette said, grabbing at his hand.

"Yes, Chette," he gently said. "I'm sorry, I truly am, but if we continue, you know you'll be left with a frightful headache. Now, count slowly to ten backwards, and when you reach 'one,' we'll dissolve the link."

"Ten, nine, eight," came the hollow, unhappy voice, "seven,

six, five, four, oh God, three, two, one," and she went limp.

Arkády clasped her frail body in his own strong arms.

"I love you, Sachette," he said. "I could never hurt you."

Arrhiána was standing quietly to one side, wiping her eyes, but in vain. The tears would not stop flowing.

"Now we must go," he said, "but we'll be back again soon. I promise."

He carried her back to her chair, and carefully placed her as she had been before, her thin hands folded in her lap. Then he kissed her once more, and turned to leave.

"Kásha?" she said.

"Yes, love," the prince said.

"When you see that bad man throw his ax at you, *fall to the left*, or he'll kill you for sure. Please, *please* remember that."

"I will, little sister," he promised. "I surely will."

CHAPTER THIRTY-ONE
"HER VISIONS ARE GENUINE"

Outside the convent, Arkády and his siblings compared notes.

"Her visions are genuine," he said, "or at least *she* believes them to be. I could find no internal or external source."

"Could she have invented them?" asked Andruin. "She's terribly lonely."

"Possibly," his brother said, "but in truth, I think she lacks the imagination.

"Rhie," he said, turning to his pensive sister, who was standing a little apart, still trying to regain her composure, "do you recall any mention in our family tree of visionaries?"

She thought carefully for a moment before responding.

"Truthfully, I can only think of one," she said, "and I know very little about her. I *think* she was called Mossy; she was our second cousin or great-aunt or something like that."

"Well, what exactly *did* you hear about her?" Arkády said, even as he raised an undetectable mental barrier against her.

Whatever the cost, he dared not relate anything about the workings of the Covenant of Christian Mages, even to someone he trusted as much as Arrhiána; or reveal Mösza's identity to outsiders. Membership on the council was a closely-kept secret, under the terms of the original pact between the Holy Roman Cæsar and the Byzantine Julian Emperor.

"Well," Arrhiána said, "well, when I was a little girl, Kásha, I remember someone scolding me and telling me that I'd better behave, or I'd turn out just like Mossy. And someone else said,

'Yes, and she'll start seeing things like Mossy, too.' It was never more definite than that, only an impression that she was very odd or off-limits, and that she had had visions and similar things when she was my age."

She waved her right hand in a circle, flashing her rings in a blend of colored light.

"Look," she said, "if you really want to know about her, ask Granny Brisquayne. She was at court then, and I'm sure she can tell you a great deal more than anyone else could at this point. Now...." Arrhiána shook herself, clutching her warm cloak about her. "Now, I strongly suggest that if we're going to visit the dowager queen today, we'd better do so before the afternoon light fades completely away."

"Agreed," Arkády said. "Won't you join us, Dru?"

"I'd love to," his brother said, "but I have an audience with Patriarch Avraäm in a little while. I'll see you both later at home, though. Please say hello to Granny for me, and tell her that I'll come by just as soon as I have a free moment."

They kissed and embraced, and Arkády and Arrhiána watched affectionately as the young hieromonk trotted off down the road. Then the siblings turned in the opposite direction and proceeded a quarter of a mile west into a district of stately manor houses. These were clustered in a well-kept cul-de-sac at the end of the tree-lined drive. Arkády's retinue of guards followed dutifully behind, *kiliçs* sheathed but at the ready.

CHAPTER THIRTY-TWO
"TELL ME *ALL* THE GOSSIP"

The third building on the left housed the Dowager Queen Brisquayne, a relict of the late King Makáry, who had married her after the lingering death of his first wife, Queen Ianthë. The daughter of Rethel Comte du Quatremère in Neustria, the Lady Brisquayne had married the Baron du Haut-Dossory at age sixteen, and then had been widowed less than a year later. The king of Kórynthia had first met her when visiting the palace of Erastus Duke of Kyzistra, who had taken pity on the pretty young widow and had provided her with a temporary living. The lonely Makáry had been captivated by her quiet grace and stately looks.

The old queen had been watching avidly for her stepgrand-children, and greeted them herself, opening wide the door.

"My dears," she said, "welcome to Tamásház." She kissed each soundly on both cheeks.

"I get so few visitors these days," she said, breathless with anticipation, "with Adeléonore and Abyssinthe coming home so seldom. Oh, they've got their own families, you know. Can you believe Adèle's expecting her first grandchild in three months?"

She barely drew breath to acknowledge their amused felicitations.

"And I absolutely *must* go to Lavallière in another month. If it were summer, I'd sail downriver to the Blackish Sea—don't you just *love* sailing—but the weather is so, so uncertain at this time of the year, that I'll probably get someone to stick me through one of those awful mirrors, as much as I dislike traveling that way. I just wonder how many folks have used one of those contraptions and wound up going nowhere at all.

"Well, don't stand about, come in, come in, now sit down, here, no, over *here!*"

Chattering away happily, she led Arkády to the deepest, most comfortable chair in her large, brightly-lit *salon.*

"And here, Arrhiána, sit over here next to me on the sofa."

The old queen bustled about, getting them settled in front of a fire crackling away against the brisk chill quickly overtaking the afternoon. She was tall for a woman, with long gray hair braided down her back in the Neustrian style, and laugh-lines creasing her face near her dark, expressive eyes.

"Emöke, where are you?" she said. "Fetch some sweets and hot tea for my guests."

"Oh, *you* know, Arrhiána," she whispered conspiratorily. "It's so *difficult* to find good help these days. I could just wring my hands in utter despair. And as soon as you've got them trained, why, off they go to some other household. Where's the gratitude, I ask you? Emöke!" She raised her voice again. "Where *are* you, girl?"

"Do sit down, Granny," Arrhiána said, patting the cushion beside her. "We don't need anything, really. We came to see *you.*"

"Well, that's very sweet of you, Rhie," the older woman said, kissing her step-granddaughter on the cheek. "Now, how have you been?"

But before either of them could answer, she rattled on.

"Tell me *all* of the gossip at court. Who's courting, who's marrying, and who's having babies! And *you*, Rhie."

She nudged the younger woman slyly.

"I hear *you've* finally come home from Arrhéné to stay. Does that mean Saint Konstantín's bells will be ringing soon for *you?*"

"Yes, I'm back to stay," the princess said, ignoring the last question. "It's not that I dislike the hills so much—it's lovely there during the summer—but I so miss being at the center of things."

"Oh, I *do* know what you mean," Brisquayne said quickly. "Even in Kórynthály I sometimes feel completely left out. All of the people that I knew back in the old days are either dead now or gone, Heaven knows where. I get terribly lonely with all of my old friends absent."

"That reminds me, Granny," Arkády said. "Rhie was telling me something about some relative of ours named Mossy who may have been at court when you were there. Neither of us knows very much about her, and we were wondering...."

"Of course I remember her!" the queen said, before Arkády could even finish his thought. "Oh, I recall her very well indeed. Her name was Mösza, and she was my sister-in-law. In fact, I think I was the closest friend poor Mosie ever had. She was a strange little girl, though. I say 'little,' even though she was my age at the time, but she always seemed much younger than her years, if you know what I mean."

Arkády nodded.

"Yes, I've known a few people like that myself," he said.

He thought of Humfried and his infantile behavior on the night of the banquet.

"I really think she was spoiled," Brisquayne said. "She was the youngest of the hereditary prince's children, born not long before he died, and she was allowed to run just a bit wild. Well, you know, people felt sorry for her. And then she had all of these romantic fancies that were, they were just so unrealistic, and she loved to play-act."

"What do you mean?" asked Arkády.

"Well, she'd make up these far-fetched stories, tales about being carried off on a white destrier by a handsome prince, or perhaps being rescued from a fire-breathing dragon by a knight of the realm, all of that folderol."

She fluttered her eyes coyly.

"I got over those sorts of daydreams *very* quickly, mind you, once I got married. And I imagine you did too, didn't you, Arrhiána?"

The princess made a little noise under her breath that sounded suspiciously like a snort.

The queen glanced over at her, then continued her story.

"But she didn't like the excellent matches that her brother, my Makáry, proposed for her, she refused even to consider them, and went off into hysterics at the very mention of marriage. I think it was just what she needed, but she never did marry."

"Whatever became of her?" Arrhiána asked quietly.

"Well, that's the funny thing," Brisquayne said, "no one really knows. During the Great War...hmmm, let me see," she paused, tapping her cheek with one delicately-tapered finger, "that was back in '64, I believe. Well, all of our menfolk went off to battle in June of that year. We women were left behind to wait and watch in Paltyrrha. But Mosie had a premonition or something—she was always having these visions—that none of the soldiers would be coming home again, and so she kept mostly to her rooms.

"And then came that terrible day in August when the news arrived that my belovèd Makáry was dead, and his two elder sons with him, and oh so many others besides."

The old woman daubed at her eyes and noisily blew her nose into a daintily embroidered handkerchief she kept tucked away in her sleeve.

"Well, Mösza just went crazy, screaming and hollering out as if the whole world were coming to an end. I mean, *I* was the one who had lost the husband, and here *she* was, tearing her clothes and pulling her hair and threatening to throw herself off the parapet, and this and that and the other. Finally, they had to sedate her, and keep her strapped to her bed to prevent the woman from hurting herself."

Brisquayne shrugged her shoulders.

"Dowager Hereditary Princess Zubayda and Makáry's uncle Víktor, the Prince-Bishop of Podébrad, took over as regents for little Kipriyán, and they packed Mosie off somewhere when it became apparent that she wouldn't recover. *I* never saw her after that, and when I asked Zubayda about it, she told me never to mention her daughter's name to her again. So I didn't. I mean, I'm no fool. Once the king was dead, I had no place at court, and they all knew it. They gave me this little house with a few servants and a small income, and provided dowries for Adèle and Sinthe when they came of marrying age, and I smiled and entertained and said nothing.

"Mosie never returned from wherever it was they sent her. But I don't complain about anything, oh no, I really don't. You see, God has blessed me with a long life and two beautiful daughters and a comfortable living, and that's about all that I could want in the whole wide world, other than a little company now and then."

She patted Arrhiána's knee.

"Oh, dear," Arrhiána said, "what a sad, sad story. You mentioned that she had dreams?"

"Well, I told you she was a bit strange, didn't I?" the queen said. "Like I said, she got all these strange notions in her head. One day, about a year before she disappeared, not long after Ezzö had invaded Pommerelia, I saw her at Land's End in the Hanging Garden, talking to the statue of Queen Landizábel. She hadn't seen me, so I just listened. I shouldn't have, really, but it was all so odd. She'd cock her head, as if she were listening to someone, and then she'd reply. I was frightened, let me tell you.

"I was about ready to creep away when she did something that *really* terrified me. In those days there was a small fountain at the center of the maze, running into a little pool. She pulled out a knife, cut her finger, and let the blood drip into the water. Then she started muttering some words that I couldn't hear, except that I'm sure it wasn't the common tongue, and an image formed on the pond. She blew on the water, and began sprinkling salt over the surface. Later on I learned that this was the *very* same day that it began to snow so heavily in Vorpommern."

Brisquayne laughed nervously.

"I talked to her not long after the news of the great storms had come to Paltyrrha, and she was quite happy about it. She told me that it just wasn't fair that cousin Ezzö should gather all the glory just for himself. *She* thought that her brother Makáry should have his share. Poo! My husband wasn't at all interested in that kind of glory, God forbid, but he thought he had no choice but to intervene. He didn't even *like* the Forellës."

"But were her visions real?" Arkády asked.

"Well, *she* thought they were," the queen said. "She would spend hours telling anyone who would listen about all of the great things that her almightiness was going to do when *she* became queen, of Kórynthia, of Pommerelia, or of someplace else. Of course, no one paid much attention to these fancies, which infuriated her. Every so often, though, she would go absolutely glassy-eyed, and say something in a monotone that would send chills running up and down your spine, and these things would sometimes come true. Mostly, though, I think it was just a little stale air mixed with a large measure of wishful thinking."

"Rhie, I've got to get back to the palace," Arkády said, before the old queen could continue.

"Granny," Arrhiána said, "we so love talking with you. Why don't you come down and see us now that I'm home? Or perhaps I can bring little Rÿna on my next visit."

"Would you? Oh my, that would be *so* much fun," the older woman said. "We should get together in March, before I head south to my daughters' place in Neustria."

She escorted them out, then stood in the doorway waving as they headed back down the road to the quay.

CHAPTER THIRTY-THREE
"JUST A LITTLE CHILL"

"She's an absolute delight," Arkády said to Arrhiána as they left. "I'm sorry we had to leave so soon, but I've a dinner to attend. And what a bizarre tale she told us about Aunt Mosie. She must have been a curious creature...."

And he chattered on in this fashion, very uncharacteristically, for some moments.

But by the time they had started downriver again on their return trip to Paltyrrha, Arrhiána couldn't help noticing that Arkády now seemed much more subdued, staring moodily at the passing shoreline as if it might tell him something new about their future.

He assumes too much, she thought to herself. *Please, dear God, do not let him die too soon*, she prayed.

In the east, roiling clouds were gathering over distant Arrhénë.

It's like to snow again soon, she mused.

And some distance further on, as her thoughts turned inward, she wondered: *Oh, Lord, I wonder where we'll all be a year from now.*

Then she was riveted to her seat as a scene suddenly seared its way through her mind, like a ray of sunshine cutting through a mass of dark clouds, and she saw stretching out before her a broad canyon with a fast river cutting through its middle, its banks filled with snow-covered mounds that she knew in her heart were the graves of Kórynthi soldiers, and she shuddered violently, quickly pulling her cloak close around her against the cold that had so quickly invaded and conquered her seemingly secure interior fortress.

"Are you all right, sister?" Arkády asked.

"Just a little chill," she said, knowing far better.

A line from *Proverbs* suddenly popped into her mind, and she unconsciously whispered it out loud.

"One generation passeth away," she said, "and another taketh its place; but the earth abideth forever."

"What?"

Arrhiána looked at him then with her head cocked to one side, appraising and evaluating, and she knew that he would never understand what she felt just then. She wasn't sure, truth be told, that she understood the moment herself.

I will watch everything that happens, she thought to herself, *and everything that we do and say, both to ourselves and to others. I will carefully note down all of our sins of omission and commission, and I will record them just as they occur, without embellishment. I will become a living record of this time and of this place. I cannot stop this war, but I can surely shame the warmongers of the future.*

I can choose to make a difference, she screamed to her silent muse of introspection. *No one can stop me! No one!*

"Nothing," she said. "Nothing at all."

Under the circumstance, it was the most and the least that she could say.

CHAPTER THIRTY-FOUR
"*THAT'LL* TEACH YOU!"

Several weeks later, on the Feast of Saint David the King, the Lady Mösza von Tighrisha, Countess of Rábassy and Shaikha of Salaleh, was considering the problem of precisely how and when and where to contact her nephew, Arkády. It was a delicate matter. On the one hand, she relished the idea of becoming the main conduit of information to and from the hereditary prince of Kórynthia; on the other, she wanted nothing happening that might compromise her own situation. There *was* a place that she had once investigated that was isolated enough, and not in danger of being discovered by anyone else; but she wasn't certain that she wanted him to have that little secret. She'd have to transit there later that morning to make certain it was still viable. She hadn't visited the site in over thirty years.

She sat comfortably ensconced in her favorite overstuffed chair, sipping her morning *tasse de thé* and nibbling at the last bit of hot buttered toast. From her window she could see the snow-covered peaks of the Jabal Khaibár, looming so close that she could almost reach out and touch them. The heart of the massif was a towering extinct volcano called the Musa-Kuh, supposedly the place where the biblical Moses had finally been laid to rest by the Israelites. It had pleased her to find a home with such a unique association with her own name.

Where her stone house was located, a third of the way up the south side of the small range, there was very little rain, although several ever-running springs provided her with plenty of fresh water. Indeed, the overflow also irrigated a small orchard, a terraced garden, and a vineyard, which kept her supplied with fresh crops and wine most of the year, except in deepest winter. The climate was rarely very warm or very cold, which suited her nature well, and there was almost no indigenous population on the hot, arid desert floor below to interfere with her activities. Her few servants, who had been provided for her as a gift by the emir of Umm az-Zakkár, seemed grateful for the chance to sleep in good beds and eat regular meals. She made certain that they stayed that way.

She felt a feathery touch wrap around her ankles.

"Sadyris," she said.

Putting down her tonic on an intricately-carved table, Mösza gently picked up the small gray cat and placed her in the palm of her hand. She stroked the smooth patches in front of her ears, and listened for a moment to her contented buzz.

"Silly kitty," she said absently, "silly little nip."

Sadyris, not being in the least bit frivolous, miaowed plaintively to let mistress know that it was feeding time, and preferably right away. Mösza rose and walked over to a darkened corner of the room, to a small wicker cage covered with a vividly colored scarf. Inside she could hear vague rustling and chirping sounds. She carefully reached in and grabbed and removed a small live field mouse by its tail, placed it and the cat slightly apart and facing each other on the tiled floor, and then stepped back to observe the miniature drama about to unfold before her.

The mouse crouched, frozen in terror, whiskers bristling, nose sniffing out the source of its danger, its bright, limpid eyes darting desperately here and there towards the remote corners of the room. Mösza watched dispassionately as the feline, looking every bit like a desert lion in miniature, stalked and pounced on the rodent, and then nonchalantly began showing off by batting it back and forth between her paws. Finally tiring of the game, Sadyris abruptly beheaded the creature. Then, without further ado, she settled down to feast.

In the background Mösza could sense the delicate wind-chimes, constructed in seemingly random fashion of pottery chips, hollow reeds of varying lengths, and shining brass medallions, as they tinkled their incessant idle melodies in perfect point-counterpoint to the *danse macabre* taking place on the floor of the *salon.*

Mösza allowed her mind to wander, recalling the first time she had been brought to this place, and what a paradise it had seemed to her then, a refuge from the cares and pressures of the real world. She had just returned from the east, young and still eager to find her way, her head crammed full of the nonsense that some men call philosophy. But things hadn't worked out quite as she had intended, and so, in the end, she had come here to the Jabal Khaibár, where she had been saved from herself by Karím ibn Taimúr, Emir of Umm az-Zakkár.

Golden Cassie, dark Neb, and gentle Puff came trotting around the corner to see what the commotion was all about. Beau the retarded, as was usual for him, showed up a few moments later. The cat paid them no attention: she had already taken their measure and found them wanting. Dogs were foolish creatures, she reasoned, put on earth solely to entertain the feline element. They stood there like idiots, their mouths hanging open, tongues dangling, and tails wagging, watching the superior being daintily parsing her supper.

Mösza loved her captive children. She gave a special hug to each one, and happily handed out treats from the cache she kept hidden deep in her apron. They all gathered around eagerly, all except Sadyris, licking her hands and begging for more delicacies from the kitchen.

"You're all spoiled," she said with a laugh, "rotten to the core."

They cheerfully agreed: anything for more treats.

"Enough!" she said, and went into the other room, where she almost stepped on a small pile of feces.

"What's this?" she asked. "Now tell me true, who's been a naughty little doggy?"

She looked at each of them in turn, but none would meet her

eyes. Their tails drooped in despair.

"Was it you, Cassie precious? Well no, I don't really think so: this is just too small. Let me taste it. Hmmm. Well, my dearies, I'm sorry to say that it was Beau-Beau again. What do you have to say for yourself, my love?"

She picked up the miniature dog with the flat pug nose and the dull rheumy eyes, and cradled him in her arms, softly stroking his curly black fur.

"Nothing? You've been a bad little boy, haven't you, dearie? You always were an obstinate one, even when you had two legs. Bad, *bad* Beau."

She put the animal down and let fly a flash of energy from a ring on her right hand. It fried him where he stood.

"Well, *that'll* teach you, won't it, dear? *Bad* dog!"

She started to say something to the others, but they had already run off as fast as their legs could carry them.

"Oh, my," she said, "such a waste. But you'll all be back at din-din time!"

Then she went off to investigate the possible rendezvous point for her meeting with Arkády.

But Sadyris just waited for her mistress to depart, and then sat up straight, as felines are wont to do, laughing silently to herself. It wouldn't be long now until she could laugh in reality, laugh right out loud at the old bitch, just like she used to, and then things would change, oh my yes, things would change a great deal indeed.

I used to care, she thought to herself, *but*....

CHAPTER THIRTY-FIVE
"IS THAT YOU, ARIK?"

The Archpriest Athanasios, meanwhile, transited that same morning to the archdiocesan chancellery at Örtenburg in Nördmark to sort through the pile of documents that had amassed during the prolonged absence of his master, Metropolitan Timotheos. These he arranged into appropriate groupings, some to be passed on to other functionaries at the Cathedral of Saint Paphnytios, others to be returned to Paltyrrha for the prelate himself to examine. Finishing his task several hours before his scheduled return to the council meeting in the afternoon, he used the *viridaurum* mirror to reach the Church of Saint Germanos in Oberpfitznerburg.

The hieromonk wasn't entirely certain of what he hoped to find there. At the least he wanted to examine the registers of vital records housed in the parish office. Perhaps he would discover something about Arik's family that might illuminate his background. In the church office he located three old, over-sized volumes bound in cracked leather, covering, respectively, births, deaths, and marriages from the past century.

In the birth register Athanasios quickly found a record dated December 24, 1139, for one "Arikos, second son of Rhouphimos and Hêliada his wife." Similar listings were soon located for Arik's two brothers and three sisters. And in the book containing deaths, he identified Arik's father, Rufím Katúnovich, who had died at the age of forty-nine on November 18, 1163, while Arik was serving in Pommerelia.

"Can I h-help you, brother?" came the quavering inquiry.

Athanasios jumped in surprise, for he had thought himself alone. Behind him stood a shriveled priest of some eighty years or more.

"I was just examining the records, father," he said.

"Is that you, Arik?" the elder man asked. "Bless my soul, I haven't seen you here in ages."

The archpriest started to demur, then paused. Perhaps the old cleric was senile, or just couldn't see very well.

"Ah," he said, "I've been busy."

"So I hear, so I h-hear," the old priest said, his head nodding up and down. "Yes, yes, you've done very well for yourself, my boy. Indeed. And I'm glad you think enough of old Father Terénty to come back again."

"I was just remembering the old days," Athanasios said. "going off to war and all. Those were terrible times, father."

"Yet we survived, my son." Terénty smiled. "It's all in God's hands, you know. Why, I can still recall that wonderful day when you finally came home. We gave you a grand welcome back then, didn't we, boy? Oh my, yes! I was saddened when you had to leave again so soon."

"I was just trying to recall, father," the archpriest said, "exactly when that happened, but as I've gotten older, my mind isn't as sharp as it once was. Did it occur in January or February, do you think?"

The old man almost cackled with glee.

"Oh, *I* remember that. It was a few days after your sister's boy was born, you know, the bas...well, you know what I mean. Such a scandal that was, too. Here, here, it's all in the register."

He grabbed the book off the shelf, propped it on a desk, and began flipping through the pages, before finally giving up.

"Well, I can't read too well anymore, can I? Perhaps you can do it for me," he stated, thrusting the volume into the startled archpriest's hands.

Athanasios turned to the year 1166, and sure enough, there was an entry he had overlooked, dated February 4th.

"Arêtas, natural son of Angela Rhouphimidês."

This could be it!

"What became of the child?" he asked.

"What child?" Terénty responded, obviously puzzled. "Oh, you mean your sister's, umm, yes. Well, I don't rightly know. Squire Armén wouldn't hear of him staying. I remember that *you* were very upset about it, and you left for good right after that. Come to think of it, I never saw the child afterwards. I remember now. The story was that *you* took him away...."

"Well, father," Athanasios said, "I'm late for an appointment, and I have to leave now. It's been good seeing you again. God go with you."

The old priest perked up.

"And with you, my son. I always enjoy having you here."

He scratched his head, muttering to himself as he wandered away.

"But I thought *you* were the one...."

The archpriest hurried back to the *Scholê* in Paltyrrha, scarcely able to contain his excitement. This was an unexpectedly promising development. He now believed that there was a good possibility that Angela was his mother, making Arik his uncle. But *who* was the father?

CHAPTER THIRTY-SIX
"THEY ARE BOTH HONORABLE MEN"

"Of course, *cher Cousin*," King Humfried was saying to King Kipriyán and the War Council of Kórynthia, "I *certainly* didn't intend to imply that either Prince Kiríll or Prince Zakháry would make unsuitable candidates for the hand of Countess Rosalla. They are both honorable and gracious men, with impeccable ancestries...."

He bowed unctuously in their direction, but they barely acknowledged his presence.

"...But since the Mährenian countess was betrothed to my late brother, Prince Adolphos, it seems only fair that the, uh, arrangements be kept in *my* family, to balance things out, so to speak. Now, as you all know, my elder son Pankratz married last year, and his wife Minerva has already borne him an heir, Prince Alexander. However, I have a younger son—*stand up, boy!*—who just passed his sixteenth birthday a month ago, and he would be a perfect match for the girl."

Prince Norbert, called "Junior" by just about everyone, stood to the right of his father, smiling at them through his crooked teeth and pimply face.

"Isn't your son a bit young for Rosalla?" asked Lord Feognóst, a cattle farmer from western Voróna.

His beefy face methodically scanned Junior up and down, appraising him like another slab of raw meat. This was not a prime cut.

"Now, it's true the princess has a year or two on my boy," Humfried said, perhaps too quickly, "but age is certainly no bar when true love or matters of state are concerned, is it, Junior? And it's not as if any dispensations were needed. Besides, a little domesticity would help settle the lad down."

"And just what would you expect in return?" Prince Arkády asked.

Humfried speared him with a glance of pure vitriol, then forced a thin smile onto his narrow face.

"Of course, we hope that the triumvirate of rulers would acknowledge my son's right to succeed in Nisyria, as they did Dolph's. However, since Junior is the son of a reigning king, we believe that the financial settlement should be somewhat, hmm, sweetened, and increased to, say, one hundred thousand gold staters."

"What!" King Kipriyán said, suddenly jerking awake in his seat.

"Well," the pretender said, "Norbertisci will have to estab-lish a new court from scratch, and that's very expensive. Nisyria is difficult to reach, and has no real resources of its own. Everything will have to be brought from a great distance. Then there's the problem of building a palace, establishing and housing a government, and all of the rest. I would think a hundred thousand would be a bare minimum."

"Out of the question," Kipriyán said. "For a hundred thou-sand they could all eat off gold plate. I'll give you Nisyria and twenty-five thousand. You can get whatever else you need from Ferdinand."

Everyone laughed, for they knew that Mährenia had few cash reserves, and would be lucky to find ten thousand to settle on the match. Humfried flushed in anger, but bit his tongue before responding.

"We thank our gracious cousin for his generosity, but we suggest that seventy-five thousand might be a more appropriate indication of his support for our joint venture."

"Thirty-five," said the king of Kórynthia.

"Sixty," Humfried said.

"Forty," Kipriyán said, "and that's *more* than generous."

"Fifty," came the reply.

"Forty-five," said Kipriyán, "and that's absolutely as far I'll go. Record it," he ordered Athanasios.

"Gorázd," he said to the grand vizier, "prepare the marriage contract."

Then, turning back to Humfried, he said: "You understand, cousin, that we'll have to get Ferdinand's agreement to this; if he says 'no,' then you'll agree to allow the candidacy of one of my sons."

"Very well." Humfried sighed. "We do agree."

Kipriyán turned to Arkády: "Where's Ustín? I want to discuss the financial arrangements, but he's not here."

Glances ricocheted from person to person around the table, but no one had seen the Master of the Exchequer.

"Call for Ustín Lord Bazhén," Kipriyán said.

And so the message went out, echoing down the long hall outside.

CHAPTER THIRTY-SEVEN
"WHO'S DEAD?"

Meanwhile, the Council turned to the scheduling of the troop musters, and decided to set a deadline of the first of May for the levies from the east, north, and south to reach Paltyrrha; those in the west would cluster directly around Myláßgorod later in the month, and those apportioned to Prince Ezzö's army would gather at Bolémia for an invasion from the north.

General Sándor, Count of Yevpatóriya in Arrhénë, expressed much concern over the timetable, saying he doubted that his eastern brigades could assemble in time; he was told to make all possible speed. Count Ygor of Zándrich also voiced his anxiety over a possible uprising of the northerners, and was ordered to leave a third of his force in Sevyerovínsk to guard the Northern Gates. But in the end, everyone around the table finally agreed that, despite the difficulties attendant with meeting the May deadline, a quick start to the expedition was far better than a late one, and would leave Pommerelia even worse prepared.

Sir Léka d'Örs, Chief Scout of the King's Guard, then made his report on military activities in Pommerelia. His spies had provided him with much information, he said. Hereditary Prince Walther had been named overall commander of the Pommerelian Army, and by King Barnim's order had hastily begun the raising of levies throughout the land. However, they could not possibly gather in any large numbers until mid-May, and then they would still have to be trained.

The present month of March was the rainy season in

Pommerelia, making the roads virtually impassable; in addition, the snows had been particularly harsh this year in the central mountain ranges, and the runoff was very heavy. Many of the fords and bridges had already washed out; Léka's agents were busily contributing their own share of sabotage to such structures.

Also, he had paid several traveling minstrels to spread rumors in Pommerelia of Kórynthi infiltration into the army there (which was true), making the raising and keeping of forces that much more difficult. Sir Léka was heartily commended for his efforts by the king, and ordered to return to Myláßgorod on the morrow.

Then Oskar von Tamburín, Royal Ambassador to the Court of Mährenia, made his report on the situation there. The Mährenians had raised seven or eight thousand men, he said, but were having great difficulties in training them as a unified force. They were superb fighters individually, but had absolutely no experience of making war on the grand scale, having participated only in local skirmishes. They were completely unprepared for large-scale maneuvering. He suggested the addition of more Kórynthi military advisers and increased training, which requests were granted by the king.

Continuing, he noted that the political situation in Mährenia seemed to have stabilized, although some dissatisfaction *was* evident among the local populace over the proposed marriage of the ducal heir to a foreign prince. The sooner that Prince Nikolaí wed the elder daughter, Countess Rosanna, the better. Duke Ferdinand's wife Johanna remained highly unpopular, both at court and in the countryside. The Mährenian army was scheduled to gather at Bublkopf by the third week of April. The passes into Pommerelia should be clear shortly thereafter....

Suddenly, the chamber door burst open with a bang. A page stood there, visibly trembling before the eyes of so many great potentates.

"He-he's d-dead!" he managed to stammer out.

"Who's dead?" asked Arkády.

"Lord B-Bazhén, Highness," the boy said. "I w-went to his bedchamber, as my master ordered, and he was sitting there, cushions propped up behind his back, and w-when he didn't respond, I t-touched him, and he was as cold as ice. And I-I ran here as q-quick as I could, sir, really."

"You did well, Körte," the prince said. "Gentlemen, I suggest that we adjourn, with the king's kind permission."

The monarch nodded.

"I want to investigate this personally," Arkády said. "Metropolitan Timotheos, I'd like you to accompany me, if you would. Also Lord Aboéty, Fra Jánisar, Lord Feognóst, and Archpriest Athanasios. For the rest, *adieu*."

Not long thereafter they gathered in Ustín's chambers. Jánisar carefully examined the body from every angle, smelling several apertures, then lifted the limp hands and pushed back the bedcovering and the minister's nightshirt.

"I see nothing unusual here," he finally told the others. "He's been dead at least eight or ten hours, probably since he retired."

He opened Bazhén's mouth and lifted his tongue, examined his ears and nose, and then with the help of Feognóst, turned him over, poking into his rectum.

"No, nothing obvious," he said. "I'd say apoplexy or angina. Can't be sure, of course, until we cut him open. Do you want a necroprobe?" he inquired, shifting back and forth on his feet rather uncomfortably.

"I seem to recall that you found nothing wrong with Andrássy, either," Arkády said, "but I still think we need to follow through on this. Aye, have it done, Fra Cantárian, but be very careful. Report to me later."

"Yes, Highness," Jánisar said.

The prince turned to the archpriest.

"Athanasios, I want you to take notes on this matter, both now and when Jánisar reports. I'll see you two later."

Then he departed.

CHAPTER THIRTY-EIGHT
"WHAT SAY YOU?"

The one known as Alpha transited to the island of Loryùppa early that evening. He had called the Brotherhood of Tighris together on several different occasions during the past month, but always there was one or more of the brethren who could not be present, and so the gathering had failed. Now, finally, he had received positive responses from all of the members that they would be attending.

He had much to tell them. The events of their January meeting were still fresh in his memory, and had left him with the unsettled feeling that they were being toyed with. He had tried to analyze in his own mind what kind of magic could have caused the effects that they had witnessed, and had decided that it represented an amalgamation of several different parapsychological traditions, two or three of which he had encountered previously, and at least one of which was unfamiliar to him. He (and they) needed help, and he would propose this evening that they seek it from some of their eastern colleagues, dispatching, if necessary, one of their own to consult with these far-distant mages. He even had someone in mind for the trip.

As he hurried down the corridor to the Enneaphon, his excitement began to build.

Yes, he acknowledged to himself, *old he might be, but he still had his wits about him.*

As he opened the metal door into the chamber, he could hear his friends discussing something. The conversation abruptly stopped. Puzzled, he looked around the room, and his heart jumped. All of the seats, *all nine seats*, were filled!

"Who are you?" he demanded of the imposter occupying his place.

"Who are *you?*" his own voice said.

"Stand aside," Alpha ordered.

"Stand aside," came the reply.

His colleagues looked back and forth in evident consternation. The height, the build, the voice were the same. Alpha felt a pain in his left side, and only remained upright with the greatest of difficulties.

My heart again, he thought. *Not now, please not now.*

He centered himself, finally regaining control over his surging emotions and his frail body.

"Brethren," he said, "we seem to have a small problem."

He heard several nervous laughs.

"I appear to have grown a twin. And I see no way to distinguish between us without letting slip the aura of secrecy demanded by our brotherhood. What say you?"

When his opposite tried to speak, the true Alpha interrupted, saying: "Let the membership decide. So mote it be."

"So mote it be," they replied as one voice.

"There can be no solution to this problem," Lambda said, "save the indefinite suspension of these meetings."

"Yes," said Mu, "one of you must go and one must stay, or we must elect a new Alpha."

"I cannot leave," said the true Alpha.

"I cannot leave," the imposter seconded.

"Then we must disband ourselves until the problem is resolved," Epsilon said, sadness evident in his voice. "I very much fear that our enemy has finally found a way to make us irrelevant to the conflict that is to come. We must each strive to fight against the chaos, to restore the order which this organization represents. Perhaps if you would sacrifice yourselves...."

But neither of the Alphas would budge from the position that he alone was the one true leader of the group.

"Then honor demands that I must leave," Epsilon said. "And when we return, *if* we return, I demand that Alpha be tested by all of us."

There were murmurs of agreement as each of the members rose in turn and filed out of the room and transited through the *viridaurum*, finally leaving only the two Alphas still facing each other.

"Who *are* you?" the true Alpha asked again.

"The Dark-Haired Man," his twin said.

The *doppelgänger* rose from his seat, and headed towards the antechamber. As he stepped into the alcove housing the great greengold mirror, he turned, crossed his arms over his chest, and added, "or anyone else you might prefer."

Then the imposter vanished, leaving Alpha gasping for air as the pain returned, stronger this time. He somehow managed to find his way to the outer passage and reach the safety of the other transit site available to him. When the ache in his side had subsided enough for him to concentrate, he focused on the shimmering metal before him, twisted the leys, and transited himself back to the Patriarchal Palace in Paltyrrha.

CHAPTER THIRTY-NINE
"THESE WERE MEN, I SAY"

The place was entirely without light. Arkády extended his senses out from his body, but could feel nothing. He could tell that he was standing near one side of a large room, but very little else. The air was icy cold. He reached his hand before him and allowed a pale amber flame to form over his combined rings, then gasped involuntarily when he spied the image of his great-aunt standing not five feet in front of him.

"You!" he said. "I...."

Then he thought better of what he was going to say.

"Yes, nephew?" the old woman said.

There was no warmth in her voice.

"Look about you," she said, "and see the fate of man's paltry creations. 'Vanity of vanities, all is vanity. What profit hath a man of all of his labor which he taketh under the sun?'"

She allowed an emerald flame to sprout from each of the five finger rings on her right hand, and raised them above her head, fully illuminating the room.

Arkády gasped again, shrinking back from the grotesque images that surrounded them. On all sides he saw the contorted, grinning faces of a hundred hideous demons, carved from black and white and green stone. In the wavering light created by Mösza's five auras, they seemed to be laughing and crying at them at one and the same time.

"What *is* this room?" the prince said, completely subdued by the horrible figures gibing at them.

His aunt laughed, long and loud, her voice echoing back and forth among the marble pillars.

"This is one of the old places, one of the hidden places, one of the forgotten places of the world, a place where men were not afraid to tap the powers divine and the forces undivine. There was a time, nephew, when men strode fearlessly into the gulf 'twixt Heaven and earth, contesting with the gods themselves for the *right* to determine their own fate.

"These were men, I say, and more than men, explorers of the infinite who dared to seize the knowledge and the power that was offered to them. In those days men dared to do whatever was necessary to expand their consciousness into the Otherworlds that so closely abut upon our own. Hell, boy, that's what this is all about. Look to where you stand."

His gaze shifted quickly to his feet. He was perched on the end of an immense, grooved altar, the center of which was fashioned all of one piece from a huge, green, circular stone set at the junction of two large, black cross-sections, stained on its surface with streaks of rust. He stepped to his left and slowly stooped, letting his hands lightly touch the brown marks, and started when he realized they were the relics of old, dried blood. Human blood.

Suddenly he had a vision of a dozen strangely-dressed men wielding long, curved knives of bronze, surrounding the naked, bound body of a struggling child impressed with the face of his own daughter, Rÿna. The leader whipped his sharp blade across the girl's throat, and caught the spurting blood in a chalice, drinking it in ecstasy. Arkády abruptly broke contact, stunned by the desecration of his oldest offspring, his rings tingling with the energy discharge.

"*What* is *this place?*" he asked again, his anger bubbling up from within.

His aunt just chortled.

"Some have called it Atlantis," she said. "The fools."

She twisted a finger under her left hand to point straight up at the ceiling.

"Up there, *that* was Atlantis, once upon a time. Down here, well, let's just say this room was old long before Atlantis ever came to be. And let me assure you, my dear, dear nephew, that no one else in the whole wide world knows where we are right now, that no one else but me and thee kens the secret of this pretty little place."

He glanced around him before turning his eyes back on Mösza. He had absolutely no idea of what to say.

"Take your time, my lovely boy," she said. "We have all the time that's available in the great green cosmos. Someone's been telling you fibs, haven't they, Arkásha? Now tell your sweet old Auntie the truth. They've been lying again, *n'est pas?*"

Arkády closed his eyes, trying to wish away this nightmare. He ran through all of the exercises that he had learned years ago to quiet his soul and regain his center. When he could picture himself clearly again, he gazed calmly upon Mösza and replied:

"'The sun also ariseth,' Auntie. And Scripture further states: 'Men come and go, but earth abideth,' as I was recently reminded. Those who erected this ruin have long since gone to their eternal punishment. They are no longer our concern.

"We can spend the evening regaling each other with fanciful tales, but I'd rather do so in more comfortable surroundings, if you please. For the moment, I have a report to make. We had another killing today."

And then he proceeded to tell her the details of Ustín's passing.

Mösza stood there impassively, drinking in every drop of her nephew's account.

"And what else did you determine?" she asked.

"Jánisar could identify no cause of death," Arkády said, "although he suspects a failure of the heart. More curiously, a brief probing showed no signs whatever of mental activity remaining in the body. This conforms with an identical reading performed on the remains of Count Alexis immediately following his passing. It's as if neither man was alive at the time of his translation. There were no residues, no memories, no thoughts of any kind. This is supposedly impossible save in one who has long been deceased; nonetheless, it happened. The physician could offer no explanation."

"Was the man murdered, or did he perish naturally?" she asked.

The prince hesitated before replying.

"Unknown," he said. "I suspect murder, but Fra Jánisar remains noncommital. I believe that the absence of any discernible mental activity in the bodies is significant, an aberration typical of this killer. He mocks us. He goads us. But I could be wrong."

"Perhaps," she said. "So, nephew, you want me to report your theories to the Covenant of Christian Mages. Welladay, welladay."

She abruptly tilted up her head and sniffed long and loud.

"Hmmm," she said, not waiting for an answer. "I suspect it's about time for us to leave. The air down here is none too good, and I have other things to do. Be seeing you, my boy."

She put her left hand to her mouth, blew him a kiss, stepped backwards, and vanished.

He looked around wildly, increasing the size of his ringflame to peer into the corners of the room, but she was gone. Perhaps she had never even been there. He shuddered again. This place was unsettling. If he stayed here long enough, the grotesque images around him might start talking back to him.

He turned around and moved two steps towards the alcove. His eye was caught then by the strange transit mirror hanging on the wall in front of him, which corresponded to nothing he had ever before encountered. First, its shape was oval instead of rectangular. He knew that such things were theoretically possible for these devices, but they were rarely encountered, being very difficult to construct and especially to balance. And this one was fashioned from an alloy of gold that he had never before encountered. That gold was present in the metal was evident in the overall sheen of the thing, but it was dark, almost black with age and with...something else. The rim was surrounded by a metallic artifact that had been cast in the semblance of a long, twisting serpent encircling the entire frame, its head, just there at the apex, devouring its own tail. He could almost imagine it moving into itself, inch by inevitable inch.

An ouroboros! They never really died, he'd once been told, but waited patiently in place until someone actually touched them. Then they sprang instantly alert and alive, ready to swallow body and soul the essence of any intruder.

Arkády deliberately backed up a step and calmed himself. Then he fixed his destination in mind, and carefully extended his *ley*-ring to touch the surface of the mirror, keeping to its center. It resisted briefly, and he almost panicked at the thought of being stranded in this place for all of his days, but he gathered together his energy, and connected the twisting lines in the æther. And then he too was gone.

But the serpent just relaxed its posture, slipt the bounds of the great circle that confined it, and began making the rounds of the cavern, as it had done for a hundred thousand years or so, and as it would continue to do for a hundred thousand more. It was very patient. Sooner or later they would come back. Sooner or later they *all* came back. And then he would eat.

CHAPTER FORTY
"THEN IT IS SETTLED MOST AMICABLY"

In mid-March, on the Feast of Saint Avraäm Kidunáya, Ferdinand Duke of Mährenia paid a second visit to Paltyrrha. Because of Archquisitor Bartholomæus's strictures against the use of *Werkzeugen*, or *vyéshchi* as they were called in the east, he'd had to ride south from his capital of Lovíza to Lömmez, and thence across the border into Köstrzyn, where Brantho Herzog von Pärtenkirch maintained a transit mirror at Castle Paradis. The duke was an old friend of his youth, always willing to accomodate whenever an advantage could be gained in return. Such was the ancient way of the Teutonmark.

Ferdinand hated relying on the nobleman for anything, but in this, as in so much else in his life, he seemingly had no choice. For the thousandth time he cursed his inability to father a surviving male heir. All of his sons had died young, his elder and younger brothers had sired no children whatever, and his last male relative, his bachelor uncle, Count Stanislaw, had perished some years before, leaving Ferdinand's two daughters equal co-heiresses to the Amethyst Throne under Mährenian law. Ferdinand had named the eldest, Countess Rosanna, as heir last year, but his wife still preferred the younger girl, Rosalla.

It was a terrible thing to be married to a woman who felt that she could run his state better than he could, when she neither understood his countrymen nor sympathized with their traditions. In truth, he was less an absolute monarch of the Kórynthi kind than an arbiter of disputes among the Mährenian nobility. The Nußknacker had always promoted the independence of its barons, who were able to hide away in its mountain fortresses with almost complete impunity, if they chose to do so.

Still, the old boundaries of Mährenia had gradually been chipped away by the continuous expansion of Pommerelia, and when King Barnim had proposed just last year that Princess Rosanna be married to one of his younger sons, Ferdinand had been greatly alarmed. So now he was forced to eat and consort with these thrice-damn'd Orthodox kings. What was a man to do?

Before stepping from the *viridaurum* mirror in Tighrishály Palace, he shook all over, a chill running up and down his spine. He hated traveling in this way. Then he patted himself down to make certain everything was yet intact.

"Thank you, Sir Kiriák," Ferdinand said, bowing most graciously to his Kórynthi escort.

I mayn't like them, he thought to himself, *but no Kürbeiser will ever be caught acting discourteously to others.*

Waiting for him at the other end of the transit-route was Gorázd Lord Aboéty, the grand vizier, who saluted him.

"My Lord Duke, welcome to Paltyrrha. The king awaits you," he said, leading the way.

Ferdinand paid closer attention this time to the *décor* of the place, which bespoke a richness and luxury that poor Mährenia could only dream about. Along this broad, brightly-lit, sumptuously carpeted corridor, for example, were empaneled the colorfully tiled murals of some of the elder kings of Kórynthia and their exploits, the tales etched in cuneiform in the old tongue. Here he saw a captive count groveling in the dust before King Tighris himself, and over there he spied the unfortunate Arbogast, the notorious last sovereign Duke of Arrhéně, being executed together with his family (all save one!) by a triumphant King Néstor. Most instructive, indeed. He was happy that Mährenia was located so far away from its new ally.

They entered the chamber of the High Council of Kórynthia,

although the only ones present on this occasion were the king, the Hereditary Prince, Lord Gorázd, and two of the Forellës, King Humfried and his father.

More marriage games, the duke thought wryly.

"His Serene Highness Ferdinand VIII, Duke of Mährenia and Ptolemaïs and Lord of the Prüffenmark," the herald said.

At the majordomo's indication, Ferdinand sat himself at the head of a solid, highly polished black oak conference table directly across from King Kipriyán.

Prince Ezzö was seated to Kipriyán's immediate left. The late pretender stared vacantly across the room and out the window at nothing in particular, although he did glance up when the newcomer took his seat. Ferdinand had no especial love for the Forellës, but he thought he knew better than anyone else in the room just what the man was feeling; it was not easy to lose a belovèd son.

Prince Arkády was located to his father's right. He was neatly attired in a brown tunic striped with black and ochre, and seemed alert and prepared for the meeting to come.

This was a man to watch, the duke acknowledged to himself, grudgingly admitting that the prince would make a fine king one day. And to think that he was just the eldest of five adult boys. Kipriyán was fortunate in his sons, indeed.

King Humfried was sprawled over two chairs at center table, just to the left of his father. His burgundy shirt was agape, clearly showing his hairy chest, and his hair was mussed. He belched once and yawned. Ferdinand caught a whiff of sour wine wafting down the table.

Gad, the man was a pig!

Outwardly, though, the Mährenian ruler kept his opinion to himself, and maintained a studied air of polite expectancy. Lord Gorázd hovered nearby, awaiting directions.

"Ferdinand," Kipriyán said warmly, "it's good to see you again. You know everyone else here, I believe."

He swept his hand around the council table.

The Duke of Mährenia bowed his head respectfully.

"Believe me," he said, "when I tell you that I am the fortunate one, my brother."

The king shuffled through some papers before him.

"You've heard, I'm sure, of the unfortunate accident suffered recently by Prince Adolphos, younger brother to King Humfried," he said.

"My daughter Rosalla was *most* grieved to receive news of the passing of her intended," Ferdinand assured him. "We extend our deepest sympathy to her father and his family."

He bowed again towards Prince Ezzö, who lowered his head in return.

"Indeed."

Kipriyán let a studied pause expand the momentary awkward silence that permeated the chamber.

"Then perhaps she and you might be receptive to a furtherance of our alliance."

He turned to King Humfried, who straightened in his chair slightly.

"Thank you, *cousin*," the pretender said, smirking. "As you may know, our younger son, Prince Norbert, remains a bachelor. Therefore, to cement our future relationship, we propose an affiliation of family between him and your daughter. However, since this connection will reach closer to the throne than before, we will require a dowry of twenty thousand staters, in addition to the other terms already proposed."

Ferdinand was privately amused; Humfried reminded him of some of his robber barons.

"With all due respect to our brother, and even as we acknowledge our desire to further the ties between us, we must remind you that Mährenia does not have the resources of great Kórynthia or even of broad Pommerelia. Therefore, we propose that the sum remain the same as previously offered, ten thousand gold staters."

He smiled as he finished.

Humfried went white, controlling his anger with obvious difficulty.

"Those terms were adequate for our brother, of blessèd memory, who had no other prospects, but our son deserves rather more."

Ferdinand threw up his hands in resignation.

"Alas, that we cannot provide more, but as the old saying is oft rendered, one cannot bleed blood from a turnip. However, let us propose the following alternative to our brothers of Kórynthia and Pommerelia, to wit, that the town of Cartágö in Pommerelia be given to the newlyweds of Nisyria, and the town of Dürkheim be granted as a wedding present to Prince Nikolaí and his bride in Mährenia. Should you both agree, of course."

He smiled most benignly once again, a cat among the sparrows.

"I, I...," said Humfried, caught completely by surprise.

"Agreed!" said Kipriyán, banging his fist on the table. "Let it be written," he ordered Lord Gorázd.

Humfried had no choice but to acquiesce.

"Then it is settled most amicably," said Ferdinand. "Our daughter Rosalla and Prince Norbert, a *most* felicitous joining. Shall we drink to the occasion?"

King Kipriyán clapped his hands, the door opened anew, and refreshments were served.

"We'll have the documents ready for signing after the banquet tonight," he said.

"Excellent vintage," Ferdinand said, letting the golden contents of the crystalline glass catch the light. "Aztrookian?"

"You know your wines," Kipriyán said. "Now tell us, if you please, how your preparations are coming for the invasion of the Prüffenmark."

And they spent the rest of the meeting discussing the details of troop movements and rendezvous points.

CHAPTER FORTY-ONE
"THIS HAD TO BE HIM!"

That same morning the Archpriest Athanasios finally found the time to visit Saint Alexios's House, the official archives of the Holy Church in Paltyrrha. He knew that Arik Rufímovich had joined the Silent Souls of Saint Svyatosláv between January and May of the year 1166. It should be a simple matter to confirm that fact in some official record. Although the chronicles of the order were kept at the mother house, as he himself had already witnessed many years before, copies of the accounts and master rolls of the brethren were presumably also sent to the patriarch each *annum* to ensure that the proper tithe was paid to support the central government of the church.

He found a series of bound leather volumes for the Silent Souls housed on a remote shelf in the archives, having entered the building, as usual, on the "Holy Metropolitan's business." Everyone here knew him, and no one paid the hieromonk much attention anymore.

Much to his disappointment, however, a full census of the brethren of Saint Svyatosláv's was only reported decennially, in years ending with the number "5." In the year I Kyprianos III (1165), Arik was not yet a member. Ten years later, far down the list of seniority, was recorded one *"Harikhos Rouphimou o hieromonakhos ep' onomati Timotheou."* In between, the registers only noted occasional mentions of this or that postulant entering the order, interspersed with financial and other records. He suspected that these lists were incomplete, and in any event, failed to find Arik mentioned anywhere in the crucial years of 1165 or 1166.

Something in the latter volume did spark his interest, however. In July of 1166 the Abbot Jován Csigály had noted a deduction from the annual sum due to the mother church in Paltyrrha, "of ten *staters* for the support of the child Afanásy." Such subtractions continued through the year 1177, when the boy was removed by Arik from the monastery just in advance of the attack by the heathen invaders from Nörrland. The notations had stopped for six months in 1177 during the siege of the abbey, but the new abbot, the Archimandrite Phálen Domník, had faithfully recorded one final deduction early in 1178, reflecting expenses incurred in supporting the child during the fiscal year 1176/77.

Since Athanasios had not come of age for a few more years, until about 1182 (he did not know his exact birthdate), he wondered if the *Megalê tou Genous Scholê* would record a similar deduction of expenditures, and went searching for the records of that institution. Sure enough, during the year 1177/78 the school had requested a rebate from the mother church for "the food, clothing, and education of the acolyte, Brother Athanasios, until he doth come of age."

This had been denied by the church administration, on the grounds that the child had already been accepted for advance training, and was thus ineligible for further financial support. The *Scholê* had appealed, citing a record on page 344 of the *Order Book* of ACCESSION YEAR Kyprianos III, or the second half of 1164, stating that the child would not come of age until "the XXVIIIth day of December in the XVIIIth year of the reign of King Kyprianos III," or 1182, and was guaranteed an annual stipend until then.

This had to be him!

Alas, that also put his date of birth at December 28, 1164, thereby removing Arik's sister Angela as a possible mother.

However, here was a lead that he could follow further! Carefully replacing the volumes that he'd examined back on their proper shelves, he promptly hied himself, robes flying, out of Saint Alexios and down the street to the State Archives in Saint Ptolemy's House. There he impatiently went through the procedure of identifying himself and the documents he needed. As he waited for the young, newly-appointed clerk to recognize his official status, he took a few moments to steady his pounding heart and wipe the sweat from his brow.

Finally, permission was granted. With hands shaking, Athanasios pulled the *Order Book* in question, hoping against hope that at last he would hold his birth record in his hands. But once again it was not to be. Page 344 had been very carefully torn from the volume. There were not even any remnants of the page left in the gutter! He felt quite sure that the sheet would have answered all of his questions. That someone had wanted to leave those questions unanswered was now perfectly obvious to him. Whoever he or they had been, they had carefully hidden him away, eradicating almost all trace of his existence from the written records.

Not quite all, however. Then something else occurred to him. He went back to the *Order Book*, and checked the surrounding pages. Nothing. However, the brief index in the front of the book recorded several other page citations, evidently financial accountings or other miscellanea relating to the execution of the order. These also had been meticulously excised. So had the accounts from the *Order Books* for I Kyprianos III (1165) and II Kyprianos III (1166).

But in III Kyprianos III (1167), the expense noted for the support of the child by Saint Svyatosláv's Monastery was carefully recorded, as were all the expenditures for Afanásy or Athanasios in subsequent years. And in the book for 1168, Athanasios almost missed the most important record, a supplemental accounting from November in which an extra reimbursement was requested for expenses incurred "for restoring the health of the sick child Maksím *alias* Afanásy." *Now he had a name!*

But despite several more hours of searching, he could locate nothing else, and finally had to run to the cathedral to say his scheduled mass. He made it a *celebratio* of thanksgiving.

CHAPTER FORTY-TWO
"I CAN'T FIND THE BELL"

As the morning meeting between Duke Ferdinand and King Kipriyán was winding down, an aide entered the room, and whispered a message to Hereditary Prince Arkády.

"Pray excuse me, gentlemen," the latter said, and hurriedly left the chamber.

He ran to his apartments in the residential wing, where he found his wife Dúra in the children's room.

"What is it, Drúsha?" he managed to gasp out.

She stepped back so he could see. Little Prince Arión was writhing in pain, rolling back and forth in his tumbled bedclothes, his pale body visibly racked by periodic spasms.

"Why haven't you summoned Doctor Melanthrix?" Arkády asked.

"*I can't find the bell*," she said, almost screaming the words, "and he's not in his quarters. No one knows *where* he is."

"Then send for Jánisar," Arkády said. "I'll locate Melanthrix. And have the servants search for that thrice-cursed bell!"

Arkády rushed out, yelling for his guards.

But the bell was in the garden with Rÿna, who had thought it a lovely little silver playtoy, and was now merrily ringing it for her dolls, Louisa, Sylyána, and Bánya, who were stoically sitting on the bench in front of her.

"See, Ouisa," she said, "it makes such a marvelous tinkling sound."

She rang it several more times, and looked at each of them

in turn.

"That means it's supper time," she said imperiously, "and you'd better come when I call, or you'll get nothing to eat."

Rÿna had laid out a sumptuous picnic for her friends, with miniature utensils, cups, and place settings for each imaginary playmate.

"Now let's all put on our napkins very nicely, just like me," she said in her very best "Márissa" voice. "Sit up straight, please."

She carefully propped each of them erect.

"Thank you, my lords and ladies. Let the feast begin!"

CHAPTER FORTY-THREE
"YOU WILL NOT GOVERN *ME!*"

Far to the southeast, in the mountains north of the city of Antukhia in the fabled land of Asshyria, Doctor Melanthrix received the message the child was inadvertently sending, jerking his head as the sound of the bell reverberated in his mind. The telltale had been set by him years ago so that he could be called from any part of the globe by Prince Arkády or his wife.

He who was known to the world as E-Ulmash-Shakin-Shumi noticed the movement, and tuned his third, his inner ear, to the sound.

"Hearing noises, are we?" he said dryly. "You haven't answered my question, doctor."

"We must leave you soon," the philosopher said. "But we will emphasize again, honored ones, that while we do appreciate and acknowledge the fact that we learned much here during our student years, still we are not presently subject to your laws or your control, and we cannot allow you to interfere with our practice of the *psai* arts."

"A complaint has been formally lodged against you," he who was known to the world as Shuppiluliumash said a little more forcefully, "by one who is respected by all of us here. He claims that you have illicitly used your knowledge and your powers to interfere with the workings of another magical tradition. What say you to these charges?"

The one who was known to the world as Melanthrix looked

anxiously about the room at the eight mages who sat there, one at each point of a crossed star, then declaimed in his strange high-pitched voice, a bit louder than he intended: "Where is our accuser? We do not see him here. Let him appear and we will respond. Until then, we must state to you again that you have no jurisdiction over Doctor Melanthrix, that you may not tell us what it is that we shall or shall not do. We utterly reject your authority."

"Do you?" said she who was known to the world as Harrabichi Kadavube Adi-Raja Bibi. "Then why have you come before the Fellowship of Saint Yabhalaha bar Qayyuma?"

The silver bell rang again, in all their minds this time, as if to punctuate her words. Melanthrix visibly began to fidget, while the eight focused on its plaintive cry.

"We came out of respect for your wisdom," the philosopher said, more diplomatically this time. "We came to *honor* your learning."

"Yet you show no respect for our authority?" said he who was known to the world as Tribhuvanadityavarman. "You *know* the law," he insisted, holding up his hand as Melanthrix attempted to interrupt. "From time immemorial the community of mages has agreed that the workings of the enlightened ones shall be subject to the authority of the select. We gave you our secrets. *Now give us our due!*"

"It...it is not the same," Melanthrix said.

"*It is!*" he who was known to the world as 'Abd aj-Jalíl Rahmat Iskándar Shah said. "You must either humble yourself before this fellowship, or choose another. You are not a law unto yourself, nor may you...."

"*Enough!*" Melanthrix said, clearly angry now, and more than willing to show his true face. "We will listen to this fool-ishness *no more!* You will not govern *me!*" for the first time using the personal pronoun. *"No one will!"*

And with that he vanished...*pffft!*...from where he stood.

He who was known to the world as Kadashman-Kharbe

exchanged exasperated glances with his brethren, took a deep breath, and said: "My friends, this insolence cannot pass unchallenged. The one who is known as Melanthrix has been charged with the crime of commingling. How say you?"

"Guilty," came the simultaneous responses from around the table.

"Then we must take prompt action," he said.

The bell tinkled in all their minds again.

"Ah, I see a way to do this that cannot be anticipated or blocked. Open your minds to me and join in this making. Let justice prevail in its own time and according to God's law."

And so it was done.

CHAPTER FORTY-FOUR
"IT MUST HAVE BEEN GOD"

Melanthrix reached the apartments of Hereditary Prince Arkády a few moments later, dreading what he would find. He had stopped first at his own quarters in the residential wing of the palace, picking up his box of medicines before hurrying to the aid of the sick princeling. He could not bear the sight of silently suffering children, for it brought to mind his own lonely childhood, and how often he had cried alone in the night for a succor that never came.

The guards quickly shooed him through the door.

"My boy," Melanthrix said when he spied the writhing body, "my poor boy."

The philosopher fumbled through his bag of potions, bringing out a small, dark bottle filled with a smoky substance that was something between vapor and liquid. One could see it roiling through the glass. Holding the child's head steady with his left hand, he popped the cork of the phial with his right, and carefully eased a drop or two into Arión's mouth. The prince gagged and tried to spit it out, but Melanthrix held the boy's mouth and nose pinched shut until he instinctively swallowed.

For a very long moment, nothing changed, but then, very gradually at first, the child's body began to relax, and the lines of pain etched into his forehead receded, smoothing the skin to its normal state. Suddenly he was sleeping naturally.

Doctor Melanthrix carefully put the stopper back in his bottle, stowing it away in the box of medications. He withdrew another, lighter phial which he handed to Prince Arkády.

"Give him a sip of this when he wakes. No more, mind! And another sip in the morning. We'll return then. He almost passed the boundary this time, Highness. Why did you wait so long to call us?"

In the background Dúra was beside herself with grief.

"We lost the bell," she said. "We can't find it anywhere."

"What!" The philosopher was aghast. "But it rang. *Someone* called us."

"It must have been God," Arkády said, "or...."

A sudden thought occurred to him.

"Where are the children?" he asked, looking around the nursery.

Four-year-old Prince Siegfried had been playing quietly in the corner with his toy soldiers. Hearing his father's stern voice, he bawled out, "'S'not me! 'S'not me!" and started snuffling into his sleeve, anticipating punishment.

Little Princess Numméla, two years his junior, stood silently with her thumb jammed into her rosebud mouth, taking it all in. Picking up a corner of the faded raggedy blanket which went everywhere with her, she dragged it over and handed it to her brother to comfort him.

"Ssst, Siggy," she said, patting him protectively on the shoulder. "No cry now!"

Suddenly Arkády had a vision of an earlier time. He saw Arrhiána comforting him after he had taken the brunt of his own father's anger. As the eldest child, more had been expected of him, more asked. He had often fallen short of King Kipriyán's mark, or so it had seemed to a small boy. In those days he had sworn to himself that he would never treat his own children in a like manner. His features softened as he bent down and hugged Siegfried gently.

"It's all right, son," he said. "Papá's not angry. I was just worried about Ari, that's all. Run along now and play with your sister."

"Mellie," he said, handing her the blanket, "always look after your brother, just like now."

"I will, poppy!" the little princess said, planting a sloppy kiss on Arkády's cheek.

Smiling broadly, he nodded to Márissa, who herded the golden-haired tykes towards the door.

"But where's Rÿna?" he asked, glancing about.

CHAPTER FORTY-FIVE
"IT'S JUST NOT FAIR"

"I don't know, sir," Márissa said, as the two little ones scampered away in front of her like puppies, all unhappiness forgotten. "In the garden, perhaps. That's her favorite spot."

"I'll find her, Kásha," Arrhiána said.

She had been watching the tender scene between her brother and his children with affectionate amusement. She too remembered those bygone days when her belovèd Kásha had stood there, time after time, stoically withstanding the rage their perfectionist father had directed at him for some supposed slight. Now she jumped up, eager to be of service, and hurried from the room.

The princess checked several places in the palace where she knew Rÿna liked to play, but she wasn't there. She finally found her, just as Márissa had suggested, at Land's End in the maze of the Hanging Garden.

"Auntie Rhie!" the little girl said. "We're having a picnic, Ouisa and me. But Bánya's sick, so he has to lie down under the cover," pointing to one of her dolls all swathed with cloth.

"I know, dearest," Arrhiána said, giving her niece a special hug, "but your father wants you to come home now. Ari is sleeping, finally. He's going to be all right. What's this?" she added, picking up the silver bell.

"Oh, that's just a toy I found on the floor near Ari's bed," the little girl said. "And it's the right size for Louisa. See?"

She took the bell and put it in the doll's diminutive hand.

"I don't think that's a plaything, Rÿna," Arrhiána said. "Your mother was looking all over for this, and she'll be very cross that you took it without asking."

Two tears started down Rÿna's cheeks, one from each eye.

"No one ever wants to play with me, Auntie, and I can't never do nothing right."

She sat down with a "huff" of expelled air.

"It's just not fair," she said with a little *moue* of discontent.

Princess Arrhiána knelt down until her eyes were on the same level as her niece's.

"No, it's *not* fair," she said, "but that's the way it is in the world. Some things just aren't very fair, particularly when grown-ups are concerned. I'll tell you what, though. If you promise me that you'll never, *ever* play with this again, or take it away from Ari's bedstand, I won't tell your mother where I found it. Agreed?"

"All right," Rÿna said.

She very solemnly drew herself up to her full height, and crossed herself.

"Cross my heart and hope to die," she said.

"What's that?" Her aunt reached out to examine a mark on the palm of Rÿna's right hand.

"It bit me!" the little girl blurted out.

"Bit you?" Arrhiána asked with concern.

Rÿna nodded.

"I was ringing the bell to call my friends to tea, and they wouldn't come, neither, so I just kept ringing and ringing, and suddenly it just *bit* me and made my head tingle. My hand really *hurts*, Auntie," she said plaintively.

"When was this?" Arrhiána asked, intently examining the reddish-brown hourglass burned into the girl's skin.

"Umm, I don't remember." Her niece crinkled her brow. "A little while ago, I think."

Arrhiána smiled, and her clouded face was suddenly transformed into that of a beatific saint. She tenderly pressed her smallest ring into the child's hand and then raised Rÿna's tiny palm to her lips and kissed the bright stain. Immediately the redness began to dissipate until only a faint outline of the mark remained.

"Oooh!" Rÿna said. "That's so much better, Auntie. Thank you!"

Arrhiána rose again, and walked over to Queen Landizábel's statue, staring pensively into the gentle stone face and eyes, so much like her own.

"Dearest," she said finally, turning back to the little girl, "how would you like to visit your Aunt Chette and Granny Brisquayne with me this afternoon?"

"Oh, could we? No one ever takes me anywhere," Rÿna said. "Oh, Auntie Rhie, I do love you."

"I love you too, dearest," her aunt said, kissing her niece tenderly on the forehead. "Come now, let's go ask your father."

CHAPTER FORTY-SIX
"THEN LET THIS
BE THE BINDING"

Back in Arkády's apartments, the prince was thanking Melanthrix for his ministrations to Arión.

"Sirrah, name but the price, and I'll render it if I can," he said.

The old philosopher suddenly looked weary beyond his years. He wiped his glistening forehead with a pale hand.

"There is nothing on this earth that you can give us that we would ask for ourselves, Highness," he finally said, "save that which we have already given you. If you would grant us just one boon, then let it be this: *do thou for me what I have done for thee.*"

"I don't understand...," the prince said, puzzled at the formal language.

"That does not matter," Melanthrix said. "*Dost thou agree?*"

Arkády paused. He made it a practice never to take an oath frivolously, particularly when the terms were not clearly stated. In this instance, however, he had made a verbal commitment that he felt obliged to honor, both as a Tighris and as a father.

"I do agree," Arkády said somberly, holding out his hand.

Melanthrix spat into the palm of his own hand, and extended it to the prince.

"Then let this be the binding," he said.

Arkády took the proffered hand without hesitation, and shook it. A tingle traveled up his arm to his heart, chilling his very soul.

"Now we must take our leave," the philosopher said, withdrawing his hand and bowing deeply. "As we promised, we shall return on the morrow. Keep the boy quiet. And rest assured, King-to-Be, that your son has not yet reached the end of his time on this plane."

He turned and left the chamber with that jingling, swaying gait that so marked his progress, exiting quickly before Arkády could say anything further, and almost running headlong into Arrhiána.

"My most gracious lady," he said, before disappearing just outside the doorway.

"What a strange scarecrow of a man," the princess said, shaking her head. "There's something about him that strikes me as wrong, somehow. And that *thing* hanging from his nose!"

"At any rate," she said, before Arkády could comment, "I found your daughter, and she's just fine. I also discovered *this*."

She held out the missing bell.

"Thank God!" her brother said. "Dúra will be so relieved. Was it Rÿna?"

"I promised not to tell," Arrhiána said, smiling, "and if you punish her, she'll think I didn't keep my promise to her. So you can't say anything. Besides, she didn't know it was anything important."

Arrhiána paused, trying to decide how best to present the problem to her brother.

"Kásha, I'm very concerned about something else concerning Rÿna. While she was playing with the bell, the thing 'stung' or 'bit' her somehow, leaving a distinctive mark on her palm. An hourglass."

"Was it magic?" Arkády asked, immediately on the alert.

"Perhaps...," his sister said, "but if it is, I can't find any indication of a compulsion in her. And *that* concerns me even more. I did examine this little trinket, and there's a telltale wrapped into the silver, which we already knew, but it's been, umm, *altered* somehow, I think. I don't have the words for what I sense there.

Not evil exactly, not good either, just something very, very different from the magic we're familiar with.

"Kásha," she said, "I really want to take her to see Granny Brisquayne and Sachette this afternoon."

"Whatever for?" her brother asked.

"First, of course, because I promised Granny last month that I'd bring Rÿna to visit her before she left for the birthing of her great-grandchild," Arrhiána said, "and second, because maybe one or both of them can tell us something about this mark. Granny's seen more of the world than you or I can imagine. And Sachette? Well, let's just say she's not truly *of* this plane."

"You'll have to go alone, then. I can't possibly spare the time to visit Kórynthály today," the prince told her. "Father has scheduled a hunt for Duke Ferdinand this afternoon, and I must be present, along with our brothers."

Arrhiána snorted.

"And, of course, hunting is more important than your daughter's well-being! Then please let *me* take her, Arkády. Sometimes we womenfolk have more of a sense of how to deal with these things anyway."

"All right, all right, Rhie."

Arkády put both of his hands in the air in surrender, as he so often did with her.

"You win, little goose, you *always* win."

He laughed out loud, a delightful sound to Arrhiána. It was good to hear him laugh for a change.

"Besides, it'll do her good to get away from this place of sickness," he added.

"And *you* go have your fun with your hunting and horses and men's games, brother." Arrhiána smiled lovingly back at him.

"*Dear* sister, what *would* I do without you?"

He shook his head, still grinning.

"Now I must run, or father will *really* be mad!"

CHAPTER FORTY-SEVEN
"A MEDIUM RAT"

After their noonday meal, the Princess Arrhiána and her niece, the Princess Grigorÿna, prepared to transit to Saint Ióv's Church in Kórynthály.

Arrhiána shooed Márissa away, and supervised her niece's choice of dress herself. Together, they settled on a favorite of Rÿna's, a pale blue satin dress embroidered across the bodice with delicate pink rosebuds, and trimmed about the waist and sleeves in fine Bremenburgan lace. The effect was charming, setting off her bright blue eyes and golden-red curls.

Arrhiána had brushed Rÿna's hair out carefully, combing through the tangles, and smoothing her charge's wild tresses.

"Ouch!" the little princess said, as Arrhiána applied the brush. "Ooh, Auntie, that hurts!"

"That was a *big* rat's nest, wasn't it, Rÿna?"

Arrhiána tried to be a little less vigorous in her attack.

"Is this one for a baby rat or a medium rat?"

"That was a medium rat," the little princess said, then added, "Oh, I wish I didn't have to comb my hair out ever, or wash it, neither. Márissa always hurts when she washes it. Sometimes I wish I was a boy, so I could cut my hair short, like Ari and Siggy."

"Ssst, dearest, you don't wish that at all. Girls are much more special than boys, don't you think?"

Arrhiána gave her niece a final pat, and let her get down from the chair.

"Ready, now? Shall we go?"

Arrhiána had chosen a gown in royal blue today, sedately cut and trimmed in a pale cream which emphasized her alabaster complexion. She had thankfully given up black, more than a month having passed since poor Dolph's death. With all that had happened, she had decided not to return to a brighter palette just yet, however. She was an arbiter of fashion and decorum at court, and she took this role seriously.

Arrhiána wrapped herself in an ecru shawl knit from the fine Arrhéni wool gathered from her own flock of sheep. She bundled Rÿna in a miniature pink version which she had brought her niece as a special gift when she had returned to court in February.

Holding her niece's tiny hand tightly in her own, Arrhiána guided her onto the transit alcove, and twisted the leys for their short journey. A few moments later, the two stepped out into the vestibule of Saint Ióv's Church in Kórynthály.

"Thank you, Captain Kérés," Arrhiána nodded, as the *Gardes Élites* sprang to attention.

Giving him a letter marked with Arkády's seal, Arrhiána explained her request to the young officer, and she and Rÿna exited from the church through the great bronze doors and out into the brilliant afternoon sunlight. In the distance to the east, Arrhiána could see clouds beginning to roll in from Arrhénë. It promised to rain later.

Surrounded by their bodyguards, they stepped from the brick-paved courtyard to a broad, tree-lined avenue beyond. From there they set out to walk the short distance to the house of Dowager Queen Brisquayne. As they strolled, Arrhiána pointed out some of the landmarks to Rÿna, chattering happily with her over the beds of sweet-smelling spring flowers beginning to push their brightly-colored heads through the rich, dark loam.

Kérés in the meantime dispatched several of his men and a *jinrikisha* to the convent to fetch the Princess Sachette hence in response to the order signed by the hereditary prince.

CHAPTER FORTY-EIGHT
"IT FEELS LIKE A BUTTERFLY"

"My dears!" said Granny Brisquayne, as she welcomed her two young guests with kisses and hugs, "oh, what a pleasant treat this is for me. Oh, let me look at you both. What a pretty dress, Rÿna. Why, Rhie," the old woman burst out in amazement before thinking, "I do believe she's the image of Mösza, isn't she? She's going to look just like her, don't you think!"

Arrhiána stiffened, and looked from her grandmother to her niece.

"I, I'm not sure, Granny," she said, hesitating. "I never really knew her."

"Who's Mo-Moëssa, Granny?" the little girl asked.

Granny laughed a little uncertainly, recalling what she had told Arkády and Arrhiána during their earlier visit.

"Why, she was your great-great-aunt, my dear. That was a very long time ago, of course."

"Where is she now?" Rÿna asked.

"Why, I just don't know!" Brisquayne said, less vibrantly this time. "She didn't tell me where she was going, did she? Now," she added, changing the subject, "I wonder if we might have some sweets around here for good little girls. Hmmm. Emöke!"

"Yes, lady," said the servant, abruptly appearing at the door to the salon.

She was a rather plain little serving girl with a pinched, frowning face, wearing a dark, severely tailored gown and crisp, white apron.

"Ah, there you are, Mokey! I haven't seen you for hours and hours," the old lady said. "Bring some cakes and candies for my little great-granddaughter, and tea for the princess and me," she added, glancing at Arrhiána, who nodded.

"Very well, lady," Emöke said dully, ducking her head as she plodded her way down the hall.

"I give up on her," Brisquayne said, with a resigned shrug of her narrow old shoulders. "Heaven knows I try to teach them some manners, but it's quite impossible. And do they ever thank me for it? No, of course not.

"Oh," she said, quickly changing the subject again, much to Arrhiána's amusement, "did I remember to tell you that I'm leaving next week?"

Arrhiána nodded affirmatively.

"Of course I did, silly old me," Granny said. "I must go south, you know, for the birthing of my great-grandchild. Let me see, that'd be your second cousin, Rÿna," pulling the little girl to her side and patting the child affectionately.

There was a sudden commotion at the front of the house, and the queen's doorman appeared to announce the arrival of Princess Sachette, called Sister Vibiana in convent. She entered accompanied by Captain Kérés, who guided her to a chair, then withdrew, bowing respectfully to the ladies.

"Chette!" Arrhiána said, "how good to see you again so soon."

"Oh, thank you, Rhie, for getting me out of that place, even for a brief time." Her sister smiled. "Thank you, thank you."

Arrhiána moved to her sister's chair, and embraced her fondly for one long moment.

"I don't think you've talked with Kásha's daughter Rÿna in quite some time, have you?" Arrhiána said.

She stepped to one side and urged her niece forward.

"Is my little angel truly here?" Sachette stretched out her arms. "Oh, may I see her?"

"Of course you may, dearest," her sister said. "Rÿna, stand very still, please, and let your aunt touch your face with her hands."

Like a sculptress feeling the shape of the clay that will soon become a work of art, Chette ran her hands gently over the child's soft, flowing locks, then moved to the front of her head, quickly outlining her brow, eyes, nose, cheeks, and mouth, and leaving nothing but love behind.

"Oooh," said Rÿna, "it feels like a butterfly."

Sachette giggled.

"You have such a beautiful face," she told the child. "I can *see* you in my mind's eye."

"Now, touch her right palm, Chette," Arrhiána said.

The young woman allowed her two hands to flow down, following the contours of Rÿna's arm, until they finally settled on her outstretched fingers.

"Well, Rÿna," she said, "I think all five are still there."

The little girl laughed gaily, a sound like the tinkling of silver bells.

"But what's this thing here?" Sachette asked.

"Oh, something just stung me in the garden today," Rÿna said.

"Well, that wasn't very nice, now, was it?"

Sachette continued to explore with her fingers the curves and valleys and swirls of her niece's palm, the leys of her life.

"It cuts across *everything*, Rhie, her whole line, here and here."

She held the tiny hand open so that Arrhiána and Granny could examine it more closely.

"So I see," Arrhiána said quietly, centering herself and keeping careful control over her emotions.

"*Who* could have done such a thing to her?"

"It's a making," Granny said, in a no-nonsense tone of voice.

"A *what?*" both the younger women asked simultaneously.

"A making. It's a kind of magical working they do somewhere in the east," the older woman said. "I've only seen a few of them in my lifetime, and that was many years ago. Here, we'd call it a *geas* or a compulsion, but it's not the same thing, really.

It binds to the flesh and then stays there until called upon, if ever. Certain conditions have to be met for it to act. That's about all I know of such magics, except that there are more things under the sun, Arrhiána, than you may have dreamt of in your philosophy."

"Can you remove it?" Arrhiána asked.

Granny sighed and shook her head.

"Only the one who imposed it can take it back. Eventually, of course, it will work itself out, do whatever it will do, and then fade away."

"*What* will it do?" Sachette asked.

"Well, that I can't answer, my dears," Brisquayne said. "I wish I could."

"I'm scared, Granny," Rÿna said. "I didn't do anything bad, really I didn't."

The old lady folded the child into her arms, patting her comfortingly for a moment or two.

"I know you didn't, child, and I don't want you to worry about it. This will probably be nothing. It won't hurt, it won't change you, and when it acts, you won't even know it happened. Now, let's just see if we can find some of those sweets. Mokey? Where are you, girl? I swear, she's as slow as syrup in January, that one."

CHAPTER FORTY-NINE
"WHO? WHO?"

Later that same afternoon, King Kipriyán took his honored guest, Duke Ferdinand, hunting east of Kórynthály in the Börzsö Forest, a large, well-stocked game preserve maintained exclusively for members of the Royal House of Tighris. Accompanying them were King Humfried and his sons, the Princes Pankratz and Norbert, the Hereditary Prince Arkády and his brothers, the Princes Nikolaí, Kiríll, and Zakháry, Gorázd Lord Aboéty, Lord Feognóst, and numerous retainers.

The day was brisk as they rode out, and the hunters wore heavy, double-woven woolen cloaks over sturdy leather hunting jerkins and breeches to protect themselves from the chill. The king looked especially regal astride his favorite black stallion, Marauder. The spirited steed plunged and reared, but Kipriyán kept firm control. He was a master horseman, and he took great pride and pleasure in showing off his skills to his cohorts.

Angry, dark clouds in the east threatened rain as the party entered the woods, and an invigorating breeze scented with pine and damp earth fanned their cheeks, which were reddened from the cold. Silver flasks of strong, searing liqueur were passed about, and there was an air of *camaraderie* and good humor amongst the group, now that the negotiations concerning the alliance had been settled to everyone's satisfaction, everyone, that is, if King Humfried's wishes were discounted.

Because the hour was late, the king had arranged for a line of beaters to drive the animals through the trees towards the hunters. They waited impatiently for the game to come to them, armed with bows and lances, a few hundred yards inside the southern edge of the preserve. The necessity for silence kept the conversation low and desultory. Not long after they took up their station, a light rain began to fall, slowly soaking through the umbrella of leaves to drop onto their cloaks and gear. A mist began to rise in the underbrush.

A crashing could be heard in the distance, moving closer, ever closer, and the king held up his hand in warning. The men notched arrows into their bows, ready to let fly as soon as something—anything—moved. Suddenly, two panic-stricken does jumped right at them, seemingly from nowhere, snorting vapor out their twin nostrils like miniature dragons, their wild, white-rimmed eyes rolling here, there, desperately seeking a sanctuary which did not exist.

The snick of bowstrings and whir of arrows filled the air. One of the deer crashed to the ground, mortally wounded, blood gushing from its mouth. The second, however, miraculously managed to escape its supposedly inevitable death, and was soon lost in the brush.

"Damnation!" Kipriyán said. "Missed that one."

The servants dragged the bleeding corpse away from the scene of its demise while the men reloaded. The rolling fog had thickened now, reminding the king of the great Åvarswood, where he and three hundred of his men had been cut off and trapped by the barbarians some fifteen years before. That had been as close as he had ever knowingly come to death, save for the attack on Marysday. The great, moss-wrapped trees and oozing, impenetrable mist had hidden the enemy until they were right in their midst. Then it had been every man for himself, in a swirling cacophony of thrust and parry, using the huge trunks as allies to guard one's back. Just sixteen of the rangers who had started out that day to scout their way north had survived the ten-mile trek back to their main force. He wouldn't make *that* mistake again.

All at once three more deer were upon them, leaping through

and over the underbrush and around the great boles of the ever-greens. One doe went down immediately, bristling with arrows, kicking out spasmodically in her final agony. Her companion, a large buck, dark as a horse and sporting ten points at least, took a shaft deep in the muscle of its left shoulder, then swerved to avoid Humfried's mount. The beast stumbled over a root as it turned, and drove its lethal antlers right into the belly of Kipriyán's steed, one prong catching the king's left leg in the calf. The combined *ménagerie à trois* crashed to the ground in an unruly heap, breaking Kipriyán's right leg cleanly below the knee.

Nikolaí promptly spurred his frightened mount forward and drove his lance into the beast's heart, killing it instantly. Arkády leaped from his saddle, quickly drew his dagger, and slashed Marauder's throat to stop his convulsive kicks from further injuring the king. In his mind, he blessed the noble stallion who had served his father for so long and so well.

Sleep soundly, old warrior, he breathed, *sleep forever in peace.*

Together, he and Nikolaí carefully eased the intertwined carcasses back from the monarch's legs, holding them as still as possible to prevent further injury. Blessedly, the king had lost consciousness from the pain.

"Kir," Arkády said, "ride to Kórynthály and alert Jánisar. Zack, summon the beaters. We'll need help carrying father back to the wagons."

To Nikolaí, he said, "Here, help me stabilize his energy. Why did this have to happen now?"

Overhead, a lone white owl watched the proceedings dispassionately from his aerie, one eye thoughtfully closed, knowing full well that the humans below were too preoccupied with their own petty concerns to bother with his.

"Who?" he asked. "Who?" he repeated again. But no one bothered to reply.

CHAPTER FIFTY
"HE MUST TELL
ME WHAT HE DID"

In the wee hours of the morning, Prince Arkády was wakened from a sound sleep by a pounding on his door. As he tried to wipe the night haze from his eyes, his servant quietly approached his bed.

"Highness?" he said. "I'm sorry to disturb you, but...."

"Thank you, Tyrvón," the prince said, "tell them I'll be there in a moment."

Arkády quickly pulled on a tunic over his night clothes, trying not to disturb Dúra, and hurried to the vestibule of his apartment. An obviously frightened officer stood there, his greatcloak dark from the rain.

"Captain Kérés, sir," the soldier said, saluting. "I'm in charge of the detachment at Kórynthály."

"What's happened, captain?" the prince asked.

"Uh, I didn't know what to do, sir," the officer said, ducking his head and shifting his weight from one foot to the other. "You see, one of my boys reported a disturbance in the tombs, and when I checked what was going on, well, I saw the king there."

"The king!" Arkády blurted out.

"Yes, sir," Kérés said. "I was as surprised as you are, sir, but the king's the king, and it's not for me to say, now, is it? But when I saw him crying and carrying on and such, and talking to someone who wasn't there, well, I thought I'd better tell you right away. I mean, I'd thought you'd like to know, sir, seeing as how he was injured today and all."

He cleared his throat nervously before continuing.

"Of course, sir, if you just want me to ignore this...."

"You did exactly right, captain, and I won't forget the service you've done me tonight," Arkády said, lost in thought. "We'll need Fra Jánisar and...no, belay that! Tyrvón, ask one of the ladies to fetch Princess Arrhiána, and have her meet me in the transit chamber down the hall. Captain, you're with me."

He strode off with Kérés in his wake.

A few moments later the trio emerged at Saint Ióv's Church in Kórynthály, and exited out the back door onto a boulevard that extended well into the distance, lined on either side with the stately tombs of the Tighrishi. All three carried a torch, for the moon was now hidden completely behind clouds that dribbled down a constant haze of light mist. Everything glistened with the wet, reflecting back a myriad of small points, as if a thousand eyes were watching them avidly from the dark. Far down the avenue Arkády could see the flicker of a single light. He had a pretty good idea of where they were going.

The newer mausolea were located at the end of the *Boulevard des Tombeaux Tighrises*, and it was there that they found King Kipriyán, prostrated before the great monument to his father. In the flickering light of their torches Arkády could see the inscription etched in Greek onto the marble façade:

"Makarios Vasileus Kôrynthias"

"*Father!*" said Princess Arrhiána, concern etched in every syllable, "whatever are you doing here? You're soaked right through. You were badly hurt today. You should be in bed recovering your strength. You'll catch your death."

Slowly the old monarch crawled unsteadily to his feet, using the tomb as a prop. Pain lined his face as he turned to face them.

"I, I must talk to him. I have to know. He must tell me what he did. He knows."

"Knows what, father?" Arkády asked.

"He knows about the Dark-Haired Man," Kipriyán said, looking wildly around in all directions. "So does Grandmamá. He did something naughty during the war, but I can't tell you what it was, oh no. And Grandmamá, she and Great-Uncle Víktor told me about it afterwards, and they said they had taken care of it, but that I'd have to watch myself all the time, have to watch for the Dark-Haired Man. I've been a good little boy, haven't I? I've been very, very careful, just like Grandmamá said. But they didn't tell me *where* to look, and so I have to know what they did. *I have to know!*"

His eyes suddenly went very wide.

"Father...," Arrhiána said.

Arkády motioned silence with his left hand, slightly jerking his head back at Kérés, who was standing respectfully to one side.

"Captain," he said, "please wait for us in the church."

"Yes, sir," was the muted reply, and the soldier trotted back down the avenue.

"Father," Arkády said, sighing deeply, "does this have anything to do with Aunt Mösza or her visions?"

"*Ayyy!*" Kipriyán said, shrinking back along the face of the tomb.

He made the witch sign with the fingers of his right hand.

"That bitch! That ingrate! She was never anything but trouble."

Then he seemed to regain some of his composure.

"What did she do, father?" Arrhiána asked.

He leaned heavily against the stone fronting of the monument.

"I was told that she dabbled in arcane lore, that she refused to marry the man she was promised to, and, finally, during the great war, that she killed someone for no good reason. They banished her from Kórynthia forever on pain of death. Good riddance, as far as I'm concerned. Grandmamá wouldn't even talk about her after she left."

Kipriyán lurched to one side, favoring his left leg, and nearly fell; Arkády immediately leant him a shoulder.

"Oh, God, I don't know what I'm doing here, son," he said. "I had to get out of that tomb, and this seemed like the only place to go. You know, I'll be interred here soon enough myself, sleeping with the rats."

"Oh, father!" Arrhiána said, "don't say such things."

"Daughter, I can feel the world closing in on me."

The king wiped his hand across his eyes, clearing away the mist dripping from his bushy brows.

"Everywhere around me are plots and counterplots. I know there's someone behind all of this. I can sense it in my heart. My father could tell me, if he were here. My grandmother knew. But I was too young. And now he's coming after me. Is it not written, 'The gods visit the sins of the father upon the children'?"

"Come, father, it's time to go home," Arrhiána said. "Come with us and we'll take you back to the warmth of your own hearth and family."

She tugged on his arm.

Like an old, bedraggled sheepdog, limping and damp, the king docilely followed her back down the boulevard to the church, where Kérés was waiting for them.

"Take him back through and get him settled down, Rhie, if you please," Arkády said, before turning to his other problem.

"Captain," he said, "I'm afraid I'm going to have to tamper with your recollection a bit. You understand why."

"Yes, sir, of course, sir, that's no trouble, sir," the soldier said, eager to please his master.

"All you have to do is relax, Kérés," the prince said. "Just relax and allow me to touch your forehead, here."

After several moments' work, Arkády saluted the guard officer.

"Good work, captain," the prince said. "I don't see any sign of the intruders now, but I do appreciate being informed about the situation, and I'll see that you get a commendation for your initiative. We can't have any of the tombs being defaced, now, can we?"

"No, sir!" Kérés said, saluting in return.

"Carry on," the prince ordered, and returned to Paltyrrha.

But in the darkness among the tombs another presence strolled down the broad avenue of the dead, looking neither right nor left, but stopping at the same place where Kipriyán had briefly rested. One hand reached out to trace the name cut into the cold stone facing, leaving a faint glow behind.

"Makáry!" came the faint cry.

"Makáry!" the surrounding tombs echoed back.

But to the question or to its reply, nothing was rendered, nothing set by.

EPILOGUE
"WHO ARE THEY OFFERING ME THIS TIME?"

Anno Domini 1241
Anno Juliani 881

Queen Grigorÿna looked up from her desk and said, "Yes?"

"I'm very sorry to disturb you, Your Majesty," the Majordomo Baron Kornik said, "but the delegation from Polonia is here. What are your instructions?"

"Concerning the usual business, I presume," she said. "Who are they offering me this time?"

"Prince Iwán, I believe—although I don't really know that for a fact," he said.

"King Amorek's second son, eh? Well, at least we seem to be moving up the list. They must be desperate."

"The Polonians would very much like to annex Kórynthia to their realm. It would give them access to the Southern Sea."

"Indeed," the monarch said. "Well, of course, we would also like to add Polonia to our realm. Perhaps I should tell them that. No, on further consideration, you can inform our dear northern friends that we are highly insulted—even scandalized—to be offered only a *second* son, and not the heir to the throne himself; and that therefore we will *not* meet with them until the offer is appropriate to our station and rank.

"Now, is there anything else?"

"Minister Donatos would like a moment of your time later this afternoon, if that's possible, Madam," Kornik said.

She glanced over at a notepad filled with nearly indecipherable scribblings. "Yes, we can see him just before afternoon Prayers. Please pass along the message. Now, you may leave us."

"Yes, Majesty," and he bowed out of the small room.

Grigorÿna sighed as he closed the door after him. She'd only been Queen for three years, but already the burden seemed almost unbearable at times. And always there was that lingering question, permeating every discussion, every briefing, every Council meeting. She had to keep stringing them along until it was too late to turn back.

She returned to the manuscript that she'd been reviewing, her unfinished history of the Great War. If only she'd had her father's wisdom, or even her grandfather's—well, at least up until the.... There was just so much about the period that she didn't remember and couldn't know. After all, she'd only been a child of eight then. Most of the principals were gone now, and those that weren't rarely wanted to discuss what had happened to them during that awful year. Some horrors simply can't be resurrected.

This was her life's work, not the day-to-day matters of state, however important they might be. Those who forgot history were doomed to relive it, over and over again; and she was determined to record the events of the war exactly as they occurred, whether or not they reflected well on her forebears. This particular conflict must not be fought again. Not ever.

But what to do about Killingford? That was the real problem: how to relate the events of the greatest battle ever fought in Eastern Nova Europa fairly and succinctly, without bias to either side—although there was enough blame left lying on that blood-stained field to spatter the souls of everyone involved, even those whose motives had been relatively pure, like her father.

She hesitated to take the next step, because of the risks

involved. Not that she was afraid for herself, oh no. The Queen Grigorÿna had lived a very long life during her short, four decades of existence, and had seen too much of real evil to be frightened of mere death. She shuddered even now at the thought of the more tainted members of her own family, several of whom she had herself planted among the royal crypts—or in special places even further removed from the world of man.

No, the problem, as always, came back once again to the matter at hand. At this time, and in this place, there was no one yet groomed to succeed her, although the number of would-be candidates seemed to proliferate almost daily. She had someone in mind, of course, but still....

Well, sufficient unto the day is the evil thereof.

She would have to try the "Working of Recollection" if she wanted to get the details right about Killingford. It was so very important, both to her and to history (she believed), to do this one thing correctly, to preserve the story of those events so that others would never have to walk those killing fields themselves.

But even to attempt the spell was risking the loss of one's persona. She needed knowledge, and she needed help.

And suddenly she knew just where to get them!

AFTERWORD
"THE WAY TO NOVA EUROPA"

This was my first extended work of fiction. It poured out of my soul in a flood of enthusiasm and joy, and remains one of the most pleasurable creative rushes that I've ever experienced. That the book exists at all is due to Katherine Kurtz, who'd bought my idea for the *Codex Derynianus*, and later suggested that I try my hand at writing a novel set in the Deryni universe.

For a variety of reasons that reflected the beginning of the changes that have since taken place in the world of publishing, that project never materialized in the way that either of us had hoped; and the result left me with a finished manuscript that remained floating in Limbo for a great many years. It would be "on" again and then "off" again, on and off, off and on, and neither I nor she could do much about the situation. Finally, after many years of waiting, it became obvious to me that the book would not be published as written—and at that point I recast it as a novel in my own created fantasy world, Nova Europa.

Ultimately, I did three rewrites of the book. During my hospital stay in 2003, I had a great deal of time to think about "Life, the Universe, and Everything," and I told my dear wife, during the five-minute intervals that "they" would allow her and my daughter to visit, that if I didn't survive, I wanted my three long fantasy novels to be published "as is." Well, it obviously wasn't my time yet; when I walked out of CCU three weeks later, barely ambulatory, I was determined to preserve what I could of my creative work.

The Dark-Haired Man and *The Exiled Prince*, as they were then called, were polished and published in 2004, and *Quæstiones* followed a year later. All three books were humongous creations, 600 printed pages in length in trade paperback, or about 183,000 words each. My dear friend and academic colleague Dr. Jorun Johns agreed to handle them at her imprint, Ariadne Press, bless her. And then the books pretty much vanished without any trace whatsoever, despite my best efforts.

Two of the fantasies received glowing notices from Tom Easton at *Analog*, and all three books garnered a scattering of other reviews that added some very flattering comments, but to no obvious effect. I started a fourth novel, *O Infinite Smile*, but (so far, at least) it has never managed to progress beyond the first few chapters. Then, too, in subsequent years my limited energy for creative writing was eaten away by the other assignments I received—to pen two Phantom Detective novels, and to write a trilogy of novels, the first of which was loosely adapted from H. G. Wells's *War of the Worlds*. These too made very little impression upon the world of letters; they were left as mere litters of words.

Finally, however, I had an idea for another Nova Europa volume, *The Fourth Elephant's Egg*, which I finished in the Spring of 2010 after two years of intermittent work. It emerged from its shell at a size slightly larger than the first three novels in the sequence. But there were some distinct differences.

The looser, more collequial style that I developed for the Wells's pastiches and for my short YA SF novel, *Knack' Attack*, seemed very suitable for *Egg*, So, in spite of the serious themes explored in that novel, I managed to maintain the skein of humorous interplay that I found so winning in several of these other works. Thus, *Egg* was both like and unlike the earlier books in the Nova Europa series.

Even so, my agent felt that it was too long to market in the present publishing environment, and so passed on pushing the book. Another one of my major creative efforts was left an orphan, and I was left wondering what I should do with this novel—and with all of my other long fictions.

After months of discussing the matter with Mary (my life companion) and several of my literary buddies, I came to the conclusion that the only way to make these novels viable again was to recast them into shorter pieces, as trilogies.

I started with *Invasion!* (the Wells project), which had originally been written as three novels, but had only been published in omnibus form. It was a fairly simple matter to break the book apart, and issue the pieces as they were originally penned—as separate books. John Betancourt kindly agreed to publish these and my other works through Wildside Press.

Next up was *Egg*, which, like ancient Gaul, could also easily be broken into three parts, under the titles *The Cracks in the Æther*, *The Pachyderms' Lament*, and *The Fourth Elephant's Egg*. I added new Prologues and Epilogues as needed to provide additional continuity. That left me with the three previously published long fantasies.

I started anew with *The Dark-Haired Man*. This was the most tightly plotted of the early books, but I could see several fracture points where the original narrative could be divided into sections, provided that I added the appropriate bridge material. However, I'd moved in a very different direction with my fiction in the intervening years since penning the first draft of this novel, and that left me in a quandary. Should I recast the book, or simply re-edit it? I decided upon the latter course.

Even at this early stage in my career as a purveyor of tales, I tended to write in discrete, three-to-five-page scenes, usually separated from the surrounding text by a row of asterisks. In later works I made these into actual chapter breaks—and I've now done so here as well. I also headed each of the dozen chapters in the original text with quotes from classic literature; I've dropped those in this version. Finally, the chapter titles themselves were all taken from chess terms or themes; I've instead employed lines of actual dialogue, which is my current practice in the other fictions.

The result, I think, helps break up the very dense sections of text that filled the original book, which should make all three parts of the reconstituted trilogy (now called THE HIEROMONK'S TALE) more accessible to present-day readers. I certainly hope so. I also edited the text lightly throughout the book, but chose not to mess around overmuch with the actual plot, which still unfolds (I firmly believe) with overtones of Greek tragedy. The King of Kórynthia is a deeply troubled, even doomed, character.

My dear friend and creative writing teacher, Fran Polek, lived long enough to see the manuscript but not the published book; we visited him and his wife, Jan, at their home in Spokane, Washington, in the Summer of 2001. He maintained a profound interest in my work as writer and editor, and I owe him more than I can say for the words of encouragement that he offered me at Gonzaga University during 1965-1969.

When I started my first book, *Stella Nova* (which later became *Contemporary Science Fiction Authors*), in the Fall of 1968, it was Fran and several of his English Department colleagues who scraped together some money to help support my efforts. Their boost at that time was a key element in my subsequent development as a writer and editor. So I rededicate this novel to Dr. Polek, with a reminder to all educators everywhere: what you say to impressionable young students *does* make a difference.

And now, gentle readers, I hope you enjoy my very first incursion into the wilds of Nova Europa. May it not be your last!

—Robert Reginald
San Bernardino, California
4 June 2011

ABOUT THE AUTHOR

ROBERT REGINALD was born in Japan, and lived in Turkey as a youth. He starting writing as a child, and penned his first book during his senior year in college. He settled in Southern California in 1969, where he served as an academic librarian for forty years. He currently edits the Borgo Press Imprint of Wildside Press, and has also penned more than 125 books and 13,000 short pieces. His recent works of fiction include twelve Nova Europa historical fantasies (2004-11); six science fiction novels: The War of Two Worlds Trilogy: *Invasion!*, *Operation: Crimson Storm*, and *The Martians Strike Back!* (2007/2011); two Human-Knacker War SF novels: *Knack' Attack* (2010) and *"A Glorious Death"* (2011); and *Academentia: A Future Dystopia* (2011); two Phantom Detective period mysteries: *The Phantom's Phantom* (2007) and *The Nasty Gnomes* (2008); a comic mystery, *The Paperback Show Murders* (2011); a horror novel, *Hell's Belles* (forthcoming); and four story collections: *Katydid & Other Critters: Tales of Fantasy and Mystery* (2001), *The Elder of Days: Tales of the Elders* (2010), *The Judgment of the Gods and Other Verdicts of History* (2011), *Dead Librarians and Other Shades from Academe* (2011). He has also edited the SF anthology, *Yondering* (2011) and the mystery anthology, *Whodunit?* (2011). You can find him at:

www.millefleurs.tv

And watch for the other
volumes in this series:

THE HYPATOMANCER'S TALE TRILOGY:

THE CRACKS IN THE ÆTHER (Book One)
THE PACHYDERMS' LAMENT (Book Two
THE FOURTH ELEPHANT'S EGG (Book Three)

THE HIEROMONK'S TALE TRILOGY:

MELANTHRIX THE MAGE (Book One)
KILLINGFORD (Book Two)
THE DARK-HAIRED MAN (Book Three)